Praise for *Kilb*

"What this book demonstrates, with its subtle, teasing tone, its habit of subverting cosiness with sudden stabs of grotesquerie, is an awareness that you can show the myths of modern Ireland in happy tandem with the reality."

—*The Independent on Sunday* (U.K.)

"An entertaining encounter with Irish rural life and characters. . . . Witty dialogue, quirky characters and an energetic pace make this a joy to read."

—*South Wales Argus*

"A zany novel all about zany Irish people in a zany Irish backwater."

—*The Tablet* (U.K.)

"A bagatelle of bucklepping fun."

– *The Irish Times*

Praise for *At Swim, Two Boys*

"Ambitious and absorbing. . . . What elevates *At Swim, Two Boys* . . . is the intensity with which O'Neill presents its central love story (an honest and moving one, whatever your orientation) and the vivid reality of the novel's characters."

—Bruce Allen, *The Boston Globe*

"Intimate yet epic in scale . . . as playful as it is powerful."

—John Hartl, *The Seattle Times*

"A funny, sad, and stirring marvel. . . . Some of the loveliest dense prose this side of *Ulysses*. . . . Transport[s] the reader into an epic that knows when to be intimate or sweeping, when to be sardonic or wrenching."

—Steve Murray, *The Atlanta Journal-Constitution*

"A beautifully crafted love story . . . compelling, touching."

—Emily McDonald, *Chattanooga Times Free Press*

"Language that moves like the tides that beckon pale, bookish Jim and his love, the more rugged Doyler. Written in a rough and dirty brogue, with a constant playful invention, O'Neill's language comes happily close to his master's."

–Emily Drabinski, *Out*

"A remarkable achievement . . . vastly entertaining and gripping. . . . *At Swim, Two Boys* is simply a superbly written love story filled with prose to savor."

–John Doyle, *The Globe and Mail* (Toronto)

"O'Neill's tour de force is an intelligent, informative work that will join the greats of the Irish literary canon."

–Brian Ellis, *The Times* (U.K.)

"A work of wild, vaulting ambition and achievement. . . . His writing is rich and allusive (think Joyce, Wilde, Flann O'Brien), his language is blisteringly exuberant, and his vision is both generous enough to take in the sociological sweep of a nation and acute enough to create one of the most psychologically accurate and moving love stories in recent literature. In short: Wow."

–Mark Harris, *Entertainment Weekly*

"A story of such tenderness, wit, and metaphysical conviction that you might well be tempted to have it placed on your breast when the earth takes you."

–Murrough O'Brian, *The Independent on Sunday* (U.K.)

"Remind[s] us of the dexterity, scope, and imaginative energy of which the novel is still capable."

–Graham Caveney, *Daily Express* (U.K.)

"Mesmerizing, sophisticated, intense, nearer to the truth of our lives than most established writers dream of. . . . There is no crisis in fiction except for those who choose not to read it. Don't miss out."

–Richard Canning, *The Independent* (U.K.)

"This rich, complex, and beautifully written book towers above the hype and publicity, marking out its author as one of the most powerful voices in contemporary Irish fiction."

—Jane Perry, *The Observer* (U.K.)

"A dangerous, glorious book: the kind that is likely to make absolutely anyone cry and laugh in public places."

—Michael Pye, *The New York Times Book Review*

"As a tender coming-of-age tale, vivid cultural portrait, and a story of courage in love and in war, this remarkable achievement lives up to its literary lineage and should establish Jamie O'Neill as a novelist of the first rank. By turns delightful and heartbreaking, *At Swim, Two Boys* is a breathtaking ride."

—Elizabeth Flynn, *Lambda Book Report*

"A truly historic masterpiece . . . a powerful Irish novel that uses a Joycean mastery of language, astounding historical detail, and an engaging love story to raise questions about freedom, love, patriotism, and desire."

—Stephen McKinley, *Irish Echo*

"In exquisitely sculpted prose, debut novelist Jamie O'Neill takes the defining moment of modern Irish history, the Easter Rising against the British, and makes it seem as though it had never been written about before. . . . Possessing great humor and an elegiac quality that makes one mourn lost youth and poor Ireland alike, O'Neill's saga achieves a kind of richness of scope and ambition that makes one reluctant to come to its tragic and inevitable close."

—Robin Hemley, *Chicago Tribune*

"The best literary news out of Ireland since the maturity of Roddy Doyle."

—*Kirkus Reviews* (starred)

"The music of Jamie O'Neill's prose creates a new Irish symphony."

—Peter Ackroyd, author of
The Plato Papers and *London: The Biography*

"The secret is out, James Joyce and Oscar Wilde had a child: his name is Jamie O'Neill, and his novel is a big, character-filled Edwardian triple-decker."

—Felice Picano, author of *Like People in History*

Also by Jamie O'Neill

At Swim, Two Boys

Disturbance

JAMIE O'NEILL

KILBRACK

or

Who is Nancy Valentine?

SCRIBNER
NEW YORK LONDON TORONTO SYDNEY

SCRIBNER
1230 Avenue of the Americas
New York, NY 10020

First published in Great Britain in 1990 by Weidenfeld & Nicolson
This Scribner trade paperback edition 2004
Published by arrangement with Simon & Schuster UK Ltd

Text set in Baskerville Book

Manufactured in the United States of America

1 3 5 7 9 10 8 6 4 2

Library of Congress Cataloging-in-Publication Data
O'Neill, Jamie.
Kilbrack, or, Who is Nancy Valentine? / Jamie O'Neill.
–Scribner trade pbk. ed.
p. cm.
I. Title: Kilbrack. II. Title: Who is Nancy Valentine?. III. Title.
PR6065.N4194K55 2004
823'.914–dc22 2003065911

ISBN 0-7432-5595-X

To W. E. P.

CHAPTER ONE

O'Leary Montagu closed his book. He was so happy. Already he could feel the edge of a tear moisten in one eye. He didn't force it, however. At these times, he knew, it was important to let the tears fall naturally. Concentration, even awareness, tended to interfere, corrupt. He laid the book aside, let his head rest against the cold window. His gaze settled on the fields outside. Their number, the rhythm of them, he found calming at first, then mesmeric, so that soon he was lost to all knowledge of tears, had forgotten even to forget them.

Those fields, he was thinking, the green acres of Ireland that reached leisurely over the land, how clever they were. The way they followed the land's lie, dipping for hollows, climbing for knolls, folding here and there to avoid a copse or the turns of a winding stream: yet always they contrived to end at a gate or a hedgerow. Receding, they gathered together, as though for comfort, losing first their colour then themselves in the fading purple hills. A passage came to him from the book he had just finished. 'And the bald bulb of

Slievenamon rose proud in the distance, damp through the mist as my own eyes had I allowed the tears to fall . . .'

'Excuse me.'

O'Leary Montagu shook himself. His cheeks were wet. The tears really had fallen. How strange, he thought, then immediately he corrected himself. The Mistress, who had penned the book which only moments before he had laid aside – he made a quick mental note for his diary:

Diary Memo: On train, whilst travelling to Kilbrack, completed thousandth and twenty-third reading of—

—anyway, the Mistress wove regularly these spells of abstraction. He could often pause minutes, sometimes hours, upon a reading, oblivious to the world, lost entirely in the contemplation of beauty. So evocative was her pen—

'Excuse me, young man.'

O'Leary Montagu's thoughts froze and his head stiffened against the window. It came to him, slowly but deliberately, that others had joined him in his compartment. He dared not look, not immediately. He had been crying, howling to the heavens for all he could recall: had anyone noticed? His face was reddening; the dampness on his cheeks began to burn. His hand ached for a touch that would give courage.

Without moving the tiniest unnecessary muscle, he stole a hand inside one trouser pocket, inched dreadfully his fingers, until – yes, there it was: the pliable, knobbly orb that was his talisman. He sighed. He was safe, encouraged in the face of the world.

'Young man! I am talking to you.'

O'Leary arranged his face to the semblance of a smile, turned slowly from the window. 'Ah,' he said generally, uncertain whom to address. 'I'm afraid I was' – he swallowed – 'affected rather . . .'

In front of him sat a thin little man, thin-faced in a bowler hat. O'Leary wasn't sure but from the corner of his eye he thought he'd caught the fellow watching him almost pop-eyed with curiosity. As soon as he'd turned, however, the thin little man had averted his eyes and now was studying his shoes as though all the most interesting bits of the world were contained within them.

Beside O'Leary, lolling her head half in sleep, was a young woman dressed all in black. A nun, he surmised, but then he wasn't so certain. She was rather a modern nun. She wore no wimple, and the ashtray they shared was nearly full with half-smoked cigarettes. O'Leary didn't smoke.

Opposite her sat a stout woman in a cumbersome coat. She was leaning towards him, diagonally across the compartment, and now she stretched out her hand and tapped her fingers on his knee. 'Young man,' she said again.

O'Leary fumbled with words. 'I'm – er – sorry,' he began. 'I was affected rather. On account of the – er—' He wondered should he explain about the book. On the whole, no, he thought. Strangers rarely understood. They didn't have the patience. Such a shame, really.

'That book,' said the lady.

'Book?' repeated O'Leary. Jubilation flashed across his face. Could it possibly be that this stout lady, a chance meeting on a country train, understood about the Mistress?

He had been holding the book aloft. She could easily have noted its title. The notion, however, still seemed improbable. Hitherto, in all the world, O'Leary Montagu had encountered not one other soul who had ever even heard of Nancy Valentine, mistress of letters, let alone appreciated her darling prose. And yet, he reminded himself – then he decided to be more practical about it. He made another mental note for his diary.

Diary Memo: And yet, I am in Ireland, travelling through Tipperary, the very cradle of the Mistress and her work. Surely it is to be expected that here in all the world—

'You understand about the Mistress?' he asked breathlessly.

The stout lady looked confused. She pursed her lips, and by an unlucky muscular empathy, the cheeks of her bottom pursed too, so that they squeaked on the leather bench. The thin-faced man beside her sneaked a tiny snigger, without once looking up from his shoes. She lanced him a withering eye, then gathered her astrakhan closer to her bosom. 'I understand nothing,' she said, 'save that that book—'

'Exactly,' O'Leary broke in, desperate to encourage her. '*Ill Fares the Land*, a masterpiece of memoiric—'

'Young man, I am not interested in the title.'

O'Leary's face fell slightly.

Diary Memo: Met lady on train who believed titles of books irrelevant. Is this creditable?

'But surely—'

'But surely nothing,' she said. 'That book which you have presently finished—'

'By all means, borrow it.'

'Will you stop interrupting me!' She made to rise but so cumbersome was her coat, she dropped her handbag by mistake.

Diary Memo: Met volatile woman on train, apparently fellow devotee of Nancy Valentine. So long have I sought a fraternal spirit – in this case sororal – a chance to exchange opinions, converse intelligently, what have you. She displayed, however, a marked bent for sermonizing. Mistook my encouragement for interference. Find myself confounded by the antics of these . . .

The thin-faced man darted his eyes to the stout lady beside him, then over to O'Leary. But as soon as O'Leary met the quivering black dots of his pupils, he hunched his shoulders, returned instantly to the study of his feet. Still, though, O'Leary believed he could catch the trace of a grin on his face. He gave the impression that it was not the conversation that captivated him, not that at all. It was his shoes. They preoccupied him, as though he were alone in all the train, with only his feet for company. And there was something droll about a shoe on a foot. The very notion of it tickled him. That was why he grinned.

The conversation was not going at all the way the stout lady had envisaged it. She retrieved her handbag, then gripped fast on the armrests of her seat, heaved herself upwards. 'Young man,' she said. Her coat fell loose about her, and she stood glowering at O'Leary like—

Dracula uncaped, he thought. He reached a sly hand into his trouser pocket. The soft orb he found there reassured him slightly. He had already recoiled as far as his seat would allow. 'Madam, if I have offended you—'

'Young man, you will remove that book from my daughter's lap. This instant!'

O'Leary Montagu arched his gaze till it fell on the young woman asleep beside him. When he had finished reading, he had closed the book gently, his regard as much for its melancholy beauty as for the tattered cloth that contained it, had laid it aside. And there it lay still, Nancy Valentine's *Ill Fares the Land*, nestling comfortably on the girl's lap, heaving softly with her every breath.

'Ah,' said O'Leary.

O'Leary Montagu – tall dark and normal as Mary once had described him – contemplated his reflection in the train window. 'Ah,' he sighed, despondently.

All he had sought to do was retrieve the book from the girl's lap. Whereupon she had leapt awake and slapped him smartly on the cheek. He had tried to explain, but all the girl had said was: 'Mother, will you stop interfering!' And she stormed out of the compartment.

And although O'Leary was in favour, always had been, of symmetry in his life, he had not expected the stout lady to follow her daughter's example and clout him stoutly on the other cheek. She muttered something, castigating herself or the world, then crashed through the compartment door, chased down the corridor calling, 'Livia! Livia!'

Even now he could hear them arguing. Their voices, usually a murmur, every now and then rose to a pitch of distinction.

'Of course you shall marry!'

'But I wish to be a nun!'

'Ah,' sighed O'Leary. He gazed at the unparticular fields outside as they whizzed through his reflection, his fingers soothing one swelling cheek, resting, then soothing the other. Mother and daughter had each slapped him on his scars: the two streaks of scars where the doctors had bungled his surgery. Eleven years ago, that was. After the accident. The scars were unfortunate, but not particularly ugly, he had allowed at the time. They bestowed some definition on an otherwise blankish countenance.

It wasn't the first time the Mistress had got him into trouble. Most definitely it was not. The volume of memoirs might well outpeak all other pinnacles in English letters, but he had to admit were it not for the Mistress, he would not now have a criminal record, be branded a sexual deviant in the files of the Metropolitan Police, barred for life from most positions of grace or eminence: scarred for life he was. Oh yes, the entry of Nancy Valentine into his life had not all been roses, not by a long stalk.

'If it weren't for the Mistress I wouldn't need to carry constantly in my trouser pocket—'

The thin-faced man emitted a tiny giggle. O'Leary glanced at him anxiously but the fellow seemed in a brown study still with his feet. He nodded now in their direction as though he wished to explain and then share with O'Leary the wild comedy of bows in shoelaces.

My God, thought O'Leary, I'm talking to myself now. He began a Diary Memo on the subject, but really the anxiety about his talisman was too acute for that. He reached his hand into his trouser pocket, fidgeted maniacally till his fingers rounded on the giving contours of the pliable, knobbly orb. It was a lemon jiffy. He let his hand roost on it a while, and his face relaxed to a brooding hen's. Just by pressing, he could tell, the jiffy wasn't even half empty.

'What about children?' came a portly voice booming down the corridor.

'What about me?' came the dawdling reply.

My God, thought O'Leary, closing his eyes. And I've got to go out there.

It was true. The touch of the lemon jiffy had worked its usual tergiversant magic: reassurance, followed by excitement of the bladder. He shambled to his feet, an awkward operation for his hand was still stuffed deep inside his trouser pocket, his grip ever tighter.

The thin-faced man in the bowler hat seemed suddenly to arrive at the notion that his shoelaces were departing. 'Good day now,' he muttered to them.

'I am going to the lavatory,' explained O'Leary flatly. The two women were still hard at it down the corridor. When he opened the compartment door their opposing clamour quite jolted him backwards. He chose the opposite direction.

The lock on the lavatory door said vacant but O'Leary Montagu had matured painfully into the caprice of this world. He glanced to his watch. He would give it the usual five minutes. Precaution, he said to himself.

Mary, of course, had tried in her usual extreme and thorough way to educate him out of this affliction. 'You need help,' she had said, and locked him in a lavatory with herself for four hours. Typical of Mary.

Diary Memo: Mary never understood me. She never will.

But was it simply precaution? Many times waiting outside a vacant lavatory for the requisite five minutes, another gentleman would arrive on the stroke of four minutes, fifty-five seconds, and happily engage the room. Then, not only would O'Leary have to wait for the gentleman to leave but also allow a further five minutes for 'precaution'. Once he'd had to endure bent almost double with frustration a full hour and twenty-five minutes to use a lavatory that had been vacant nine-tenths of that time. Precaution?

Diary Memo: The allowance of five minutes to ensure a lavatory signalling vacant lives up to its promise of vacancy is not, as one might expect, a precaution. Ex contrario, *it is a consequence of Fate's almost criminal amorality. Neurosis it might be, but a scarred soul in this unordained world is but the mark of Adam.*

O'Leary Montagu stole himself a smile. An excellent memo. It executed all he had intended when first he resolved to keep a diary. Not just the daily recording of fugitive events, public, private, what have you – interesting, amusing, vital and valuable as these no doubt were: but more, much more, the endeavour to crack the ice of the world's surface, to eschew the glacial reflection of common appearance, and to plunge instead into the nether darker waters of cold reality. Precaution? Nonsense. It was neurosis. His diary said so.

And this diary of course was one of the inestimable benefits of his introduction to Nancy Valentine. God forbid, but were it not for *Ill Fares the Land*, he might still be writing the blasted, the dreaded detective novels. And instead of that latest concise, incisive mental memorandum for his diary, he would have thought:

> 'He paused outside the john. His eyes narrowed. The lock said vacant. He glanced behind. Nobody. He weighed his chances. Checked his Rolex. Give it five, he thought.'

Or worse still, he might have butterflied back to that two-week dalliance with the plays. The plays and their tortuous lack of dénouements:

> 'Stands outside LAVATORY, Stage Centre, Back. Checks WATCH. Impatiently. Paces to Right. Turns. Paces to Left. Short, quick steps. Checks WATCH again. Sighs audibly.'

And what was the use of that?

And there was more. Were it not for his first breathless devouring of the Mistress's opus – two days' growth of stubble, half-eaten sandwich forgotten on the carpet, eyes –

though sore-red with sleeplessness – expanding to baubles of amazement, excitement, exaltation! and the couch moulding itself to his contours: for thus had he first taken of *Ill Fares the Land*'s literary feast . . . Were it not for Nancy Valentine, he would not now be writing a biography of, well . . . of Nancy Valentine.

Diary Memo: Mary never understood the Mistress and me. No doubt she was jealous. 'Silly mawkish drivel,' she said once. 'Worse than a Mills and Boon.' Another time she had advanced the opinion: 'You treat that book like the Bible.' But I got her on that one. 'Tautology,' I said. 'Bible means book.' She never understood me. But she'll come back. Might take ten years or more. But Mary'll be back. Just wait and see.

'You mean that? You want me to marry the likes of that?'

'Of course not, Livia. It's a *gentleman* I want you to marry.'

They had found him palely loitering outside the vacant lavatory.

'Ah,' he began. From the looks on their faces, disparagement on the girl's, horror on the mother's, it seemed at last they had found something on which to agree. 'I'm sorry if—'

But having concurred, if only on O'Leary's unsuitability for marriage, they were happy to forget their agreement, along with O'Leary himself. They embarked on some other disputation, which seemed to involve the girl's father, her 'sainted father' as they both referred to him. O'Leary was hurt, naturally, to be discarded so promptly—

Diary Memo: Spurned once more, a cur out of the way.

On the other hand, the women were clearly in a pother. Perhaps it was safer this way. He glanced to his watch. Another three minutes and twenty-two seconds to go.

Diary Memo: Whilst training to Kilbrack, peculiar thing happened in the corridor . . .

The diary memo trailed off after a while, as O'Leary found himself increasingly caught up in this strange couple's argument. It seemed that the daughter, dressed already in canonical black, was intent on becoming a nun. The mother wanted her to marry, the daughter refused. That much was fairly straightforward. It was the manner in which they argued that captivated O'Leary. The girl leaned languidly against the mahogany casement of a window, drawing almost disdainfully on long black cigarettes. The mother, meanwhile, kept both her hands gripped to the handrail, her handbag dangling from one wrist and banging into the other, supporting her frame while she endeavoured to stamp one or the other of her feet. The daughter, Livia, spoke little and that in a kind of patient drawl. Her comments, however, indolent though they came, displayed a remarkable compass, even depth. Florence Nightingale was quoted, along with Saint Clare, Joan of Arc and Mao Tse-tung. Meanwhile, as though to confirm how knowledgeable was this daughter, the mother harangued the very timber of the train with the names of all the private convents and colleges she'd been sent to. 'Finishing school in Locarno, Livia? Of course you shall go!'

Livia then digressed on some erudite disquisition that seemed to contrast the relative attractions of gargoyles and madonnas in European art. A disquisition that was punctuated by her mother's rehearsal of all the gym slips and evening coats, indoor shoes and outdoor shoes with which she'd had to furnish her ungrateful daughter. O'Leary was quite taken by the young woman's eloquence, until after a while it came to him that she had stopped. Worse still, that the mother had stopped also. With a fateful dread he realized they had introduced him once more into their convolutions.

'Is she?' insisted the mother.

'Oh Mother,' said the daughter. 'Leave the poor thing alone.'

'No, I wish to know.' And finally she managed actually to stamp her right foot. 'Well?' she said.

O'Leary knew that he must answer this difficult woman. This time he would take no chances. 'I'm sorry?' he said. He glimpsed his watch from the corner of his eye. Only fifty seconds more.

'Is my daughter a gargoyle?' said the stout lady impatiently.

It was safest, O'Leary decided, while he tried to think of an answer that might please both of them, to keep his gaze on his watch. He had to tap the face, so incredulous was he that a second could endure so long.

'Well? Say something.'

Once more O'Leary turned to face them. His hand was already half-way down his trouser pocket, when—

Diary Memo: My God!

His hand stopped, froze like his thoughts earlier in the journey. His eyes had met Livia's. She was watching him, bemused slightly. His eyes focused. His eyes widened. He saw her.

Diary Memo: For one moment I actually saw her . . .

He recoiled. It was like glimpsing the—

Diary Memo: It was as though I had exited some forlorn Stygian cave and glimpsed for the first time the primordial radiance of the—

His eyes squeezed involuntarily shut at the sight of her. She wasn't just beautiful, she was glaringly so. Even with his eyes shut, he could still see her. He could still see her black hair loose like a gypsy's. Her midnight eyes gleamed a languid defiance, restrained only by the indolence of her slow-blinking lashes . . .

Diary Memo: Waiting outside lavatory, on train, travelling to Kilbrack, on a Wednesday, an afternoon, eight minutes and thirty-seven seconds to three o'clock, aged thirty-six, I found love . . .

And in that second's age of blinded vision he could still see the arc of her chin resting on her turned shoulder. She wore, nay hallowed, a simple cotton dress. True, it was austere and canonically black: but the merest implication of her breast underneath resexed two thousand years of conventual tradition.

Diary Memo: She appeared before me, the languid legend of Livia . . .

He did not turn to her mother. There was too much wonder in his eyes. He spoke. 'She is beautiful.'

'There!' exclaimed the stout lady. Perhaps she tried to clap her hands, O'Leary didn't know: whatever, her handbag clattered to the floor again.

Livia smiled. O'Leary felt the warmth of her gaze suffuse his being. The scars on his face, his receding hair, the suit that was frayed and crumpled: no matter. Under Livia's perfect gaze, even O'Leary felt assured. She was about to say something. He could tell by the tiny, almost ironical, quiver in her lower lip. Whatever it was, she changed her mind. She tipped a long finger of ash. It floated through sunbeams to the floor. She said to her mother, 'Though no madonna, neither am I a gargoyle.'

'If he wants to call you beautiful, let him.'

'Very well. Call me beautiful.'

'So!' exclaimed the stout lady. She'd cracked the nut. 'So

you want to be called beautiful? Well, if you want men to call you beautiful, why won't you marry one?'

'Mother, I intend to be a nun. You made me a Catholic to spite my father—'

'Your sainted father,' the mother corrected.

'And now I'm of age I intend that you pay for it.'

'Livia . . .' pleaded her mother. But it was too late. Livia had pushed open the lavatory door and disappeared inside. The bolt turned. Engaged, said the lock.

The stout lady seemed close to fainting. She tugged harder on the handrail to support herself. She shook her fallen head. 'As ye sow,' she said and sniffed. She remembered O'Leary. She raised her head, pursed her lips once more accusingly. 'As ye sow . . .'

O'Leary was staring at the engaged lock on the lavatory door. Instinctively he glanced to his watch. The second hand was just approaching four minutes and fifty-five seconds.

Back in the compartment, he pondered his predicament.

*Diary Memo: It would appear that the problem (*quaestio*) that presents itself here concerns the question (*quaestio*)—*

No, that wouldn't do. Why must he always aspire to – what was that word? He sighed. The problem was that only moments before he had fallen desperately in love with the most beautiful girl imaginable. But soon his train would be arriving at Clonmel where he must alight for the long hike to Kilbrack. Would he ever see the girl again? He knew nothing of her destination, hadn't even enquired after her surname. Was love so fresh, so young, to be thwarted so—

From down the corridor he heard them returning. The door opened, Livia leaned her head inside. 'Oh,' she said. 'You again.' But O'Leary didn't hear her, for an angel had whispered her name in his ear.

The mother tottered up behind. 'But what has a mouth-organist to do with my daughter's refusal to wed?' she wanted to know.

Livia arched her eyebrows, then closed the door after her. 'Not the mouth-organist,' O'Leary heard her drawl as they retreated further up the corridor. 'I mean Alfred Adler, the psychoanalyst.'

Diary Memo: She returned, my heart raced. She departed, the world ceased.

'They're arguing.'

O'Leary opened his eyes. It was the thin-faced man in the bowler hat who had spoken. He was still staring at his shoes, still intently, but now there was more of a quizzical bent to his mien. His face straightened. 'They are,' he confirmed. It was as though he had garnered this information not from the evidence of his ears, but from some oracular faculty native to his shoes. 'And what is more—' he glanced up, then down again to make absolutely certain '—they'll be arguing the while till they arrive at Kilbrack.'

'Kilbrack? Did you say Kilbrack? K–I–L–B– . . .'

The sudden animation in O'Leary's tone, the manner in which he jutted forward his chin, the way his eyes gleamed, and those dangerous scars on his cheeks: the thin little man retreated into the seat. He glared down at his shoes, as though accusing them, as though it was they had engineered this predicament. But in the end, with all O'Leary's persistence, he had to nod his head. 'Yes,' he confessed, for there it was written clear as day in his laces. 'Kilbrack.' And he hung his head low.

'Ah,' said O'Leary. So they travel also to Kilbrack. Ah . . .

The thin-faced man cursed his rotten cess. How he missed his pocket knife. Oh, St Brendan the Voyager, what an eejit he'd been to leave it at home that morning. Travelling all the way to Waterford and back for his weekly supply of medicaments, didn't he know he'd be naked without his knife? His stout sharp Swiss-made pocket knife, from Switzers in Grafton Street, his mother had given it him. A knife was the only way to look a man in the eyes. Without it you were naked. His mother had told him that. He felt in his jacket pocket for the hundredth time, but still no knife. Oh, St Brendan the Perilous Coracle Voyager, what an eejit had he been.

O'Leary Montagu had forgotten for the moment about his own talisman, the lemon jiffy in his pocket. So they shared his destination. No need therefore for haste. Plenty of time to plan and gauge and execute a campaign of conquest.

Diary Memo: A successful campaign of conquest.

Kilbrack. Was it happenstance? Coincidence? Or had the

tricky hand of Fate dealt him a poker hand by mistake? One thing was for certain: the Mistress had introduced into his life yet one more lapis of delight. He felt shame now that he had berated her earlier, as though it could ever have been she who'd earned him his criminal record and his reported sexual deviancy. Those couldn't be placed at Nancy Valentine's door. Those were in the hands of Fate, the tricky dealer.

'I'm sorry,' he said to *Ill Fares the Land*, lying beside him on the vacant seat.

''Tis all right,' said the thin-faced man in the bowler hat.

O'Leary remembered he wasn't alone. 'So – er – you know – em . . .'

'Ah, sure I know them well,' he replied. Perhaps if he engaged this stranger in conversation there'd be less risk of personal injury. 'They do always be arguing. The pair of them. Together. At it cat and dog. In and out. Day and night. Mother and daughter. Arguing.'

'I see.'

'Like Kilkenny cats they'll be at it. All the way to Kilbrack.'

'But they can't actually live in Kilbrack,' said O'Leary doubtfully. 'Surely?' Of course they couldn't. Kilbrack was a blighted, accursed land. He had the evidence of Nancy Valentine's memoirs to assure him of that. 'Bereft of a soul, save the souls of the dead, a shell where once stood homely grandeur . . .' It was all described so painfully in the book.

'I know the place,' owned the thin-faced man. 'A terrible whereabouts. Shocking. No place for an honest respectable gentleman. No place at all. Steer clear of Kilbrack, take my advice. Not that I would advise you of course, begging your honour's pardon.' And he tipped his bowler hat.

'But Kilbrack is precisely where I'm bound.'

'Ah,' said the thin-faced man mournfully. 'Well then.' He heaved a long breath. 'You can ride in with me so.'

CHAPTER TWO

THE DAY HAD begun with a funeral, mused O'Leary Montagu, as his head crashed once more into the threadbare upholstery of the Ford Popular: it'll likely end in one too. They were travelling at most at twenty miles an hour – though he wasn't sure: the speedometer would quiver only about the five-mile mark. The thin-faced man in the bowler hat, for all his lengthy study of his feet, seemed to have curiously poor manipulation of them. He would peer perplexedly downwards as he switched from brake to clutch to accelerator as if searching for the bass notes on a church organ. At most they were advancing at twenty miles an hour, so the violent careering and jerking, the swaying from side to side of the road, seemed on the whole unnecessary.

'Look out!'

'Yes,' replied the thin man as the van scraped past. ''Tis a grand day all right. By the Snakes of St Patrick himself.'

As funerals went, the morning's ritual had been a worthy affair. Of course, O'Leary would expect nothing less from

Mary. Mary was never a girl for half-hearted measures. It was only natural her funeral should be an expression of her inner thoroughness. Mary's parents had cried, the young priest had given a sermon of fulsome praise. At the graveside an older priest, a friend of the family, had intoned in Tridentine Latin. Bells had rung. The clods of earth had resounded on the coffin lid as the grave-diggers commenced their burial. A spotted flycatcher had chirped from a yew tree nearby. Even O'Leary had felt a tear trickle from his eye, touched by the time-honoured ritual of it all. He wasn't, of course, for one moment taken in. If Mary didn't want to see him again, that was her affair.

Diary Memo: Mary never understood me. She never will. What pains the more sadly though is that she could believe I would be taken in by so destitute a ruse. It insults one so.

There was a sudden blaring of horns from behind. The thin-faced man cursed, muttering lowly to himself, and swung the car on to the grass verge so that the open-topped Bentley could pass. And as it passed there drifted to the Popular the tail-end of an increasingly familiar conversation.

'Exactly, Livia,' came the stout lady's quavering voice. 'You're much too young for chastity.'

O'Leary strained to catch Livia's drawling reply or a glimpse of her languishing pose. He sniffed through the window—

Diary Memo: Motoring to Kilbrack, I caught the faintest whiff—

But she was gone, swallowed by the cloud of dust and exhaust that sailed in the Bentley's wake.

The thin-faced man began searching through the pedals again and they were back on the road. ''Tis not right,' he said in a mean grumble of a voice.

'I'm sorry?'

'A pharmacist would study as long as any doctor.'

'I'm sure he would.' O'Leary was too preoccupied with thoughts of Livia to bother overmuch with this abrupt change of subject. 'How much further before we reach Kilbrack?'

But the thin little man would have none of it. 'Do they think there are fewer and less strict examinations for a pharmacist, is that it? Less burning of the midnight oil, is that the root and branch of it all?'

'I'm sorry, but do you think could you concentrate a shade more on the road?'

'As if a pharmacist wouldn't need to know, tripping off his tongue, at the tips of his fingers—'

Apparently not, O'Leary answered his own question despondently.

'—the ins and outs and the intricate byways of the pharmacopoeia, Irish, English and American to boot, as well as any doctor would, I ask you?' His feet on the pedals seemed to strive for a crescendo. 'I repeat, what would a doctor know that any pharmacist worth his salt wouldn't know before him? As if a prescription would prove of any value at all if the pharmacist wasn't pre-cognizant of the properties and true significance of each and every drug prescribed. I ask you?' The feet now were skating *glissando* over the pedals. 'And the likes of them'd treat you no better than common trade!'

'I think,' moaned O'Leary, clutching his stomach, 'I'm going to be sick.'

At the best of times O'Leary disliked travelling by car. It was on account of the accident eleven years ago. Now, though he didn't actually vomit, he retched, spitting bile and spittle on to the grass verge. And all the while the thin-faced pharmacist stood over him expounding how in France and other continental countries of a civilization at least as old if not older than their own Anglo-Celtic variety a patient afflicted with an illness, minor or major, be that as it may, would welcome the advice of a pharmacist, and not spurn him and ignore him on every given occasion, social and professional, what have you.

'Could I have some water?' asked O'Leary plaintively.

'The likes of them'd want a doctor's prescription before they'd take any water from me,' the pharmacist retorted. 'And that's no lie.' Stepping back into the car, he added in a more conciliatory tone, '"Tis only a short hop now to Kilbrack itself. You can drink your fill there.'

He started the engine and they continued onwards, the thin man's feet pedalling a dilatory fugue, himself unfolding his crusade for social recognition for the common pharmacist; O'Leary bumping his head this way and that on the upholstery. Attempting to forget or at least to ignore the vicissitudes of his travels, he gazed out the grimy window, concentrated on the passing scenery.

'And returning home that evening,' the words of the Mistress came back to him, a passage from the book, 'an evening leaf-late in August, an August of rustling russet, I halted by a thorn tree for the catching of my breath. The sun through the treetops was leprechaun's gold. That evening I believed in miracles . . .'

So beautiful, thought O'Leary. Perhaps it was this very road the Mistress had taken. He glanced behind through the rear window of the Popular. Below them was the Suir Valley and disappearing into the distance the chimneys of Clonmel. They passed a thorn bush, the sun through its braches like leprechaun's gold. How beautiful. If only I could believe in miracles.

Everything was as he knew it should be, everything in its place, all was as he had pictured. Past that bend, over that ridge, and they would be descending into the valley of the Brack, with Kilbrack itself close against its bank. So intimate was he with the Mistress's memoirs, that this land was as familiar to O'Leary as the scratches of fate on his own palm.

It was a strange book, mystical and melancholy. It told of an idyllic childhood in the big house, Knight's Kilbrack. How the young Nancy Valentine grew up to womanhood, and was set fair for a contented life, happy amongst her kith and kin, holding her rightful place, when – well, when disaster struck. The exact nature of this disaster was never explained, or at least O'Leary, though he pored over the text, could never quite grasp its cause. It seemed that daughter and father fell out, and the young girl was forced to quit her beloved home.

Many years pass, and many wanderings, until the daughter, Nancy Valentine, inevitably returns. The scene that greets her ''twould rend an honest man's heart'. Where once rose the grandeur of Knight's Kilbrack, now a broken shell points stark to the twilight. Ragwort crowds the fields. Dank weeds and nettles cloak what once were the homes of friends. And wandering through this desolation, the Mistress might touch upon some cracked though fashioned stone: in an instant she is transported to happy nights by the fire at Nellie Maguire's pub, or to family prayers at the Cuthberts' Rectory, or to a night-long ceilidh in Bridie O'Toole's cottage that she shared with her brother Jim, or to old Downey weeping at the bedside of his dying mother. Until the sting of a nettle or the prick from a thorn reminds the Mistress inexorably of their passing. The village is no more. Her friends all are dead or departed. Ghosts alone stalk the lanes.

And then, amidst this ruination, in the final and most heart-rending portion of the book, the Mistress glimpses a wizened and blind old man, bent upon a stick. She asks what news, and the old man tells his tale. Without a seed, the house had failed; without the house, the village was dead. 'And d'ye know for why?' demands the blind and wizened man, raging with his sorrow. 'For love was forced to quit her home.' At that very moment Nancy Valentine recognizes the veteran for her own father, who had exiled her so many years before. But the father has grown wild and demented with the years. The daughter's heart is human, it softens with regret and forgiveness. She seeks to kiss her father, to speak him good cheer, but too late, the old man dies at her feet.

Whereupon, Nancy Valentine turns her back to the shell of her childhood, her mien to the hard world beyond, and she vows nevermore to return to that 'ill-fared land' . . .

The tears had come once more. He wasn't crying, he was sure. It was closer to weeping, the soft tears concurring with the damp still of the air. He sniffed, patted the book in his jacket pocket. 'So sad,' he said.

'No call for remorse,' the pharmacist replied, matter-of-factly.

'I'm sorry?'

'They got what was coming to them.'

O'Leary eyed him queerly.

'O'Driscoll, J. A., MD, of Glenville, County Cork,' the man intoned. 'Drunk in attendance, violation of Hippocratic oath; *Cork Examiner*, 14/7/1968, Page 3, Column 2.' It appeared he was engrossed in a long recitation of all the doctors he had read of who'd been struck off for malpractice. 'Kenny, Patrick Joseph, MD, Cork Road Estate, Waterford, in the county of that name . . .'

O'Leary let him drone on. He decided it was time he worried about Livia. What could she be doing, so beautiful a young lady, travelling to the desolation that was Kilbrack? He did not know. He tried now to picture her in his mind, but strangely he could conjure no memory. The words he had used to describe her – languid, languishing, beautiful – these he remembered exactly. But the images that these words should convey escaped him entirely. He felt like an old man trying to catch a spring breeze. Worse, the more he concentrated, the more clearly came to mind the contrary picture of Mary. It was intolerable.

Diary Memo: Refuse to contemplate Mary.

Besides, it was her funeral. If Mary didn't want to know him, it was her funeral. And it was all so symptomatically thorough of her. Ever since she had nursed him in hospital, eleven years ago that was, after the accident, always her insufferable thoroughness. And even when the hospital had run out of patience with him, had discharged him, impossibly incurable, they had said; no, that wouldn't do Mary – oh no – move in with me, I'll see you won't suffer. And for ten years he had suffered patiently her insufferable thoroughness.

Until two weeks ago.

Diary Memo: It was all of two weeks ago. It was evening. I had just remarked to Mary upon an engaging resonance I'd felt in bed that morning whilst reading Ill Fares the Land, *as was my custom. Had the Mistress read Thoreau's* Walden, *I asked myself. Each certainly echoed the other's sentiments. I believe at the time Mary was ironing, or performing some such household chore. She had finished work at the hospital. The evening meal was cooking. Lamb, if my memory serves me. 'Mary,' I said, 'it occurred to me this morning that Nancy Valentine might have been influenced by Thoreau – chronologically it could hardly be vice versa – in particular by* Walden, *Thoreau's noted description of a self-sufficient life in the woods.' I waited, expectant of response. Calmly, Mary put down the iron, untied her pinafore, folded it: then dropped it delicately to the floor. 'I'm leaving,' she said.*

And she had meant it.

Diary Memo: I followed Mary into the hall. 'Mary?' I said. 'I am going home,' she said. 'I am going home to Ireland, to my parents in Dublin, and I am leaving you for good. I hope I shall never see or hear of you again.' All this she delivered in a calm, collected voice. I responded in like. 'Why, Mary, have I incommoded you?' 'O'Leary Montagu,' she replied, 'I have known you for eleven years, the last ten of which you have slept in my bed. You know what they call me at work? The Virgin Mary, that's what they call me. I have been nurse, maid, and nursemaid to you. Frankly, I'm bored.' 'Writers bore you?' I enquired. 'O'Leary, you're not a writer. You're a neurotic.'

Yes, she had called him a neurotic. She of the extreme thoroughness, she of the insufferable assiduity, she who had invented her own funeral even. Her audacity bore no thinking.

Diary Memo: I waited by the front door while she packed a bag. 'So, you think me neurotic?' I enquired. 'You've never written a word,' she said. 'You just talk about writing. You don't write: you think writing. Show me one word you've ever written. You can't, can you? Of course you can't. Remember the detective novels? They were bad enough. For the last six years it's been Nancy Valentine this, Nancy Valentine that: if Nancy Valentine farted we'd get a four-minute warning. You're a neurotic. You just talk. And I'm bored with your talk. I'm sick of it. You've driven me to drink.' She shook the empty gin bottle. 'I'm neurotic myself to put up with you. And I'm sick to death of that bloody woman's ridiculous memoirs. Goodbye.'

And she had meant it. And it was typical of her thoroughness to go to such extremes. Her parents had connived with her, dredged up some doddery old priest, friend of the family, he'd dragged in some curate friend of his, probably owed him a favour, and yes, O'Leary had gone along with it, the charade, the impoverished ruse – if that was the way Mary wanted it, he'd play along, of course he would, no ghost at the banquet he. And when he'd got the telegram, he'd crossed over on the night boat, he'd landed in Dun Leary, he'd dressed all in black, black tie, black shoes, and he had promptly gone along to her funeral.

'Pathetic,' he said.

'And there's worse,' agreed the pharmacist. 'Two medical students from University College, Dublin, caught soliciting young women, improperly motivated, the worse for drink, in FitzWilliam Square, Dublin, *Evening Herald*, 23/4/1971, I ask you.'

They had climbed the far ridge. Unfolded now below them was the valley of the River Brack. Soon they would glimpse Kilbrack itself. The Ford Popular groaned at the summit of the ridge, hesitated a moment, and then, like an old mare sniffing hay in its stable, it bolted down the mountain slope.

Nancy Valentine believed in miracles, but O'Leary Montagu knew only of Fate. Tricky-handed Fate, he called it. You would be crossing a road. It was night. A car would come, a great black car, hit and run you down. You'd wake a fortnight later to a new world: a new name, a new life.

Tricky-handed Fate, O'Leary called it. And he distrusted it like a dog in a rabid country.

And what might Fate have in store for him in Kilbrack? The tricky hand had been busy enough that day and no mistake.

'Poynings, Hannibal,' said the pharmacist, 'sail-boarding in surgery. *Aran Isles Gazette . . .*'

Diary Memo: It was while mourning beneath the yew tree, the grave-diggers' slow spadefuls of earth resounding hollowly on the coffin lid, an ear half-cocked to a flycatcher's chirping, that the notion befell me.

'Sail-boarding in surgery hours, I mean,' the pharmacist corrected himself.

He had no money, or more accurately, no income. He could hardly expect Mary to continue supporting him from 'the other side' – as she would put it. That wouldn't be playing her game. Her apartment in London was on the market. Her father had told him: 'Good morning, Mr O'Leary Montagu. You will not be surprised to hear I am the only beneficiary of my daughter's will.' An immediate sale was expected. It was yet another indication of Mary's impossible thoroughness.

Quo vadis now, he had asked himself.

And of course, once more the Mistress had come to his aid. He had the volume of memoirs with him. He had plenty of paper – O'Leary never ventured far without a small stationers' supply of foolscap blocks. He had only one change of clothing with him, money enough for one week only – maybe two at a pinch; but at least he had a half-full lemon jiffy in his pocket. Fate, he thought; and why not?

He hadn't waited to bid farewells to Mary's parents – they had, besides, proved none too pleased with the ease with which he had seen through their charade – he hadn't even waited for the old priest to finish his intonations: he dashed out of the graveyard, caught the first suitable train south. At long last he was about to achieve the goal of all his labours: the biography of Nancy Valentine had begun.

'So,' he said now, while the pharmacist took a break from his recitation. 'You know Kilbrack well, do you?'

'Know it?' replied the pharmacist. 'Sure, I was born there.'

O'Leary eyed the man with a new respect. 'In Kilbrack?'

'I buried my mother there, sure.'

'Ah,' said O'Leary. He understood now the man's journey. One more grave in a land of graves. 'You're visiting the cemetery.'

'Cemetery? Not at all. I live there sure.'

'But you can't. Nobody lives in Kilbrack. The place is dead.'

The pharmacist eyed him warily. By St Fiacre, patron saint of taxis, why didn't he have his Swiss-made pocket knife with him? He'd end up cut to pieces one of these days, his blood red on the green grass of the verge. That verge there, he thought: my blood and all. By St Fiacre.

And yet, what else was he to do? Whoever heard of a stranger coming to Kilbrack? No man in his right mind would visit Kilbrack, given any say in the matter. What was he up to, so? On some business or other. Oh, he'd been right all along to keep his eye on this queer one. His mother had told him that. 'Keep your eye on strangers, JD. They carry disease and never mean you good.' Good, sound advice, but his mother was famed for that, famed throughout the barony. What could the man be up to?

O'Leary Montagu, for his part, was racing through his mind. Characters from the book swam before him. There was the old man in the big house, Nellie Maguire in her pub, Bridie O'Toole, stout Mrs Cuthbert – 'Stout?' he cried aloud – and Livia, her daughter – 'My God, Livia!' – and thin old Downey, with his undying love for his dying mother, sporting always his bowler hat—

'What's your name?' he demanded of the man beside him, as the Popular drew up outside a closed pharmacy. J. D. DOWNEY, MPSI, the sign outside read. DISPENSER OF MEDICAMENTS AND ADVICE, with 'ADVICE' underlined three times.

O'Leary nearly fainted. The village was supposed to be a ruin, the people dead or departed. It was in the book.

But Downey was unaware of the cause of O'Leary's torment. He was thinking what a queer explosive character he had in the seat beside him. Why, back in Clonmel at the railway station toilet, he'd gone up to the urinal to relieve himself and there was this man with the scars all over his face. And no sooner had Downey approached than this fellow had reached into his pocket and attempted secretly to squirt a lemon jiffy into the urinal, missing the porcelain but soaking Downey's feet in lemon juice. To boot. By St Rock the Healer, whose feast day it was, he was a queer customer altogether.

CHAPTER THREE

O'LEARY MONTAGU PEERED into the gloom in the corner. Faintly he could make out a vast mass of a giant of a person. He could feel the gaze, intense and suspicious, like a ray of cold moonlight, staying him.

My God, he thought.

But as his eyes grew accustomed to the gloaming in the pub, the giant, like an amoeba, dissolved into just a little old lady with a mistrustful face and a little old man nodding off beside her.

'Bridie,' he said falteringly. 'Bridie O'Toole. And Jim.' It was like greeting old friends. Except these were supposed, long ago, to have died. The woman was watching him. Her gaze was – a touch – discomfiting still. Why wouldn't she blink? 'Hello?' he ventured.

Now she blinked. Her lips trembled apart and her voice came lowly and slowly, closely as fell her gaze. 'I suppose and you've come to purchase the place,' she said.

'I'm sorry?'

'Never mind that. You've come to purchase the place. Say now, or roast for ever in hell.'

O'Leary glanced tremulously about him. There was only one thing he could think to say. 'I'm sorry?' he repeated.

'And so you should be. The TV. The gambling machinery. The rock and the roll machinery. The devil's contraptions, the load of them. We'll have none of that in Kilbrack. I'll tell you that for nothing.'

She spoke almost spitting out her words. And indeed spittle did follow upon her every sentence. It dribbled down her chin, thin rivulets of it, down on to the table. He could see her more clearly now. She had wiry grey hair which darted out, thin strands of it, in odd directions, as though electrified, or petrified, or – O'Leary wondered did he even dare think it? – unwashed. Her eyes too seemed electric, green and steadfast—

Diary Memo: Goring me.

A door opened behind him, and a woman in dressing gown, curlers and cigarette smoke shuffled in behind the bar. 'Customer,' she said flatly.

It was Nellie Maguire. Again O'Leary had the unsettling sensation of greeting a long lost friend. 'Nellie Maguire's place, open all hours . . .' Open still, he thought.

Diary Memo: On entering Nellie Maguire's, was confronted by unsettling resonances. These are no ghosts. This is no ruin. Could it be in all these years, I have misunderstood, misinterpreted, the Mistress's text? Could it truly be—

But he hadn't time to finish, because Bridie, slicing the air with her tongue, announced. 'He's here buying the pub.'

'Well,' said Nellie. She stubbed out her cigarette. 'Not before time.' She retrieved her butt, lit another cigarette from its embers, pulled half-heartedly. 'I was beginning to doubt if anyone read the classifieds any more.' She eyed him distantly, her eyes – too heavy to glance – rested on his hand-grip. ''Twould appear you mean business anyhow. If you'd sent to inform me, I'd have made the effort.'

O'Leary rallied his wits. 'No, I'm afraid I rather believe—'

''Tis too late now, worrying your head,' said Nellie resignedly. 'What you see is what you get. G-and-T?' She reached for a glass. Then she sighed. 'Whiskey do you?'

O'Leary glanced at the optics. The gin was empty. Not only that but wisps of ancient cobwebs trailed from it. 'Er – water,' he said.

Nellie sighed. 'No money at all?' She lit a new cigarette from the butt of her old one.

'About—' O'Leary counted the cost of his train journey '—eighteen pounds and a penny.'

She stubbed out her old cigarette in a handy saucer. ''Twas too good to be true. Should've known, so I should.' She slumped down on the bed.

She had shown him around the private quarters of the pub, indicating in an offhand way the kitchen – 'a small scrub'd see it grand' – the sitting room – 'small point dusting now' – and her bedroom – 'You'll excuse the mess,' dismissing with a wave the riot of pink, white and sky blue petticoats. 'They must belong to someone. Can't think who.' And now they had come to the guest's, the spare, bedroom.

And it was only here now in the guest's bedroom that O'Leary had managed to impress upon the woman his impoverished circumstances. 'Not that it isn't a fine proposition,' he assured her.

'It is?' she enquired, doubtfully.

'But I'm afraid I'm rather down on my uppers.'

Nellie Maguire sighed again.

Diary Memo: Old now, but she was beautiful once. Oh yes, you can see, she was beautiful in her day.

'Trust Bridie O'Toole to tease out the wrong end of the stickeen.'

'She does appear rather rash,' O'Leary agreed.

''Tis beyond me, the worry of the place.' She looked about abstractedly for the saucer, couldn't find it, tipped her ash on to the linoleum. ''Tis too much for a woman alone. And I never married. I never did.' A smile of resignation crossed her face, as though she were talking about her bad luck with the pools. 'Though not for the want of offers. I'll tell you that for free. I was a fine-looking girl once upon a time.'

'I believe you.'

'I used be pretty. Men? Had them queuing up, so I did. But there was only the one man for me. I saved myself too long. And he married away. Why am I telling you this?' She shrugged. 'What harm. Men? They'd queue up for me. You mightn't believe it now, but I used be pretty once upon a time.'

'Oh, I do believe you.' And wasn't there a passage

somewhere in *Ill Fares the Land* that recalled her youthful charms? Now, such sadness in her eyes, such weariness in her voice: what desperate tragedy must have befallen her to furnish so desolate a soul? And all slumped lowly on the bed. 'You were a fine good-looking young lady,' he avowed.

She smiled weakly. 'The way you talk, you'd swear you were here yourself.'

'In a way, I feel I was.'

Nice man, she thought. Shame about the face. Such ugly scars. Medusa would faint at the sight of him.

'Though no madonna, neither am I a gargoyle.' Thus had Livia appraised her looks. And O'Leary, watching himself now in the mirror in the guest's bedroom, owned that the description could well sum up his own looks. The languid legend of Livia of course, in her modest way, had been prevaricating. She was beauty absolute. But his own features, he confessed, could well be considered to epitomize restraint.

Except of course for his scars.

Diary Memo: Perhaps the scars are a shade too long, a shade too wide, a shade too – well – there, for one ever to be truly distingué . . .

They would never heal. Even the surgeons had admitted that. They would never close up, heal, disappear. He'd never look like a soldier of brave and distinguished service, a valiant duellist, never play the ardent – if unfortunate –

sportsman, a thin line on his cheek evoking gallantry. He'd always look like he'd just stepped away from a car accident, a particularly gory hit-and-run affair. Life is so undemocratic, he thought.

He pulled himself together. I am thirty-six years old, he chided himself. Still in my prime. I'm not small. I'm not fat. My hair is still mostly black, and it recedes almost imperceptibly. I have an intelligence unrivalled in my experience. I'm in love with an intellectual and beautiful girl. Her mother wishes her to marry. I have my mission to accomplish, my biography to write. What more could a man want?

'A room,' he answered thinly, 'and some money coming in . . .'

He heard scuffing feet approaching from the hall outside, and Nellie Maguire, still in her slippers, dressing gown and curlers, still with a cigarette lagging on her lips, shuffled back into the room.

'Well, I've had a look at the books below. There's not much going in the way of wages. I'll say that outright. Though God knows, I could do with the small help. You'd sleep here?'

O'Leary had leapt to attention on her return. He nodded his head eagerly now. 'A bed and a blanket is the most I need.'

'I suppose I could stretch to a few shillings the odd weekend.' She sat down on the bed.

O'Leary wished he could slump down on the bed too. He was quite overcome with excitement. He'd never had a job before. Hitherto, it had never occurred to him to enquire after one even. He felt quite proud.

Diary Memo: That'll show Mary.

'I'm so tired,' Nellie muttered to herself. 'I don't know.' She heaved in enough breath to enquire, 'Could you start today?'

'Immediately.'

'I've given them a drink downstairs. Should keep them going. You could look in after an hour or so. They'll shout if they want anything. We're never busy. Trade – we're never what you might call brisk.' She was leaving. She stopped. 'And you're sure you can cope?'

He'd been in bars before. Of course he could cope. 'I assure you, Miss Maguire, you shall regret nothing of your decision, I can assure you.'

She didn't look terribly reassured, but she said, 'Very well. I must lie down. The days grow longer with the years.' And she shambled out into the hall. O'Leary waited till he heard her bedroom door close.

Diary Memo: Cognizant of Fate and its tricky manner of dealing, nevertheless I feel entitled . . .

And while his diary memo trundled on ponderously so, the smile that slunk across the scarred terrain of his cheeks said simply, Jackpot!

Thin-faced Downey sat down at his counter. He switched on the bare bulb above, took out from his pocket the brown paper package. He was about to unwrap it when he hesitated, glanced to the door. Had he locked it? He was sure he had. He started to unwrap the package. Or had he? He got up from the counter, tip-toed to the street door, tried the handle. It was locked and bolted. Of course he had locked it. He had known all along.

He didn't fear intruders – didn't he have his stout Swiss-made pocket knife on the bench in front of him, hurriedly retrieved from his other jacket? It was just that the business of the brown paper package was a difficult and intricate affair. The division into dosages required the whole of his professional attention.

He unwrapped the package, carefully. The powder was likely to blow anywhere, all over the shop, so refined was it, no more than dust really. He prised open his pocket knife and began cutting the powder into the recommended number of dosages.

It was altogether an unusual affair, he had to admit. And he was never quite sure if he had the right end of the stick at all. The medicine was rare, no doubt about that. So exceptional, so expensive was the medicine, that the customary outlets for pharmaceutical supplies had ignored it altogether. He had to go to extraordinary lengths for its procuration.

Downey winced his nose slightly. To tell the truth – a thing which J. D. Downey often did. He was mindful of that, ask any soul in Kilbrack. His mother had warned him to be. Notwithstanding that, however, tell the truth, he never felt entirely at home in those places, pharmaceutical outlets, no matter whether he could get the special medicament there or not. He didn't know what it was. Silly really, but he never seemed to have the right card on him, that was all, the correct identification.

He looked up at the portrait of his mother on the wall. She was surrounded by saints. 'Or the right Latin,' he said sorrowfully to himself.

Anyway, when the lady had first come to him and described the properties of this wondrous medicament, he had been astounded. Why had he never heard of it before? 'Doctors won't prescribe it,' she had told him. And apparently, the truth of it was – according to what she had told him anyway – that so wondrous were the cures worked by this medicine, that were doctors to prescribe it, they'd be out of business within the week. Lock, stock and barrel. It was a conspiracy of silence, a cartel of mean-mouthed self-preservers, living off the backs of the sick and the dying. Oh, St Rock the Healer, how – 'Typical!' he said aloud. For Downey knew his doctors, knew them well. And the money-grabbing, self-preserving gombeen men that they were.

'I could have been a doctor myself anyway,' he muttered, eyeing keenly the blade of his knife. 'What all the fuss is about I don't know. Any gossoon with breeches on could make a doctor. Bloody la-di-das. They treat you worse than common trade, so they do.'

He looked down at the open package and the powder neatly divided, as if wondering who had put it there. 'Anyway,' he muttered, and continued on with his dosages.

She had known where to procure it. Expensive and rare

though it was, she had known one place in Ireland, one man in all the four green fields who might have a supply. And so, every Wednesday Downey made the journey by train to Waterford. In a dowdy pub by the docks he handed over the envelope she would give him and in exchange the foreign-looking gentleman with the funny accent would give him the brown paper package.

And how it did work! Wednesday evening, she'd walk in here all down and out, and she'd leave with the skip of a ten-year-old.

'Bloody doctors,' muttered Downey. 'Denying the populace their just medicament. By the hokey! By the Tongs of St Dunstan himself!'

He had finished cutting the powder. Each dosage he scraped into a little paper envelope, rather like a Beecham's Powder, and stacked the envelopes in four neat piles, twenty all together.

'I'd have made a good doctor too,' he said. 'If only I'd scraped the Latin highers.'

There was a knock on the street door. 'Who's there?' he called.

''Tis only me.'

'Where is he now then?' asked Bridie coldly. She'd hardly moved a muscle in her seat since the lanky-legged stranger had entered the pub nearly two hours before. Even when she spoke, her lips only trembled.

'Who?' said Jim beside her. She had nudged him, waking him on his thirty-ninth wink.

'She's gone out, and he's upstairs,' said Bridie.

'Aye,' agreed Jim.

'What's he want coming here?'

'Who?'

'If it's not buying the place he's at, what's he at at all, I want to know.'

'Well,' said Jim.

'Lanky streaky fellow all dressed in black, is he a guard or what is he?'

Jim shook his head gravely.

'An insurance investigator, a taxman inspecting fiddles on returns, a gauger come to see about optics and the right measurements, a Customs man on the track of bad liquor, which is he? Nothing good and that's for sure.'

Jim nodded his head, then shook it, then nodded again. It was a mystery.

'And there's more. What was in the bag he fetched upstairs? Nothing heavy and the way he could lift it. And I'll tell you something for worse. There was a book in his pocket.'

'A book?' This was serious.

'Sticking out. I saw it. Clear as day. A book.'

Jim poured the dregs of his pint bottle of stout into his glass.

'And the way he knew our names. Bridie, he called me. Bridie O'Toole.'

'Bridie?' repeated Jim.

'And Jim he called you.'

'Jim?' – as though he was grateful to be reminded of his name.

'He's done his homework true enough.' What else might he know? Rotten cess on the man, troubling her at her age. Hadn't she enough on her plate as it was? She sipped her whiskey. 'Whatever his profession,' she continued, ''tis a dangerous calling and the scars on his face and I'll tell you something more—'

But she didn't tell anything more because outside she heard footsteps approaching; and with a nudge to Jim, she fell stiffly silent. The door opened. Nellie Maguire breezed in.

'Well,' she said nodding, and rubbed her hands together. 'Well.'

'He's upstairs still,' said Bridie.

'Well,' said Nellie brightly and sniffed a loud crescendo up her nose. She'd forgotten she had a guest.

Upstairs in his new room, O'Leary Montagu lay on his bed, his hand worrying the jiffy in his trouser pocket. It seemed unfair somehow that after all those years of study, of preparation and perspiration, with all the vicissitudes of his life and of Fate, after all this, that he should journey finally to Kilbrack to commence his great work, the biography of Nancy Valentine—

> *Diary Memo: Not a biography merely, but a detailed semantic and semiotic analysis of the Mistress's style, an exegesis, an eisegesis too, of her work—*

Yes, he knew all that. It just seemed unfortunate that he

should arrive here and discover that he had misunderstood all along the very meaning of her words.

Fate, he said resignedly to himself. The tricky dealer.

At first glance – or rather, upon the thousandth and twenty-third reading even – he had thought the Mistress was describing a world that was no more, a deserted village, bereft of human breath. But how wrong could a man be? It was obvious to him now – how could he have been so illiterately naive? – the true intention of her pen was to convey something, a resonance, a notion, whatever, altogether different. It was so obvious.

Diary Memo: Scilicet!

What that different notion, resonance, something actually was, he feared he didn't yet know. It would require another reading, the thousandth and twenty-fourth. But he wasn't down-hearted.

Diary Memo: Ex contrario. *My visit to Kilbrack has proved already within three meagre hours of greater fruitfulness than ever I had dared to hope.*

For the evidence of his eyes gave him not only the opportunity – he always had that – but actually the encouragement to reread the book again and yet again, to sit once more at its banquet, savour yet again the Mistress's darling prose: and all with new eyes, new ears, a fresh tongue, a newborn sensibility. Oh, lucky man, he thought.

Diary Memo: Annus mirabilis!

He would have leaped off his bed immediately and grabbed for the book, devoured page one in an instant, so eager was he to begin: except a new thought suddenly struck him.

My God, he thought. If all these people, Bridie and Downey and Nellie Maguire, yet live and abide in Kilbrack—

His heart was racing, his eyes aglow. He struggled to capture his cascading thoughts in a diary memo:

Diary Memo: What if—

But the notion was too exciting, too outlandish, for pedestrian concision. He rode a waterfall, not traversed a bridge. What if . . . the Mistress herself yet lived, breathed still to this very day in Kilbrack! My God! thought O'Leary Montagu.

'My God,' he said aloud, and jolting upright, snatched his hand from his pocket. Lying on his bed, tossing and turning his way through his literary dilemmas, he had chanced to look up at the door. And there in the doorway observing him, her gaze fixed on his hand fumbling his groin, stood Nellie Maguire.

Her eyebrows were arched. There was no hint of reproof, however, in her voice. 'I see you're making yourself at home,' she said.

'Yes, yes,' O'Leary jabbered. She thought I was – she thought I was – God knows what she thinks of me.

Stranger than I imagined, Nellie was thinking. Poor man,

with a face like that, no wonder he's only his own whirlygigs to play with.

'I was wondering was there a grocery about?' he asked quickly.

'Grocery?'

'In case I should run out of jiffies. See?' He managed to withdraw the jiffy from his pocket. He held it aloft almost triumphantly. 'I usually keep one handy.' My God, he kept saying to himself.

'The place is on its last legs, grocery-wise,' she said cheerily.

'Last legs?'

'There's no grocery in Kilbrack. Not since Downey's mother died.' Her head nodded in the direction of the pharmacy. 'Tell the truth, I'm only staggered to have a guest. Nobody comes here to Kilbrack these days. Guest-wise, that is.'

'But, Miss Maguire, I'm not a—'

She flapped a hand. ''Tis a ghost town, Kilbrack.' She smiled happily, content with the world and its ways. And sniffed.

My God, thought O'Leary again. He blinked. With the shock of her coming, he hadn't noticed. But looking now, he saw a miracle. It was a woman transformed. Her cheeks were rosy, a light shone in her eyes, no longer careless, but carefree. Her hair hung in loose golden curls around her shoulders. And she had dressed in – of all things – a catsuit. A florid pink and blue catsuit with a shiny scarlet belt about her waist. It was a woman transformed. For a moment he doubted it was the same person at all. But yes, it was Nellie Maguire all right. Except two hours ago she had shuffled a beldam of sixty winters. Now she couldn't be one second beyond thirty – thirty years young, frisky and alert, impatient. 'You must have been tired,' he said.

'Tired?'

'That rest has worked wonders.'

What's he blethering on about, she wondered. Her eyes trailed over the shelf, the table. Three leather-bound diaries, she counted; six blocks of foolscap, seven reporter's notebooks. On the table stood three bottles of ink, blue, black and red, a fountain pen, pencil and rubber, and in the centre, in pride of place, a cloth-bound book. She gave him an artful smile. 'You're a writer, are you?'

'Why, yes,' he said, pleased. 'How did you know?'

She winked craftily. 'If 'tis incognito you want, 'tis incognito you'll get. A little R and R from the traffic of the world. I know how you feel. That's the way we are here, guest-wise. Mum's the word.' And tipping her nose with a finger, she left the room. 'By the way,' she called cheerily before her door closed behind her, 'I'm off spring-cleaning my bedroom. But should you feel at all thirsty, help yourself at the bar. We don't stand on ceremony here. Bridie or Jim'll show you where. Truth be told, I'm not used to paying-guests at all.'

'But Miss Maguire, I'm not a paying-guest. I'm your new barman.'

But Miss Maguire had gone.

O'Leary Montagu replaced the lemon jiffy in his pocket, fiddled with it ponderously. What odd behaviour. And what a transformation in the woman. Everything about this village seemed odd to him, improbable almost. He contemplated a moment longer, then snatched his hand from his pocket.

And what a thorough curse was the tergiversance of common lemon jiffies, he thought, as he made his usual five-minute dash for the lavatory.

When Downey had dropped him outside the pharmacy, three hours before, he had taken a fitful tour of Kilbrack. The village was a clump really of three or four dwellings, pressed together where the road – little more than a lane – forded the River Brack. The buildings looked old, time-worn, but they were still habitable. Weeds grew in cracks in the masonry, paint peeled. But at least there was masonry, at least a memory of paint. The only recent construction was the Catholic chapel in a field off the road. Rain had stained its bare concrete walls, so that it had taken on an appearance of disregard, equal to the abandoned Anglican church on the other side of the lane which truly was in ruins.

Through all this – quietude, O'Leary judged was the word – the River Brack flowed quietly on. Unparticular ducks gathered at the ford, but as O'Leary had no bread, they soon disregarded him. As far as the eye could see, feathery trees, alders and willows, marked the river's course. The scene seemed idyllic. He was surrounded by pastures, lush with the long green grass of Ireland. True, there were weeds, and few cattle grazed: but the fields were hardly crowded with ragwort, as the Mistress had told.

And yet, though the village certainly wasn't dead, still there was an air of despondency about it. As though it was uncared for, unkempt, like a widow's hair when she's grown too introspective. Dulled by the river's flow, O'Leary had felt something of this desolation in his own heart. A magpie had landed on the grass. One for sorrow, he thought. And O'Leary had waited as he always did, wondering how long must he delay till the mate would alight, bringing joy.

CHAPTER FOUR

STOUT MRS CUTHBERT dried her eyes, then took the pot off the stove.

'Really Mother,' said Livia. 'You mustn't take everything so seriously.'

'I educated you,' she said. 'And God knows, for all the gratitude I get . . .' The pot was too heavy to carry in one go from stove to table. She rested it on the draining board, caught her breath.

'No Mother,' said her daughter reasonably, 'you badgered my father—'

'Your sainted father.'

'—into paying for my education.'

'And God knows, I paid for it then and I'm paying for it now.' With a heave she lifted the pot on to the kitchen table.

Livia poured the wine. She sniffed at it, pleased. She had chosen a Rioja, robust enough to defeat the worst of her mother's cooking. She tested the temperature of the bottle. Timed to perfection.

Mrs Cuthbert doled out the stew. Livia blenched. Cabbage, she wondered. Kippers?

'I never thought your education would lead to this. What was it all for?'

'An interesting speculation,' agreed Livia, eyeing the stew disinterestedly. Rabbit?

'I don't know what it's led to with you. Flying off to a convent. If I'd any sense I should have left you there.'

'Wine, Mother?'

Mrs Cuthbert waved the bottle away. 'And you talk of being a nun. You wouldn't last five minutes in a convent.'

'You seem to forget, Mother, that at the age of ten, when my father was dying, and to prove to Father Michael the sincerity of your intention – viz. apostasy from the Anglican and baptism into the Roman faith – you whisked me away from my happy school in England, deposited me in a convent in Wicklow. And all by post. I dreaded the morning's delivery. Where next, I would ask myself. What if she went Buddhist?'

'You're not eating,' said Mrs Cuthbert.

'What is it?'

'Stew.'

'And so, Mother, after eight years in Wicklow, it is precisely in a convent that I feel most at home.'

'I sent you to Locarno too.'

'To a Catholic institution. Where, I might add, the tastes though certainly Roman were more catholic than RC. You really should try this wine.'

'Do you realize I spent all day yesterday, all this morning

too, on the telephone to every convent in Ireland, asking for you? I felt a fool.'

'I did tell you I was going to a convent, Mother.'

'Am I supposed to believe that?'

'It's the normal practice.'

'Daughters going to convents?'

'Mothers believing daughters.'

'Believe you me, if I hadn't found you, if I hadn't hurried all the way to Waterford, dragged you back here, to your home where you belong, you'd regret it. You'd regret it for the rest of your days.'

'You didn't drag me, Mother.'

'And you'd blame me. Who would you blame? Your Father Confessor at convent? Sister Cecilia? Ms Lacoste in Locarno with her pince-nez and her red stockings? No: I'm the goose would get the blame.'

Livia poured herself another glass. 'I was coming back today anyway. I only went to Waterford to enquire if they had any vacancies. As it happens, I was out of luck. But there are plenty more convents. Nunneries, abbeys, *béguinages*.' She sipped the Rioja. 'The world is filled with opportunity.'

Mrs Cuthbert stood up stoutly. 'I can see, Livia,' she said, 'that it's time I put my foot down.' She tried, as usual, to stamp her foot. But having stood up, this necessitated her putting all her weight on one leg. And with her legs wedged between table and chair, it was an operation beyond her balance. She looked puzzled at her feet for a moment. Then sat down and stamped. She stood up again, opened her mouth. But she had forgotten what she was going to say.

She sat down, defeated. 'Why you just can't get married, Livia, I don't know.'

The grandmother clock in the far corner of the pub struck eight. O'Leary Montagu looked up from the bar. How time passes when you're working, he thought.

He had seven glasses of stout in various stages of fullness on the counter. Now he added an eighth. It was better. Not quite right, but definitely his efforts were at least beginning to look like stout. He began on a ninth.

'Lights.'

O'Leary shivered. 'I'm sorry?' he said.

From her seat in the corner, Bridie was watching him. She held his eyes a moment, then said, 'The lights go on at eight.' The same slow deliberate delivery.

'Oh. I see.' He searched around him for the switch.

'Here,' said Bridie. And without moving her face, her torso, without straying her eyes, she reached out a hand to the wall behind her, pressed the switch. A red-lamped light on the window-sill came on, bathing one side of her face in a healthy pink complexion, paling the other to a phosphorescent greyness.

Not dead, but dying, thought O'Leary, dreadfully.

Jim suddenly awoke from his nap. 'What's that?' he asked.

'Eight o'clock,' said Bridie beside him.

'Do you say? Well.' He picked up his large bottle, weighed it in his hand, poured some stout into his glass. 'Well,' he said, and fell back to sleep again.

O'Leary shook himself nervously, trying to avoid Bridie's gaze, and returned his attention to the glasses of stout lined up in front of him. He had tasted each one and each one had tasted different, none of them good, most of them undrinkable. One was pitch black, another creamy white, one had a head three-quarters down the glass, another had no head at all. I've been in pubs before, he chided himself, I've seen stout poured. It's easy.

It was also perverse.

He picked up another pint glass and began pouring once more from the tap.

Everything else was elementary. In fact there were only large bottles of beer and shots of whiskey to contend with. The pub certainly wasn't overstocked.

Mary had always drunk gin and tonic. Small measures at first, but later on during his sojourn, she had taken more and more to gin. In the end, it was all gin. No tonic, no ice, no lemon. Sometimes no glass. She was a peculiar girl and no mistake. She had blamed him. You're driving me to drink, she would say. But the truth was, as O'Leary himself had pointed out, she had no outside interests. Literature, she averred, alluding to Nancy Valentine and *Ill Fares the Land*, bores me stiff.

He thrust his hand into his trouser pocket. There were no slices here for Mary's gin and tonic, but he had his lemon, safely there, his jiffy. Too true he did.

His hand shot out. Damn, he cursed.

Livia blew out a long whiff of uninhaled cigarette smoke.

She hated cigarettes. She hated smoking. The smell of it on her clothes annoyed her in the morning. It annoyed her in the evening. Ashtrays she found particularly offensive. But some things one just had to do. She offered it up as a sacrifice.

'You won't smoke cigarettes in a convent,' her mother rebuked her from the sink.

'In a convent I shan't need to.'

Mrs Cuthbert shook her head, suspiring, returned to the washing-up. With a splash, she threw Livia's wine glass into the murky water. If it weren't for that girl's education, she knew, she could afford a maid. A real maid, probably live-in, they had plenty of rooms, spare rooms. She'd wear a black uniform, perhaps some white lace, not too frilly, around the collar. A young girl would do, somebody local, a townie from Clonmel. She wouldn't have to be trained. Mrs Cuthbert could see to that herself. She knew all about maids. Yes she did. They'd had maids at home. Maids? You couldn't count them. Tweenies, scullions, chambermaids. All in their livery, black and white, a frillier one for grander occasions. Two footmen, a butler, Papa's valet, never mind gardeners. An army of gardeners. That was how to live. That was how she was brought up to live. And then she had married that sainted man, that stupid sainted Arnold Cuthbert, the Reverend Arnold Cuthbert, damn him to perdition. She would never forgive him. Not if she lived a thousand years, she couldn't forgive him. And she squeezed his neck in her fingers, squeezed it . . .

Till Livia's wine glass cracked in her hand. 'Now look what you've made me do.'

'Are you bleeding?'

'Of course I'm bleeding.'

Livia examined the outstretched finger. 'It's only a scratch. I'll fetch a plaster.'

Mrs Cuthbert leaned exhausted against the sink. 'I'm bleeding, Livia. I'm bleeding inside. My heart bleeds.'

'Sit down, Mother, I'll put a plaster on.'

'Do you think a plaster could staunch my broken heart?'

'Aren't we being a touch melodramatic? It's only a scratch.'

But Mrs Cuthbert grabbed a fierce hold on her daughter's arms. 'Livia,' she pleaded. 'On my bended knees I beg you' – and she made a motion as if actually to kneel – 'Livia: marry!'

Livia closed her eyes slowly, made a wish, opened them again, lost her faith in wishes. Her mother was still half-kneeling before her. She pulled her upright. She smiled, sadly, almost comfortingly. Her mother seemed so old of a sudden. Her smile faded. Hard to think that old woman there had murdered her father.

'Come on, Mother,' she said. 'You sit down. I'll finish the dishes.'

'I didn't send my daughter to finishing school in Switzerland to have her washing up at a sink.'

'All right,' said Livia. 'You wash and I'll dry.'

'I'll sit down.'

And Mrs Cuthbert sat down. If only Livia would marry. With all her education, her refinement, her sophistication, her blood: she could so easily restore their fortunes. They would be gentry again. There would be money, there would be respect, invitations to balls. Her third cousin Valentine would recognize her again in the street, and remember that it was canasta she came for on Thursdays, not to see about the bats. And there would be – she looked around the kitchen – there'd be funds for paint on the ceiling. If only Livia would marry. If only Livia would surrender this nun nonsense and marry.

The right man, of course.

'That's funny,' said Livia, staring out the kitchen window.

'What?'

'That man on the train.'

Mrs Cuthbert could hardly believe her ears. Man! She nearly tripped, fighting her way to the window. 'Where?'

'In Maguire's back yard.'

'Oh yes.'

'Under the yard lamp. He's standing outside the toilet.'

'Lavatory,' Mrs Cuthbert corrected mechanically.

'Lavatory,' repeated Livia equally mechanically. 'I thought I recognized him. It's that ugly fool from the train. The one with the scars.'

'So it is,' said Mrs Cuthbert.

'What's he doing?'

'Has he looked this way?' she asked hopefully.

'He keeps checking his watch. God, but he's ugly. Even in this light. Fancy him turning up in Kilbrack.'

Not at all, thought Mrs Cuthbert. Not at all, and she had a glint of hope in her eye, hope that for so long had been foreign to her countenance. Hadn't he said on the train that he thought Livia was beautiful? Hadn't he?

And now he'd followed her all the way to Kilbrack. It was love. It was obviously love. Mind you, it had to be said: he certainly wasn't an oil painting. But only superficially. He was well spoken. Delivery is so important. He'd been in a car crash, poor fellow. Scars weren't hereditary. He dressed like gentry, faded. It wasn't quite what she'd have chosen herself. But if a skinny, lanky fool with scars was how God chose to answer her prayers – well, at least God had been half-listening. That'd show third cousin Valentine.

'What's he doing now?' she asked.

'Nothing. He's just standing there.'

'He's waiting to use the lavatory.'

'Of course he's not. The door's open. You can see there's no one inside.'

'He keeps checking his watch.'

'He's been there nearly five minutes. Wait.' Livia turned to her mother. 'He's gone into the lavatory,' she said, astounded.

But Mrs Cuthbert wasn't listening. She was gazing in awe at the kitchen ceiling.

'What a funny man,' said Livia and returned to the sink.

'Thank you, God,' whispered Mrs Cuthbert.

O'Leary Montagu closed the lavatory door behind him, pulled down his trousers and sat on the seat. He sighed.

The light was on, the door was wide open, anyone could see there was nobody inside. Yet still he'd had to serve his five minute's 'precaution'.

The doctors had told him: 'You are a sorry creature who moves on predestinate grooves, like a tram. You are an obsessional neurotic. Good day.'

It had all begun in the parade of shops, down the road from Mary's apartment. All of six years ago, that was.

Diary Memo: At that time it was all detective fiction. Before that it was the accident. It was Nancy Valentine who introduced me to the craft of memoir-writing and diaries. All of six years ago. And it was all of six years ago that I was first introduced to Nancy Valentine.

He checked back over the diary memo. Not very concise, he thought. Out of practice.

It was a Monday. Mary had been on night shift. She was at home, sleeping. He crept into her bedroom. He didn't like to disturb her, so he just sneaked some money from their kitty. On Mondays, a street market with bookstalls was held outside the parade. O'Leary liked to peruse the literary section. At the time, he collected books of the *Teach Yourself Detective Fiction* ilk.

But they had nothing new in stock. Down-hearted, he wandered through the stalls. At one, there was some sort of commotion going on. A youth was dashing away. Apparently he had pinched a book and scarpered. The police had been called. Stealing books, O'Leary had mused at the time. Why had he never thought of that?

Leaving the parade, he felt a natural need to visit a lavatory. There was a public convenience in the middle of the street. He descended the stairs, entered the Gents.

There was hardly anybody there. A middle-aged man stood at the urinal. O'Leary approached, unbuttoned his fly. Suddenly there was a rush beside him, a youth shoved him, pushed him into the middle-aged man. He felt a fumble in his jacket pocket. He turned. But the youth had gone, disappeared. The middle-aged man smiled at him. O'Leary smiled back, embarrassed. 'Here?' the man said. 'I'm sorry?' said O'Leary. And the man reached out his hand to O'Leary's fly.

It was then that the three policemen pounded down the steps. ''Ere, what's going on 'ere then?' one of them called.

'Bloody perverts,' said another. And they grabbed the middle-aged man and O'Leary Montagu as well.

'It was him!' squealed the middle-aged man.

'I'm sorry?' said O'Leary. It was all very confusing. He tried to shrug the policeman off, but in doing so a package slipped out of his jacket pocket. It skidded on the tiles. O'Leary looked down. It was a book. A plain cloth cover. Nancy Valentine, it said. *Ill Fares the Land.*

One of the policemen picked it up. 'Well,' he said, sounding pleased as punch. 'Fancy that. Bloody pervert's the bloody bookthief.'

'Right, sunshine. It's the paddy wagon for you.'

And thus had O'Leary Montagu been introduced to the memoirs of Nancy Valentine, mistress of letters.

Diary Memo: Less of an introduction: it was a baptism of fire.

He sometimes felt he could put up with the criminal record.

What's a criminal record these days – in creative society? The brand of a sexual deviant? Mary could vouch otherwise. Livia would soon find out. It was the obsessional neurosis that hurt. The lemon jiffies for urinals, the five minutes' 'precaution' for closets. Ever since that moment, he couldn't use a lavatory without waiting five minutes outside to ensure beyond any possible tiniest doubt that it really was vacant. He couldn't urinate at a urinal if there were others present. If he stood there dry, other men eyed him suspiciously, or worse still, suggestively. So he carried a lemon jiffy with him at all times, and squirted that through his fly instead.

O'Leary Montagu sighed. He pulled the chain.

Thin old Downey felt in his pocket for his knife.

'He's outside,' said Bridie.

Downey's fingers tightened on the handle. 'Who?'

'The incognito man.'

'Outside, you say?'

'Five minutes.'

'Five minutes?' His thumb inched along the blade.

'More.'

'Well.' He looked about him. His eyes narrowed. 'What incognito man?'

'He's come to stay.'

'Well.' He eyed the bar warily. 'Who's serving?'

'He's outside.'

'Who?' said Downey.

'You gobshite, you. O'Leary something's his name. He's come to stay.'

In his pocket, Downey's knuckles turned white with the fierceness of his grip. He looked around him, jerkily. 'Who's calling me a gobshite?'

'Shut up,' said Bridie. 'He's outside on the bog, gone ten minutes. And she's upstairs, sleeping in her bed. She said he's a writer, I heard her say it. But I know better. I looked in his room. There's a book there all right. I crept up for to see. But he didn't write it. That book's by a woman. I read the name. Might call himself a writer, but he's working behind the bar. Working incognito, so he is.' She paused for breath. 'What d'ye think of that?'

My poor poor mother, moaned Downey, and his heart sank deeper than the pit of hell whither he was sure he was bound. By the plagued dog of St Rock the Healer, 'twas terrible straits he was in. His good name would be dragged through the courts, then the papers, his poor mother's memory shattered in her tomb. No doubt about it and no way to turn.

For he knew where the man came from. Wasn't it obvious all along? Working incognito behind the bar – sure who did he think he was kidding? For years now he'd dreaded this day. Ever since his mother had died and he'd changed the grocery to a pharmacy in her honour – MPSI he'd written on the sign. Oh those deadly letters – he'd known this would happen to him one day. There'd be a rap on the door. 'Good evening, sir. I'm from the Pharmaceutical Society of Ireland. I'm here investigating false credentials. I'd like to step in if I may.' Oh, lackaday, lackaday, moaned Downey to himself.

Was there nothing he could do? Must he accept defeat

with no shot fired in his defence? What about bribery, he wondered. Would that do the trick? 'Twould only delay his downfall at most. Besides, he had no money left hardly. He was close to the end of his mother's savings. Flattery? Was he up to flattering that streaky stranger? He doubted it. Maybe he'd buy him a drink or two, get him drunk even. He might commit an indiscretion himself. If all else failed there was always blackmail.

One thing was for certain. He wasn't about to let Bridie O'Toole in on his tribulations. She'd find out soon enough in the evening papers, God help him.

He avoided her attention and concentrated on the bar. All them glasses of stout. He'd never seen so many. And in the midst of his trials, his tongue tasted the parched edges of his lips. It was thirsty work being hounded by the Society. He could almost feel the satisfactory workmanlike plop of the stout as it would – if it could – hit the desert in his belly. 'The stout,' he said, and given his woes it wasn't half as difficult to force a smile as he'd expected; ''tis a fierce squadron of stout lined up on the counter. What's all the glasses in aid of?'

''Tis not for you anyhow,' spat Bridie, and she rinsed her mouth with whiskey and red lemonade.

Downey gritted his teeth, then switched to a grin. His right hand still in his pocket, he sauntered up to the bar, chose the fullest glass of stout. He raised it to Bridie, in tremulous aplomb. That'd show the old hag there was fight in him yet. Then he returned to his favourite place by the wall. On the wall was his favourite poster. *The All-Star Hurley Players of Ireland*, it said. He knew them all, knew every county they played for. Offaly, Offaly, Cork, Waterford . . .

He knew them all. He raised his glass to the young hurley players of Ireland, and took a thirsty swig.

'Here he is now,' said Bridie, as O'Leary Montagu returned from the lavatory.

'Hell and damnation!' cried Downey as he spewed the mouthful of stout on to the floor. 'Is it poison you're at now?'

Oh yes, to be sure, it was certainly an extravagantly peculiar place, thought O'Leary, as he poured another two pints of stout. Poured them, left them, topped them, left them, headed them, skimmed them, served – as Downey had shown him how. He raised his glass in acknowledgement to the helpful pharmacist.

Diary Memo: Local chemist is manly love.

He was certainly getting a taste for this stuff. Perhaps too much of a taste, too soon.

Diary Memo: I mean, lovely man.

He found himself too busy at this novel occupation to risk much time worrying about Livia. But once when Bridie had approached the bar, he had asked about Nancy Valentine.

'Ye'll learn soon enough,' Bridie had replied.

'Learn what?' His heart had raced.

'There's no secrets kept from Bridie O'Toole, that's what ye'll learn.' And she slid slowly back to her seat.

And though Downey plied him with drinks the night long, when O'Leary broached the subject of literature with him, all he had done was retreat to a poster hanging on the wall where he started muttering to himself, 'Offaly, Offaly, Cork, Waterford, Derry, Derry, Cork . . .'

O'Leary had the feeling he wasn't getting very far with his researches, let alone with the wooing of Livia. It was a confusing time. There was something very odd, sinister even, about Kilbrack and the way nobody answered a question straight. He felt like a detective. 'So, he was a private dick. He took a swig of his nonmedicinal stout.'

My God! cried O'Leary. Please no!

He'd a hunch about this two-bit dump, name of Kilbrack. A nasty feeling, in the pit of his stomach. But he'd dig the dirt. Sure, he'd dig it up. That's what private dicks are for, aint it?

The detective novels had returned.

CHAPTER FIVE

LATER THAT NIGHT, much later, as O'Leary Montagu climbed the stairs on his way to bed, he realized he was drunk. Very drunk. He couldn't remember if he'd locked the front door of the pub even.

And he realized he was drunk because his thoughts, rather than arranging themselves in concise diary memos, continued to slug it out with him in what Mary used to call 'a strong dose of the Detectives'.

> 'He froze on the stairs. Jelled, like a French blancmange. His eyes narrowed. He looked like some alley cat on edge. Below, you could hear a pin drop. He glanced behind. Nothing. Had he locked the door?'

'Oh please no,' he groaned. 'Anything but the Detectives . . .'

He fought frantically to steady his mind, to shape his thoughts into decent diary memos. But all that came out was:

'He stood there, like a fly on a fly-paper. He had to pull himself together. It's no duck soup being a private dick. Sure he was tough. But the job showed. He mopped his brow. Hell, he was sweating like some hog in a Swedish sauna.'

The door of course had been locked all the time. O'Leary cursed and once more made his way up the stairs to his bedroom. And all the while, he was fighting back the dreaded Detectives.

'He fought. Sure he fought. But any schmuck coulda told him. The dice was loaded. He was on a one-way ticket to noplaceville.'

One hour later, he closed his book, turned off the light, rested his head deep in his pillow. How beautiful, he thought. How melancholily beautiful. He felt so close to the Mistress. He was tired now: tomorrow would tell. Tomorrow he would visit to Knight's Kilbrack, her childhood home. And who could tell, other than Fate, what wonders might befall him there?

Before he closed his eyes, he tested his cogitation.

Diary Memo: Testing, testing . . .

Yes, it was all right. There were no more Detectives. Nancy Valentine had worked her usual magic. And O'Leary Montagu might safely drowse, to worry in peace about Livia.

'You bet,' said the Detectives.

* * *

Across the landing, in her room, Nellie Maguire lay awake on her unmade bed. She had little left. She had sold all the land, the great tracts of land her great-aunt had bequeathed her. The pub was on the market two years since, but no one would buy in this God-forsaken hole. Kilbrack was dead. She was fast approaching flat bottom of her savings. She felt old. Old and withered. She was sixty with the worry of it.

She got up, dragging her slippered feet from the bed, shuffled over to the dressing table. She cleared a space, took down the mirror, polished it with a blouse that was lying draped nearby. She opened the drawer where she kept Downey's little envelopes that looked like Beecham's Powders, chose one. Then she dismantled her leg razor and carefully withdrew the blade.

Tuesday nights were the worst, with their yawning of emptiness. Wednesday mornings could usually be relied on for a ticklish tang of expectation. But this morning she'd had hardly the vim even for that. Wednesday nights were the best. The bounty of her supply would normally disburden the heftiest of her worries. Tonight she just felt old.

She rolled up the ten pound note and sniffed the thin white line of cocaine from her mirror. And sniffed. And sniffed.

And in the first rush of menthol down her throat the world was realigned to its truer significance. She remembered the starving souls in Africa, and compared to them, what worries had she? She was alive, she was young, she was beautiful, she was happy, she was . . .

And she leapt back into her bed with the hop-skip-and-a-jump of a ten-year-old.

In his cramped bedroom above the pharmacy, thin old Downey muttered in his sleep. 'O table,' he said, and turned, sweating. 'Genitive, *mensae*, of the table; *mensarum*, plural, of the tables . . .'

For Downey was suffering his nightmare. He was a schoolboy again. On the door hung his Christian Brothers purple blazer. His shoes were polished. A clean shirt was laid out, a tie. His satchel was ready, packed only with his lunch. Tomorrow he'd need no textbooks. For tomorrow he'd sit his highers. Latin One – language and composition – in the morning. Latin Two in the afternoon – literature and Roman history. There was only the Latin left and if he passed his Latin he'd be half-way home to medical school in Dublin. Oh, wouldn't his mother be proud of him then. She'd always wanted that. A doctor in the family. She'd made him promise. And what a fine cut of a doctor he'd make too, and no two ways about it, that was for certain. He'd only to scrape his Latin.

He turned, tossing in his sleep again, his mind a riot of declensions and cases. '*Mensa, mensa, mensam*,' he muttered, '*mensae, mensae, men*—' And he woke, screaming from his jactitation, 'Hell and damnation! By, in or from: what's the ablative?'

* * *

Bridie O'Toole lay stiff in her queen-size bed, her eyes wide open, staring at the maps of dampness on the bedroom ceiling. Beside her, Jim lay snoring away. It was a good bed, iron-sprung, with a horsehair mattress. As a child Bridie had slept in that bed, along with her brother. And when their parents had died and Jim had suggested Bridie move into the parents' room, Bridie had told him where to get off. It was her bed as much as it was his. And so, now both past their fiftieth birthdays, they still slept in the same bed they had shared as children.

And now this stranger had come in their midst, asking questions, poking his nose, working incognito. Where was he from? If only the great lump of bacon beside her would shut up his snoring she might be able to work something out.

'Shut up your hootering,' she said and gave Jim a terrific poke in the ribs.

'What?' said Jim.

'Button your nose, I said.'

'Go to sleep.'

'With that racket?'

'Go to sleep, why won't you? I was busy dreaming of the seven seas.'

'None of your seven seas gob. You was snoring.'

'I was nearly happy.'

'I'll cross my eyes on you.'

'You wouldn't dare,' said Jim, fearful suddenly. 'And me poor ribs too.'

'See if I daren't,' said Bridie, and she crossed her electric green eyes.

'No!' blurted Jim, and he squeezed tight his own eyes. 'Don't cross them, Bridie! Please!' But he could feel Bridie bringing her face closer to his. And he could feel through his closed eye-lids that her eyes were crossed, eyeing him crookedly, gruesomely.

'They're crossed now, Jim. Open your eyes and see the truth.'

'No!' squealed Jim. 'Stop it, please!'

'All right, then. You'll shut up your hootering, will you?'

'I will, I will!'

'Very well.' She withdrew her face. 'You can open your eyes now. I have them uncrossed.'

And gingerly Jim opened his eyes. But he'd known it all along. He'd known not to trust her. 'Agh!' he cried. 'You fibber!'

''Tis no worse than you deserve.'

'I'll get a button,' said Jim.

'You wouldn't,' said Bridie. But less sure of herself now, she added, 'Where?'

'I'll rip a button off me pyjama tops and throw it on the floor.'

'You wouldn't.'

'I will.'

'No!'

'I'll do it now.' And he ripped a button off his pyjamas and tossed it flat on to the middle of the linoleum.

'Agh!' screeched Bridie, squeezing shut her own eyes. 'Pick it up! Pick it up!'

'I won't! Agh!' For he'd spotted her crossing her eyes again.

. . . And so they wrestled, their eyes pinched and squashed till it hurt, the one terrified of the gruesome crooked sight of his sister's crossed eyes, the other appalled at the thought of the sight of a button lying monstrous on the floor.

In her bedroom at the Rectory, stout Mrs Cuthbert knelt before the figurine of the Virgin Mary, lit by the flame of the Sacred Heart above, and she prayed as Father Michael had instructed her.

'Holy holy queen, mother of mercy, hail our life, our sweetness, and our hope. To thee do we cry, poor banished children of Eve, to thee do we send up our sighs . . .' When she'd finished the Salve Regina, she felt she had fulfilled enough of Father Michael's strictures for the moment, and could begin to pray in her own more genteel fashion. She relaxed slightly on her cushion. 'Well, Lord,' she said, 'at least he's a man . . .'

Outside her bedroom window, dimly discernible in the moonlight, she could make out, if she cared, the bare ruined spire of St Ciaran's, whose Protestant parish was her late husband's care and benefice – Kilbrack.

Cure and benefice, she thought. It had been their ruin. Anyone could see it was hopeless. Wasting money, squandering it away like that. She wouldn't have minded so much if he'd used his own money. But of course he didn't have any money of his own. Oh no, it was her coffers he'd raided, her dowry. It was wicked. That wicked man, wasting her money on that pile of rubble. God knows, he could have built fifty brand new cathedrals with all the money he'd wasted trying to repair that wrack, that ruin.

And even if he had restored it, who would have worshipped there? They and third cousin Valentine were the only Anglicans remaining in the parish. Who?

'Why, Charity, one labours for God.'

'I asked who will use it.'

'Why, Charity, it is we who will worship there.'

But she had fixed that. Of course she had. If he was prepared to see his family pauperized, laughing-stocks of the county – well, she knew what she'd do . . .

And she had done it.

'. . . And Lord, even Father Michael would agree: it would be such a waste for her to be a nun. And remember the lamps and – well, of course You remember – the lamps and the bushels. I know it's my fault she's a Catholic, but how was I to know she'd take it to heart so? Just a little marriage, that's all I ask. You've surely got enough hand-maidens as it is.' She paused for a moment. 'Oh, and don't forget, he's got to be reasonably wealthy.' She wondered a moment was there anything else. 'No, that's it,' she said. 'In the name of the Father, and of the Son, and of the Holy Ghost. Amen.'

Anway, she thought, Father Michael's due for lunch tomorrow. She'd ask him to come early. He'd sort her out if anyone would. Although, Father Michael, it was no use denying it, Father Michael had changed since he had joined the Bishop in his Palace . . . She sighed and blessed herself again. Only time would tell.

And having blessed herself twice, she climbed stiffly to her feet, heaved herself into her bed. She toed the hot-water bottle down to her feet, reached under her pillow for the bar of chocolate she kept there.

'Well,' she said. 'It's in God's hands now.'

For a prospective hand-maiden to Christ, even Livia thought it odd sometimes that instead of a Bible or some devotional writings, she kept under her pillow only architectural sketches. But the sanctimony with which she handled these wrinkled old drawings betrayed her almost religious veneration of them. She didn't open them out, just held them in her hands, pressed to her bosom.

'It's hard sometimes,' she said. 'I know I promised retribution, I know I made that solemn vow to you, your avenging angel. But sometimes it is so hard. She is only human, after all, the dust of the ground. But I shan't give in. If it's marriage she's set her heart upon, then marriage is the battle-ground and I shall never wed. She murdered your dreams till you died. I'll smother hers. I miss you, Daddy. I miss you so much.'

At the gates to the big house, Knight's Kilbrack, the two pillars, generations of ivy crumbling their stone, stood gaunt in the night. They rose proud from the lane to end suddenly in a capital supporting – nothing. The two heraldic birds had fallen years before. In the moonlight in the undergrowth they could still be discerned – armed, guardant, displayed – glowering upwards, as if poised for attack, disdaining to acknowledge their cracked and chipped wings. Oddly, these birds were not eagles or any other of the conventional charges; but were magpies, stylized to ferocity, but still discernibly birds of the field. They lay unmoved, tansy through their talons, ragwort through their wings.

Nothing could be seen of the big house. It was as if the pillars and their sentinels denied even the moonlight entry. The path led in from the gates and the derelict lodge, darker and narrower, crowded in by the pressure of thickets, trees overlapping overhead. All was dark, silent, deserted.

Save for the old mongrel bitch Nancy who smuggled through a hole in the demesne wall. She sniffed the night air. But there was nothing of interest. Far better to return to her master's bed and snuggle up to Valentine's warm body. She padded over to one of the fallen magpies, pee'd, and sneaked back into the demesne.

O'Leary Montagu tossed in his sleep. His room, unused over the years, was an unlikely mixture of damp and dust. It was chilly, but at the same time the air felt stale, unaccustomed to movement, breath. It wasn't, however, this discomfort which troubled his sleep. It was his dream.

For O'Leary Montagu was dreaming as he had dreamed obsessively every night for the past eleven years . . . of the accident.

CHAPTER SIX

O'Leary Montagu was born at the age of twenty-five – a difficult age. Now, aged thirty-six, he had known, enjoyed, endured, eleven years of life. It was on account of the accident.

His earliest memory was of hospital. He had woken to a world of bright white light with darker blobs floating or bobbing up and down in it; which little by little had coalesced into faces. Faces in white uniforms: doctors and nurses leaning over him. The faces were concentrating, concerned, intense. Shyly, O'Leary had shifted his eyes to right and left. Their eyes followed, searching. He tried a smile, apologetic. The faces relaxed. Relief exploded to sudden noise. Thunder. Could it be thunder? Thunderous applause? O'Leary mouthed, Thank you. It was some time before he realized there were medical students present, and that they were showing their appreciation of the consultant professor's expertise. And that was his earliest memory. He had slept then, but no longer comatose; next day he had woken, as usual in the world of men, to a morning, waking, living world. Except, to O'Leary Montagu, it was the first morning of his life.

The accident he only remembered in dreams, nightmares really. He would be crossing a street. It was night-time. Where, whence, whither, he couldn't tell. Of course, they had told him where they'd found him, they'd given him the address. But still he would never know it. A sudden roar, a sudden light, the brakes would screech, fail. The car – a great black battering-ram of a car – would hit him, smash his face, his head, to pulp. The world would turn red. The whole world would be bleeding, soaking him in blood.

And then he'd wake from his nightmare, soaked in sweat. The dream would be lost, forgotten, returned to that abyss of oblivion which was all his previous life.

They had moved him, that first morning, into Mary's ward. And immediately, he had fallen in love with Mary, helplessly in love. She was seventeen, fresh from Ireland. She had told him his accent sounded Irish, and it pleased him to speak like her. Far grander than my accent, she said. She called him O'Leary Montagu. Was that his name? Mary had blushed. No. O'Leary was the ward sister and Montagu the consultant in charge of his case. At the time of his accident, he carried no identification. The police had tried, but had come up with no leads. They had to call him something. It was only human to have a name. And the name O'Leary Montagu had stuck.

A dental specialist had opined from the state of his teeth that he was male, twenty-five years old, with a pronounced disregard for dental hygiene. And when they had taken the bandages off his face, Mary had watched pitifully from the end of his bed. But O'Leary didn't really mind: at least she hadn't turned away. And nearly all the patients in that ward had scars.

Thus had O'Leary Montagu irrupted into the world, in love on his first morning, full-grown, amnesiac, and scarred with the incarnation.

Nothing of his previous life came back to him. Nothing. At first the doctors had been concerned. It was unusual, not to say unprecedented. No flashbacks? No. Dreams? I don't dream. Everybody dreams. I'm afraid I don't. And the psychiatrist had anxiously noted down: 'Unwillingness to co-operate.' Smells, sounds, the television: does nothing jolt your memory? O'Leary shook his head. Nothing? Absolutely. And the psychiatrist crossed out 'unwillingness' and pencilled in 'obstinate refusal' instead.

Life absorbed him. He sat up in his bed the day long, watching the other patients heal or die, accepting Mary's nursing ministrations as tokens of her love. Let the psychiatrists and social workers talk of this other man, this poor unfortunate who apparently had suffered an accident: as far as O'Leary was concerned he was a stranger, as foreign to him as the patient in the next bed along. He had Mary, he had life. Of that stranger he could see from Mary's solicitous eyes that she thought him a poor unloved individual, nobody claiming him, nobody wanting him, an unmissed missing person. But himself he didn't dwell. He was far too busy substantiating this new world to worry about the plight of a stranger.

The vocational guidance counsellor asked him what career would he prefer to follow. 'I'm sorry?' he asked. 'Career? But I'm quite happy here.' The vocational guidance counsellor insisted and O'Leary Montagu racked his brains.

Earlier that week, the man in the bed beside him had died. Before they could cart away his belongings, O'Leary had sneaked out of his own bed and stolen the book the man had intermittently perused. It was a thrilling read. *Murder in the Big House*, it was called. Already, in four days, O'Leary had devoured the book three times. If it was such engrossing stuff to read, might it not be diverting to write the same? *Murder in the Big House* was a 'Number One World Bestseller'. The sticker on the cover said so. Who knows, but O'Leary might have a dormant talent himself for detective fiction.

He looked up at the vocational guidance counsellor. 'Writer,' he said.

'Have you written before?'

'I'm afraid I don't really know.'

The counsellor managed to stifle her laughter until the odd fellow was safely outside the door. She had loaded his arms with circulars on 'Careers in In-House Journalism'.

But O'Leary Montagu returned to his bed happy in the knowledge that he was a writer. And he was complacent enough for a whole six months until one day Mary asked to read some of his work.

'I'm sorry?'

'We're not busy tonight. Just thought I'd like to read some.'

Writer: one who writes. Ridiculous, but somehow he

had neglected to remember that a writer wrote. He felt such a fool. It was then that the detective novels began in earnest.

'What do you write about?' Mary asked him another day.

'Myself,' he answered gravely. 'You can only write about yourself.'

He didn't write. Time enough for writing. Practice came first. And so, he would lie in bed, practising writing detective novels – in his head. He was wary of the world. It was capricious. Fate, he called it. Tricky-handed Fate. It was far too wayward for his liking, deceitful even. And it didn't seem enough to plaster his few belongings with his name 'O'Leary Montagu', and the number of his bed, and the name of his ward, the name and address of the hospital, down to Earth, Solar System, Milky Way. It wasn't enough of a safeguard against this world. For this world might trip you up, careen you any time, any place, leave you abroad and naked. You would wake from another coma two weeks later with another new name and another new life.

In the hospital administrator's office, the administrator, the accountant, the lawyer, the psychiatrist, the vocational guidance counsellor, the social worker, the consultant professor and his assisting surgeons, the ward doctor and the ward sister all sat in grave conclave. There was even a submission from the Royal College of Nursing and another from the hospital maintenance staff's union complaining about the theft of biros and notebooks from workers' pockets.

Never in the august history of the hospital had such a disparate collection of individuals, classes, causes, met in such unaminous concord.

'A drain on scarce resources,' said the hospital administrator.

'A waste,' said the accountant.

'A liability,' said the lawyer.

'An obsessional neurotic,' pronounced the psychiatrist, 'showing distinct signs of chronic obstinacy, a condition previously restricted to—'

'Yes. Thank you,' said the administrator.

The vocational guidance counsellor thought him 'a dreamer'; the social worker 'an inadequate'. The consultant professor and his assisting surgeons deemed him a sorry failure, testimony not to their lack of skill but to the patient's congenital fear of a cure. 'The scars won't heal. He enjoys the attention.'

The ward sister and the ward doctor concluded, 'He's simply malingering. Nothing wrong with him. We've made him too cosy here.'

And then all together, in almighty concourse: 'He'll have to go!'

Fate had struck. But O'Leary Montagu had prepared his flight.

'Well,' said Mary, 'if things really are that bad – and I suppose they must be really,' she added, still rather doubtful, 'I've got a couch at home. It's only a stick of a thing. But you could kip down there a week maybe.

Better than the hostel. Until you find your feet, anyway.'

And O'Leary Montagu had moved into her Camden apartment. And when after the first week, he'd finally told her that he loved her – 'Oh, Mary, Mary, Mary, I love you, love you, love you . . .' – and she had laughed, laughed at him: well, at least she had laughed. She could have thrown him out.

She was a born nurse, he a born patient. She was lonely in London, missed her home. O'Leary had guessed she would be. They were content together. They belonged.

And he did love her. She was younger than he, but there was a sense in which he was only one year old. And his love for her, chaste even to a kiss, held something of the devotion an infant might feel for its mother. They slept together. The couch was too cramped for his long legs, so he complained. But sleep was all they did. Mary was tired after her shifts.

He never showed her his writing – indeed, there was none to show – but he knew she understood he was a writer. He needed his calm, his peace. She wouldn't disturb him.

Save for one evening after two years together, when they decided he must get out, see more of the world. It was her idea really. He was sure. She took him to a play. He seemed to enjoy detective thrillers: she chose *The Mousetrap*.

He left the theatre in a dream, drama exploding in his mind. He crated all his detective novels, and the library of manuals of *The Craft of the Detective Novelist* school. And with all his unemployment benefit he bought playscripts. Any plays. Every play he could land his hands on. And of course, the concomitant library of manuals: *Teach Yourself Dramatic Writing, The Playwright's Craft, Some Outlines in Dramatic Scripting* . . . all of them.

And his thoughts accordingly took the shape of the directions in a play. For two weeks he didn't walk into a room. Mary watched him. He saw that she could tell. If he came into the bedroom, it was: 'Enters. Stage Back. Slouching.' If he smiled: 'Smiles . . . Distantly.'

It passed. After two weeks he was back to the detective novels again, and he watched Mary sigh as though happier with the devil she knew.

He watched her closely, tirelessly so, as though only his vigilant eyes could keep her there with him. He was sure his helplessness must endear him, certain his unassuming soul besought a returning fondness. He would wait anxiously for her to come home from her shift and as soon as the key turned in the door, he rushed to report to her each new development in his latest plot. Sometimes he waited for her in a bar across the street from the hospital. After a drink or two, he would catch himself regaling the regulars with tales of his love. The regulars laughed. He believed it was a cosy and friendly pub – until eventually it dawned on him the customers were – well – not quite what he had thought. O'Leary felt uncomfortable in the presence of some men. Particularly those who dressed or behaved as women. He didn't know why. And he was far too busy with Mary and his love for her to ponder the question overmuch. He stopped visiting that pub, as he stopped visiting any place where deviants were thought to gather. He was tall, dark and normal, as Mary pointed out.

Cleaning, washing, cooking, ironing for him, they were a chore of course, O'Leary understood that: but she would have had to clean, wash, cook, iron for herself anyway.

Four years passed before any difficulty arose to sully their relationship. Scouring second-hand bookshops, O'Leary had come across a peculiar volume titled *The Creative Impulse: Get It Right!* He sat at home poring over it, more and more confused.

'It's a joke,' explained Mary.

'I'm sorry?'

'It's a jokey sex manual. Can't you tell?'

'Sex manual?'

Later that night, tipsy from gin and tonic, they had lain on her bed, the manual between them. It was a game at first and giggling they followed the instructions to kiss, finger, explore; to begin with fully clothed, then dishevelled, then nearly naked. Until Mary had felt rise within her body not the need for her own satisfaction but the urge to satisfy this man beside her. But O'Leary had insisted on following the manual to the letter, and upon the instruction '71: Now switch off the light' he had duly obeyed. Still clasped in her arms he had relaxed. Without the manual to guide him, he fell to sleep.

O'Leary reckoned it was round about then that Mary began to doubt his sanity.

* * *

Soon afterwards occurred the incident in the lavatory outside the parade of shops down Mary's road. And there had followed the final gargantuan spring-clean of his library. From then on it was all diaries, diary memos, and the memoirs of Nancy Valentine.

It was Fate of course, O'Leary knew. Fate had guided the young bookthief to the lavatory to deposit his stolen book in O'Leary's jacket. And reading it, devouring the pages during and after the court case, with the fines and the suspended sentences, he thanked Fate – though still wary. But what wonders it portrayed! What glories! What chords it struck! What life! That one slim volume contained all the pain, joy, loss and heartache of the history of man since first he stumbled on two legs.

'Aren't you taking this a bit too seriously?' wondered Mary.

'Too seriously?'

'It's only a book.'

'Yes, it's a book. Whence the "only"?'

He then scurried about seeking any information at all on Nancy Valentine. Amazingly, it seemed that nobody had heard of her. He tried the owner of the bookstall whence it had been stolen.

'*Ill Farts the Land?*' the man said, surprised.

'No,' answered O'Leary, wearily. He'd explained it a thousand times to Mary already. 'The t is a printer's error.' Wasn't that obvious? 'It should read *Ill Fares the* – not—' but he didn't like pronouncing the mistake. 'It's a quote from Goldsmith.' Then seeing the man's uncomprehending face: '*The Deserted Village*, line fifty-one.' Once more, under his breath, he cursed the ineptitude of printers.

The man leafed through the book. 'Privately published,' was his conclusion. 'Vanity, most like. This must be the proof copy. Sooner or later, they always end up on the dust heap.'

The misprint on the title page was embarrassing. Galling, too.

'It's a joke,' said Mary.

'It's not a joke. It's a typographical error. A child could see that.'

Besides, it wasn't the only misprint in the book. 'Passed on from generation to generation' – a phrase the Mistress used frequently in her atavistic moments – oftentimes appeared with the first a misset as an i. When, in one particularly evocative passage, she describes returning home of an evening 'leaf-late in August', the printers – criminally? indolently? – had set 'lead-like in a gust'. It was one amongst many examples. O'Leary, of course, was relieved to hear that the present volume was only a proof copy.

He tried the printers. His envelope came back marked 'Nkata'. Nkata, he wondered. Sounded African.

'Don't be silly,' said Mary. 'It's shorthand. It stands for "Not Known At This Address".'

'Ah,' said O'Leary. The mystery deepened.

It became his crusade. Not only to explore the exaltations of the Mistress's voice, that of course; but more, much more, to champion her, fight for her due recognition from the philistines of the literary establishment. Those criticasters who hitherto had ignored her genius, too chauvinistically masculine, no doubt, to allow of a female equal, let alone an incomparable better. In turns, it brought tears to his eyes and temper to his cheeks just to consider this abominable neglect.

In short, O'Leary Montagu resolved to write the biography of Nancy Valentine.

'Are you sure you're not taking all this a little too far?' asked Mary.

'I'm sorry?'

'I know you miss – I know you must miss – your childhood. You feel left out. You feel you don't belong.'

'I'm sorry?'

'Your amnesia.'

'What about my amnesia?'

He knew he spoke coldly. His ears told him. And he was aware he had never spoken to Mary in this manner before. Even in the mirror, he could observe what she must notice. In his eyes there was a glint of the haywire disciple, a spark of the fanatic in his soul.

He could tell it frightened her. 'Don't you see, O'Leary?' she said. 'You're just trying to relive your own childhood through the memories of this, what's her name, Nancy Valentine. Through her eyes, you re-invent your own history.'

'Mary, if you choose not to recognize literature, that's fine. Only do keep your interpretations to yourself.'

She cried. He heard her through the bathroom door. But he needed to keep her quiet, subdued. Lately she'd insisted on upsetting his contemplation with constant examination of his 'toilet anxiety'. By this knockdown phrase she intended, apparently, the lemon jiffy in his pocket and the five minutes 'precaution' outside lavatories.

'Why do you keep visiting them, so?' she demanded.

'I get caught,' he replied. 'It just happens.' It was too complicated to explain.

'I don't mind if you're –' she hesitated, 'in any way unusual,' she ventured one evening.

They had been playing Happy Families on her bed. It was late. O'Leary as usual was falling asleep, his head resting heavily, almost restrictively, on her chest.

He froze, then stared at her. What a peculiar thing to say. 'I'm sorry?' he began.

But then another part of him began to wonder what would it be like to tell this girl, this friend, his only friend in all the livelong world, speak to her, tell truthfully his feelings, unburden all that was terrifyingly innermost in his—

'I should hate,' he replied, 'for you to be late for work on my account.'

He began to watch Mary ever more closely. He followed her to work. He dogged her home. It became obvious to him soon that while he was conducting his own vast researches into the life, work and influences on and of Nancy Valentine, she – Mary – had commenced her own crusade: the search for O'Leary's past.

Ha! he thought.

He read her post. From an analyst colleague she received some illiterate superstitious gibberish:

> To me it appears your friend is adrift, a canoe unmastered in an endless present, a stream, so to speak, only of consciousness. He has come now to need a rock

> to punctuate this current, upon which he might rest steadfast, if only for a time. Apparently the memoirs of this woman writer temporarily – I stress that word – supply this rock, requite this need . . .

It went on, but O'Leary had already read enough. He screwed it up.

She resorted to a handwriting specialist next. The graphologist replied:

> We have here a male in his early thirties, a strong streak of stubbornness, a dreamer perhaps, certainly naive, definitely strong-willed: I picture a man lost half-way on a long journey, having mislaid his charts and compass. Or perhaps in a rage, he threw them away. Who can tell? By the way, your own handwriting is remarkably similar to his, indicating a persistence equal to . . .

And O'Leary had damned that one down the drain, too.

She put advertisements in the Irish papers. He knew this from the responses. A lady from Lisdoonvarna replied seeking his hand in marriage. And a man from North Dublin sent her details of a hostel he ran for misplaced gentle-folk 'at *très* reasonable rates, Mam, believe you me'.

She was so thorough. Insufferably thorough.

'Why are you doing this to me?' he demanded one time.

'You're sick, O'Leary, that's why. I'm trying to help.'

'You're not helping. This is interference, pure and simple.'

He continued sleeping with her. But they didn't talk any more, not in bed.

'Why are you frightened to touch me?' she might ask.

'I'm asleep,' he'd reply.

He followed her to the police station. He listened at the door. 'Which register?' enquired the sergeant patiently. 'If we don't know his name we can hardly put him with the missing persons. Can we?'

She walked sheepishly home.

'Do you ever think about God?' she wanted to know another time.

'God? You meat Fate?'

'I mean religion.'

'There's plenty about religion in *Ill Fares the Land*.'

'O'Leary, don't you wonder about *yourself*, about *your* history? Don't you want to know who *you* are? Don't you ever want to *know*?'

Dumbstruck, he stared at her. His fingers came up slowly to her face, bent, beckoning her. She followed, into his study, which before had been her sitting room. He had never invited her in before. He pointed to a row of books on one of the shelves. He tried to say something, but couldn't. He was still quivering, struck dumb by the incomprehensibility of her remark.

He gestured to the shelf of books. Four dictionaries; a complete *Encyclopaedia Britannica*, 1924; another one dated 1969 with two volumes missing; a history of Christianity in seven volumes; *How It Works: Science at Your Fintertips; The*

Illustrated Medical Encyclopaedia 'For Home Use'; and dictionaries and compendia on history, philosophy, politics, literature, foreign languages, and *European Art from 500* BC *to the Present.* The shelf sank, groaning under the weight of such collected knowledge. And pride of place, in the middle of them all, stood Nancy Valentine's volume of memoirs, *Ill Fares the Land.*

'And you think I haven't enough knowledge, enough history on that shelf for a lifetime of learning?'

'Have you read all those?' she asked, whispering in wonder.

'I'm annotating,' he answered.

'Ill Fares the Land?'

'Of course.'

'You mean you haven't read them?'

He held his temper. 'I believe, Mary, you have revealed yourself in your true colours.'

'What?'

'You're jealous of my feelings for the Mistress.'

It was a peculiar thing, but lately, for some months in fact, or even some years, even six years, he wasn't sure, but certainly he'd had the feeling of late that Mary was pushing him away. She wanted him 'cured' and out of her life. She'd said as much often enough. 'Don't you ever get bored with your shilly-shallying?' was one of her tangential comments. 'I'm sick of your bloody amnesia', was another.

That night Mary drank too much. 'You're neurotic,' she said in her cups.

* * *

The more she drank, the less patient she became.

'Memoirs? It's a joke, O'Leary. No one has "Farts" in the title!'

He attempted once more to explain about the criminal ineptitude, infamous throughout the world, of common printers. But she chose to change the subject.

'Call that literature? If it was half-way decent half-way at all, she wouldn't've had to publish it herself! Face it, O'Leary: you're mad. You're stark raving doolally!'

'I'm sorry?'

'And shut up saying you're sorry!'

She took another neat swig of gin.

In the end it came as no surprise that she wanted to leave. Oh, she would leave, yes. If only to shock him. As if an emigrant nurse's departure could ever replace the memoirs of an undiscovered literary genius. He had long suspected that she would leave. After all, that was how Fate chose to work – deviously. It was the manner of her departure that disconcerted him.

'You're neurotic, O'Leary.'

'Yes, I believe you've advanced that opinion before.'

'You're obsessionally neurotic.'

'Thank you.'

'But what am I? What am I doing here?' She spoke as though she were an actor delivering some epilogue to an audience. Her hands gestured theatrically. 'Why do I put up with him? The lazy, boring, ugly loaf. Look at him. Ten years he's slept in my bed! Ten years! I've been mothering him, humouring him, worrying about him. And what for? He can't even get a hard-on!'

She continued. 'So what am I? Of course I am! I'm neurotic too. Nursing isn't my profession. It's my bloody obsession. I'm an obsessive nursing maniac!'

There was no gin in the flat. Just as well or she'd have downed the bottle. She didn't finish the ironing. She left. She said she was going straight back home to her parents in Ireland. 'Never to see, hear or think of O'Leary Montagu and all his works or lack of them ever ever again!'

Even after the front door had slammed, O'Leary could still hear her on the steps.

'So help me God!'

After she had left, O'Leary took the lamb that she had been cooking for their dinner out of the oven. He sat down, tried to eat. He couldn't. He tried to imagine Mary in front of him. She held her cutlery badly. But for some time now he'd found it difficult to picture her, visualize her at all in fact. He got up, went into his study, took the copy of *Ill Fares the Land*, returned to the kitchen, opened it, read.

When first he had opened the book, on the very first page, it had felt like a hole was being brimmed, a cavity at long last filled. He could almost hear the swoosh of fresh air as it rushed to inhabit a vacuum unsealed. But that night, the night Mary left, he felt nothing. He pushed away the book, pushed away the lamb. And cried.

And while he cried, one part of his mind niggled his tears. 'It's a shame she never existed,' it remarked.

But out loud, he wept. 'She'll come back. She must come back. Oh Mary . . .'

Crossing the road in the stilly night, O'Leary Montagu spun awkwardly around like a puppet on too short a string, tripped spastically, turned to the roar of the engine, recoiled in the sudden glare of the Bentley's headlights. The brakes screeched. O'Leary screamed and the whole world was bleeding, soaked red with the blood of his squirming, falling body. And he awoke grasping for breath, gasping, clutching at the frantic sheets.

But all was silent in Kilbrack. The moon had set, the thick night of the country surrounded him. It was a dream. Only a dream. It was ordinary night in Kilbrack, late August in Ireland, harvest was on the wind. He closed his eyes again, his heartbeat slowed. He slept.

CHAPTER SEVEN

In Knight's Kilbrack, the big house, Valentine Brack stretched his long thin body and shifted to a more comfortable posture in his bed. In the leather-bound journal in front of him, he read, *Ill Fares the Land: Volume XXXII*. He considered this for a moment, then added, 'page one'. He rescrewed the cap to his pen, leaned back on the bolsters, and surveyed gloomily the rashers on his breakfast tray. They had congealed. He decided to cheer himself up with a little quote from his favourite poem.

'Sweet Auburn!' he began, 'loveliest village of the plain, where health and plenty cheered the labouring swain—'

The door opened abruptly and Bridie strode in. 'This room's due cleaning,' she announced and tugged open the curtains.

Valentine Brack frowned. He dismissed the untouched plate of rashers to the far side of the tray. He was about to wipe his mouth on the napkin, but then decided against it. He waited till he was certain she was watching and wiped his mouth on the bedsheet instead.

'And I suppose you've a mind for clean linen tonight,' she said.

The old man pulled a hair from his nostril. He returned his attention to his journal.

'This weather,' said Bridie. 'Rain? 'Tis bucketing.'

'Oft in whirls the mad tornado flies,' he muttered pleasantly.

'Them sheets'd never dry this weather. The damp. You'd have farmer's lung before you'd know it.' Pneumonia. Damp sheets. 'Twould kill him dead. Why had she never thought of that before?

Valentine Brack looked up. 'Near her betrayer's door she lays her head,' he chose to tell her. 'And pinched with cold and shrinking from the shower, with heavy heart deplores the luckless hour.'

Bridie eyed the long thin plank of a man in his bed. She hated him. Working her at her age. Why couldn't he be done with it and die? God forgive her! Pass over, she meant. She'd get the Labour then. She had her stamps all paid. She could lie in bed then of a morning till Nellie Maguire's might open. She saw the untouched plate of rashers. Her eyes opened and narrowed again, glinting at the sight of them. Her nostrils quivered at the smell. ''Tis a wonder it wouldn't rain through,' she said conversationally: then made a dash for the breakfast tray.

But old though he was, Valentine Brack was too quick for her. He slapped her knuckles a sharp tap with his pen.

'The tray,' she said.

'I haven't it finished.'

Bridie made a feint back to the door. 'I haven't the time for wasting. The house is leaping.'

Valentine Brack inspected the woman at the foot of his bed. He screwed half his face into a grimace of disapproval. 'Who are you?' he demanded.

'Pah,' said Bridie. 'Don't be giving me none of yer gob.'

'Where's Jim?'

'He's out beyond, weeding.'

'Weeding what?'

'How would I know? Weeds.'

He considered this. 'The country blooms – a garden, and a grave.'

'What?'

'Get out.'

Bridie made a face, but Valentine Brack had already returned his attention to the leather-bound journal. 'Where's my pen?'

'In your hand.'

So it was. 'Why are you still here?'

Bridie still had half an eye on the breakfast tray. 'This room's due cleaning.'

He thoughtfully unscrewed his pen. 'Tell Jim,' he said, 'that I wish him as much joy in the weeding, as I have had in the writing.' And he laughed to himself, sending a chuckle down his frame like a wobble in an unsupported plank.

'You're mad.'

He leaned up in his four-poster bed and ranged his attention over her cramped body once more. 'Are you the lady come to see about the bats?'

'I'm the cleaner,' she spat. 'I'm yer blasted house-keeper.'

He looked at his tray. 'Is this tray finished?'

'No.'

'Take it anyhow.'

If only she could get something on Downey she'd get that eejit of a pharmacist to slip her some poison, anything. She'd put paid to this doddering old fool. And she'd get the Labour. She had her stamps paid and all. Only this fool kept her working. Why couldn't he die like any normal man would? God forgive her again. Not die: pass over, she meant.

As she reached over to pick up the breakfast tray, Valentine Brack saw clearly the dribble trickling down her chin, the dribble stains on her house-coat. 'Dear charming nymph, neglected and decried,' he said courteously, 'remind me, do, to engage a cleaning lady.'

Bridie hissed through her teeth. ''Tis that blasted cur as does it.'

As though her word were a command, in padded the old mongrel Nancy. She went straight up to her master's bed, tail wagging expectantly, and leaped up to nuzzle into his arms.

Bridie glared at the thing. There was mud everywhere. Mud and dust and dog hairs. She didn't mind the dirt. It was the cleaning she despised. ''Tis the cur, I tell you. Keeping the place leaping with filth and fleas.' Her fists were gripped so tight on the breakfast tray that the crockery was rattling.

'Thou source of all my bliss,' said Valentine Brack, 'be so good as to return that plate of rashers to me.'

She swore – but carefully, under her breath. If she was

sacked she'd get no Labour at all. Hadn't the Father Michael told her as much? She clashed the tray down on the side-table, clanking it on the marble top. 'Rashers?' she said.

'Here.'

He selected one rasher from the plate and held it up to the dog. 'Sit,' he said, and the mongrel sat. 'I don't know why you've taken against poor Nancy so. After all, she's surely the most intelligent beast in the four green fields of Erin.'

Bridie sucked in her cheeks and her lips so far that it nearly dislodged her dentures. The fist of her free hand was jerking involuntarily, backstabbing the air behind her. She hated that man. She hated that dog. God forgive her, but she worshipped bacon.

'Thou guide by which the nobler arts excel,' he continued, 'do I detect a hint of doubt in your demeanour?'

'Pah,' said Bridie.

Poor Nancy watched the outstretched rasher, her eyes imploring, adoring, lips watering. Her tail thumped on the rug, raising clouds of dust.

'Not a sound,' admonished Valentine Brack, 'till I tell you.' He checked to see he had Bridie's full attention. Dust, dog and bacon: of course he had. 'Now,' he said to the dog. 'Who commanded the British forces at the siege of Quebec, 1759?' He raised one finger, paused for the effect, then dropped it theatrically. 'Speak, Nancy.'

And on that signal, the mongrel half-barked, half-growled.

'Good girl,' he praised, as she gobbled the prize rasher. Then, sneaking a crooked glance at Bridie, he explained.

'*Wolfe.* General James Wolfe, Victor of Quebec. Though successful, he died in the attempt.'

'You're mad,' said Bridie and she tipped the remainder of the bacon on top of him. 'You're mad. Think you're a writer? I'll tell you something. There's a lad come to Nellie Maguire's, says he's a writer. A real writer too. None of yer gobbing havers. A man with a book beneath his belt. Published and all. I saw it on the table in his room. That's what you call a writer. A real man. So there. Stick that in your old journal, if you will.'

And having swept up the tray, she pounced through the door and was off. Nancy scampered on to the bed, licking up the spilt rashers. Valentine Brack absently fondled her neck.

A writer in Kilbrack, he was thinking. A book published. Written and published. The wonder of it. And only a young lad too. This was news.

And he scurried off the bed, scattering bacon and bedclothes and dog.

'Bridie!' he called. 'Bridie O'Toole!'

Nellie Maguire sighed. 'It's some sort of note. For you, I think.'

O'Leary had watched her shuffle down the stairs. In her dressing gown and slippers, a fag again lagging on her lips, she looked the grandmother of the gay young thing of the evening before.

'For me?'

'Tall young man, it says.' She lolled her head sideways, unequal to its weight. 'I don't know,' she admitted.

O'Leary took the note. His hand was shaking. He had a hangover.

Nellie watched him while he read, his face breaking into happy surprise. She'd been right to give him the job, she considered. If her hunch was correct and he was truly a man from the Drugs Squad, it was safer to keep him under her nose. The last thing she needed was a barman, of course. The O'Tooles and Downey were her only customers. Those three could run the place on their own, often did. But with the stranger occupied below, she could more easily attend to her own affairs, work out an escape from this mess.

He had finished the note. 'Good news?'

'Yes,' said O'Leary. 'Quite excellent, in fact.'

'Well, I'm off upstairs. Don't talk to me about breakfast.' She heaved in a long breath, then exhaled abruptly. Watching her, O'Leary had the impression that half-way through breathing she realized she had no use for the long breath after all. 'Anyway,' she said and shambled off up the stairs.

O'Leary opened the note again and excitedly ran through the details once more. He was rereading it still, the seventh time, when Nellie returned.

'Good morning to you,' she said cheerfully. 'And how's my guest this morning?'

O'Leary groaned. It was preposterous. Here she was, transformed again, resplendent in another catsuit, gold lamé this time. Rings on her fingers, stilettos on her heels; bangles and chains dangled from her neck, her wrists, to clang if she moved.

'And isn't it a wonderful morning too that's in it? With

the rain pattering on the sills with the rat-tat-tat of a boogie band? Hearken to it.' She tittered joyously. 'Bacon and eggs for breakfast? Coming up.' And she danced her way to the stove. 'A touch under the weather this morning, are we? Jimjams, is it? Shocking.'

O'Leary shook himself. 'Er – yes. The stout—'

'Spoil ourselves last night, did we? Quantity-wise? What the heck. Aren't you on your holidays?' He flinched at the raucous jangle of her jewellery as she set his place at the table. 'Poor thing. You've a face like you've slept in it, agony laden. Take a trip up to Downey, why don't you? He'll fix you something, remedy-wise.'

'Downey?'

'The pharmacy.'

'Why yes, that is a good idea.' He brightened considerably. 'By the way, Miss Maguire, I hope you won't mind awfully, but that note I received—'

'Note?' It was as though she had never before heard of it.

'Yes, it was from the Rectory. Mrs Cuthbert has invited me to lunch with her. I do hope you won't mind.'

'Not at all. Popular man. The Cuthberts and all. Nice folk. Left footers, religion-wise. Used to be anyway. Can't keep pace with them now. All the same, spice's the life. By the way, how long do you think you'll be staying with us, guest-wise?'

'I'm sorry?'

'Here's your hat, where's your hurry!' And she laughed uproariously. 'If you gave me some idea how long you planned stopping, that's all, I'd know what groceries to get in. The van calls today.'

'But Miss Maguire, I work here.'

'Ah!' She tapped her crown. 'Nellie Maguire, you'd forget your – what is that thing called? Anyway, you're a writer, aren't you? I have it remembered now. Working here, are you, on your next book?' There was a shuffling outside in the pub. 'That'll be someone wanting service. This hour and all. 'Tis all go. Shan't be a sec.' Then at the door: 'By the way, thanks a million for helping out behind the bar last night. Won't happen again, I promise. But I was that jiggered, I was dead on me feet, sleep-wise.'

Diary Memo: Pendulum-wise, the moods of that woman are impossible. Have determined to seek alternative employment. Of a live-in nature preferably. The enclosed space of the bar affects my sinuses.

Hangover really.

Diary Memo: Till that happy hour, however, there is the jackpot luck of Mrs Cuthbert's timely invitation. Lunch 12.30. The other suit perhaps? . . . And Livia . . .

'My, but you certainly are the popular man today.' Nellie Maguire breezed back into the kitchen. 'That was Bridie O'Toole hotfoot from the big house. The old man above's after inviting you up for afternoon tea!'

The grey aquiline Monsignor did not turn an inch from the

view he was regarding from the Rectory's drawing room window. He said, as though to the spire of St Ciaran's itself, 'Tea, did you say, Mrs C?'

'Earl Grey, Father Michael.'

'Monsignor.'

'I'm sorry, Father Michael. I mean Monsignor.' Mrs Cuthbert poured the tea, spilling only the tiniest drop from her Crown Derby pot.

The Monsignor continued staring out the window. In silence he contemplated the overgrown cemetery, the spire rising restrained to a native sky, the fragments of stained glass remaining. The stone was crumbling, he knew – he'd had a survey done – but the foundations were sound, deep in the age-old soil. He liked that church. It was a church fit for a gentleman.

In his reflection in the window he spotted a strand odd in his oiled hair. His fingers, quick as a lash, corrected it.

'Monsignor?' Stout Mrs Cuthbert spoke in the register of a schoolgirl.

'First things first. Is it the discretion of the confessional you're after, Mrs C?'

Mrs Cuthbert eyed the straight back of the priest with an inbred awe of religious authority. 'Milk, Monsignor?' she asked.

'Lashings of it, Mrs C. Only lashings. There's a grand future in milk.'

Mrs Cuthbert poured, and the small drop she spilt she mopped with her lace hanky. 'Monsignor, it's about Livia.'

'And sugar, Mrs C. We all of us Adam's children bear the

sin of the sweet tooth, God forgive us. Sugar beet's sound. Three sugars, please, Mrs C.'

Mrs Cuthbert rattled her best bone china to the table where the priest would sit. 'Your tea, Monsignor, is on the table.'

'Grand.'

Mrs Cuthbert remembered when he was a curate. Such a nice English word, curate. His back was still straight and rigid as it had been then. Indeed in appearance little had changed to mark the earnest young curate from the authoritative Monsignor with his back to her now. Except perhaps, a whisper of a wheeze: not every time he breathed: but always before he embarked on words.

He wheezed now. ''Tis a grand church you have out there, Mrs C. I'll give you that for your heathen Protestants, they knew how to keep a decent church. Bricks and mortar: always a sound investment. The RC's is a stable compared.' He turned now from the window, his shiny black soutane swishing with the turn, draping to faultless creases.

And this Rectory too was a fine Georgian manor. In disrepair and bare inside, he allowed. But a little lucre, some small persuasion, and both church and Rectory would make a fine comfortable living. He had the money, and by the grace of God, he had the persuasion too.

'Livia, you say.'

'Yes, Father.'

'Monsignor,' he corrected sharply.

Stout Mrs Cuthbert's dumpling face collapsed slowly, inwardly, to its deepest pathos. Monsignor – it was outlandish. And if there was anything to say about the Protestants, it was that their titles were good solid English words. Monsignor. However, he was still a man of the cloth. She had been brought up to respect the cloth. And when her allegiance had been transferred to her late husband's enemy's camp, her respect had travelled with it. She had made her bed. And though she felt no longer like a crossed, insurgent wife, but like a widow thwarted, still she had made her bed; she would lie on it. It was in her blood.

She sighed heavily. 'Yes, Livia,' she said. 'Monsignor, you'll remember years ago when you were curate here in Kilbrack—'

'Of course, I remember,' he broke in. 'The Portakabin Curate they called me at the Palace.' He smiled now at the recollection of those heady young days. How pleasant it would be to return to Kilbrack, retire a while from the world's business, await the call to purple.

'You helped me through my time of need—'

'And guided you to the true faith of the Apostles. Of course I remember, Mrs C. Weren't you my first conversion? The smile was on the other side of their faces up in the Palace when they got wind of that snigget of news, I don't have to tell you.'

'I asked you to come today because—'

'To the great consternation of your husband, I recall. Arnold Cuthbert. Now there was a religious man. But for his satanic Anglican heresy, he was a saint incarnate. The Reverend Arnold Cuthbert. It has a heathen ring to it, don't you think? Reverend.' And his tongue burred disdainfully over the sound.

'Monsignor, I want you to have a word with Livia for

me. She respects you. God knows I've tried myself. Father Michael—'

'Monsignor.'

'I've tried everything. I'm at my wits' end.' The rehearsing of her woes had produced such disquietude that squeezing her fingers, Mrs Cuthbert had teased her wedding ring loose. It slipped off completely now, rolled on to the floor. 'My ring!' And she heaved herself down on to the carpet, feeling for it under the table.

The Monsignor deftly retrieved it. 'Gold,' he said appreciatively. 'Safe as houses.'

The telephone rang.

'That'll be for me. 'Tis unfortunate, I know: but constant accessibility is the touchstone of the modern priesthood.'

'It's for you,' said Mrs Cuthbert.

'I had half a mind it might be.' He accepted the telephone, examined the mouthpiece, wiped it. 'Hello,' he said. 'Hello? Hello? You will have to speak up. Where? Tokyo? Oh, Tokyo. Hello.' There was a long pause, during which the priest's handsome features blushed steadily to purple, as if in premonition of the higher office that awaited him. Mrs Cuthbert had the notion they must be particularly mortal sins he was hearing. 'Are you mad?' he shouted at last. 'Sell, man, sell! Before the markets open!' And he slammed down the telephone. He picked it up again immediately. 'God bless,' he said, and replaced it more gently. 'God protect me from fools and novices,' he said as he sat down again. He sipped his tea. 'Nice tea that. Perfumed, is it?'

'Earl Grey.'

'Very nice. Would there be much of a market for perfumed tea?'

'Market?'

'Never mind. Where were we?'

'Livia, Father Michael.'

'Monsignor.'

'Monsignor.'

'And how is the young scallywag? Take my advice, go easy on that one. She's a very clever girl that, do you know? And pretty with it. Pretty – isn't the half of it. How is she up in the marriage stakes?'

'It's the marriage stakes are the problem. I asked you to come to see if you might have a word with her. She'll listen to you—'

'Now, now, Mrs C, you'll have to let her go one day. Take it from me. Too tight a leash, butterflies on wheels, you'll strain the horse's neck. Will she be down soon? 'Tis a long stretch since we had a little theological discussion between us. I used to enjoy the odd dispute with Livia, little pagan that she is. Will she be down?'

'For lunch,' said Mrs Cuthbert.

'I think that'll be for me.'

He picked up the telephone again. 'Of course it is I. Monsignor, damn you!' After another long delay, he shouted, 'Think ham, boyo. Ham, ham, ham. And good morning to you, too.' He smiled at Mrs Cuthbert as he replaced the telephone. 'The youth of Ireland,' he said, 'our greatest asset. Did you know, Mrs C, we have the youngest population in Europe, thanks be to God and Holy Mother Church – all set to double in the twenty-first century. And what will these kiddies be eating? Hamburgers, Mrs C. Think of it. Hamburger stalls everywhere. Left right and centre, the whole shebang. The future is all hamburgers.' He fixed her with his sharpest look. 'Invest in ham.'

Mrs Cuthbert sighed.

'What do you mean, you're closed?'

'Closed for the feast day of St Hyacinth of Cracow,' intoned Downey, cowering inches away, yet snatching with the corner of his eye a quick glance at the rain-sodden pilgrim at his door. 'And 'tis no lie neither. Look, and there's a sign on the door to prove it too. You won't call me mendacious.'

O'Leary Montagu followed Downey's nod and there true enough on the knobbled glass door of the pharmacy was a handwritten sign in tiny neat italics.

'St Hyacinth of Cracow?' he repeated.

'August the seventeenth.'

Pretending to cough, Downey darted a look to the anti-burglar chain device on his side of the door. Was it still securely fastened? It was. He'd known all along. 'Closed,' he said, his hand comfortable on the Swiss-made knife in his pocket.

A squall of rain and the guttering above the shop quivered, close to overflowing. O'Leary peered up. The sign had changed since last he'd looked. There was still J. D. DOWNEY, DISPENSER OF ADVICE, with 'ADVICE' underlined three times. But it seemed he no longer dispensed any medicaments, for that word had recently been hastily crossed out, along with the initial MPSI which previously had appeared in proud and bold capitals. The entire sign was rattling loose. There was another squall of rain and the guttering gave up its overflowing ghost, cascaded its dirty water, missing O'Leary's head by inches.

'Can't you let me in a moment?' he pleaded. 'You can see it's pouring down. I'm soaked through.'

'This side of the water,' said Downey informatively, 'this weather is known as a soft day.'

'Can't I come in?'

'And what would you want coming in here?'

'Medicine, of course.'

'Medicine?' What new jiggery-pokery was this? 'Medicine for what?'

'Pneumonia if I stand out here much longer.'

'Pneumonia, is it?' said Downey, his chin jutting over the anti-burglar chain device on the door. So the incognito man wanted to test him, did he? Test his knowledge. Well, Downey was up to a test this time. He might have failed his Latin, but the man would soon discover he wasn't dealing with a failure. Nor with a total fraud. 'Now, there's a tricky knot of a malaise,' he said. 'A knot to outwit a Grecian conqueror's sword or the one word of the Lord and no mistake.'

'I'm sorry?'

'You'd best come in.'

There was an extravagant unlatching of chains, and Downey bowed O'Leary in. It was dark inside, yet still O'Leary gazed in wonder.

'Quite correct,' said Downey. 'Our American cousins

would have us term it pneumonitis, but 'twas pneumonia our forefathers suffered – and if pneumonia was good enough for them, 'tis good enough for us. Are you with me?'

'I think so,' said O'Leary. 'I'm not sure.' There were rows upon rows of shelves in the pharmacy, lined against every wall, rows and rows of dusty, cobwebbed, and most of all, empty shelves.

'A condition of the lung, *Lobar pneumonia* is common most amongst children and young persons of either sex. The pneumococcus germ enters the body via mouth or nose, finding its way to one lobe – one lobe only, mind – of the lung, producing inflammation. The resultant fever, combined with a cough, is often associated with a little rust-tinted sputum.' The thin little pharmacist stood back, grinning expectantly, hands behind his back like a schoolboy. That'd show this inspector from the Pharmaceutical Society that he wasn't dealing with a complete impostor. He knew his stuff. Of course he did. 'What d'you think of that then?'

'Extraordinary,' said O'Leary. It was the emptiest of empty shops he had ever seen in his life, uncontaminated by the slightest hint of a medicine, or indeed of anything, save dust. On the whole of one wall hung a musty poster, a home-written year-planner, that spelt out in red, green and black ink the feast days of hundreds and hundreds of the most obscure saints. 'St Narses the Gracious,' he read, 'August the thirteenth. St Joseph of Volokolamsk, September the ninth. St Gerard of Csanad, September the twenty-fourth.'

'Extraordinary,' he repeated.

'Oh, there's more still.' Downey could see his little treatise had had the desired effect. Of course he wasn't a fraud. So what if he'd failed his Latin and couldn't go to Medical School. What of it, if even the Pharmacological College had refused him entry. He still knew his stuff, could rattle it off with the best of them. Oh yes, Latin too. And Greek. He was a chemist in all but credentials, God damn it. '*Bronchopneumonia*,' he continued, 'acute bronchitis to the layman, is a close relation, Greek *pneumon*, lung, the common root to both. You'd be surprised what a man might know. Happily surprised, I might add. The treatment is penicillin. You saw the sign, I take it?'

'Closed for St Hyacinth?'

'Not at all. J. D. DOWNEY, DISPENSER OF ADVICE.'

'I did. I couldn't help but notice, however, that it's been altered recently.'

He spotted it, thought Downey. Hell and damnation. He coughed. ''Twas the village boys. Larking about, they were. 'Twas them inserted the medicament nonsense. Such malarky. Tragic what these kiddies'll get up to.'

He was grinning earnestly away, nodding his head eagerly, as though encouraging O'Leary, begging him even, to commiserate with him on the sorry state of Irish youth. O'Leary felt he had missed something in their conversation.

'Needless to say I removed the offending words – and initials, I made a point of that – as soon as the prank was brought to my attention. As you well know, I'm not a member of the Pharmaceutical Society of Ireland and hence would not consider in a thousand years dispensing medicaments no matter what their worth or urgency. Leave that to the professionals, I always say. Men with Latin tripping off their tongues.

'And by the by,' he continued, 'I believe you should be informed, what with all the saints and their feast days to observe –' he nodded in the direction of the year-planner, 'sure I haven't had the chance to open shop once, not once mind you, since I turned it from a grocery. Never. On my mother's sacred memory.'

'I believe you,' said O'Leary. There would be no point opening such an empty shop.

'You do?' Downey had not expected it to be so easy. Was the man being sweet now, buttering him up, before the final devastating onslaught? Time to display a little more learning. 'Pneumonia, you say?'

'Well no. Actually it's a hangover.'

'Sure, that's no symptom. Off with your shirt till I have a listen to your pneumons.'

It was some time before O'Leary could convince the man that it was a hangover he was suffering. By that time he had his shirt off, his trousers down, and the fellow was eagerly tapping away at his knees, testing his reflexes, so he said. It was all very awkward because O'Leary, though he had his trousers down, refused to take his hand out of his pocket where his fingers gripped tightly on the jiffy. Downey too kept one hand in his pocket. The stout Swiss-made knife with the sharpest blade in the South Riding – he saw to that – might be his saviour yet. His mother had given it him on his eighteenth birthday, the day before his Latin highers. Oh dear, thought Downey.

To cover his embarrassment, O'Leary decided to test the

water, so to speak, with the work of Nancy Valentine. But it seemed the pharmacist had never heard of her.

'What book?'

'*Ill Fares the Land*, of course. It's all in it,' O'Leary tried to explain. The man tapped his other knee, a fierce wallop. 'Your mother ran a grocery here.'

Worse it gets, thought Downey. The man's kept a book on my doings, stretching back God knows how long. They'd been spying on him all these years, the blasted Society. Oh, he'd known, he'd known.

'Look here, is this really necessary?' O'Leary asked as he bent over double, trying to touch his toes with one hand, while the pharmacist felt his spine, rambling on about muscular stress and how lumbago and fibrositis had no scientific evidence to support their existence. 'All I have is a headache.'

Downey muttered something about shilly-shallying behaviour. He told the man to dress. 'Dress,' he said dejectedly. He knew he'd failed. I've failed once more, he told his mother. The worst of it was he knew his mother wouldn't be surprised. 'Always let me down,' she had complained from her death bed. 'Doctor? Sweet Jesus and all the saints, you wouldn't make a common pharmacist.'

But suddenly Downey was forced to stand back. Stand back in amazement. By St Anthony, patron saint of lost causes, he was saved. Or was he? Perhaps. Could he try? Will I? I've nothing to lose now. St Rock and I will!

For a dazzling idea had struck him. This man, this inspector from the Pharmaceutical Society of Ireland, was in his shop. He was suffering, apparently, from a hangover.

Serves him right, Downey might have said. Teach him to drink beyond his limit. Except – and this was the brainwave – wasn't Downey – oh yes, poor old Downey, who couldn't master his Latin declensions, who wasn't a doctor, nor a pharmacist neither, truth be told, though his mother had craved with her dying breath that he be one, or at least the other – wasn't this very same J. D. Downey the sole dispenser – in all of Ireland, so far as he could tell, all the world even – of this miracle cure, this medicament that transformed in an instant a careworn gammer to a carefree young girl? What if he tried it on this inspector? In an instant his fortunes would be reversed. The inspector would have no choice but to acknowledge his brilliance. He would be hailed – J. D. Downey of Kilbrack, Tipperary – as the final discoverer of the philosopher's stone, the panacea, the catholicon that men of science and art had sought in vain for three thousand solid years!

The idea was tremendous. It quite knocked him back and he had to sit down for a moment while the full blast of his brilliance swept over him. He glanced up at his mother hanging on the wall, surrounded by all the saints. She would be so proud.

He fetched himself up to collect one of the packages. Miss Maguire liked to keep one or two with him in the pharmacy in case she ran out too soon. 'Try this,' he said, mixing the powder in some water, a quarter of a gill, he judged. ''Tis just a little remedy of my own devising, but it should do the trick.'

St Anthony and St Rock, it had better, he thought.

* * *

Five minutes later, O'Leary Montagu stood, froze, in the middle of the street. He checked his Rolex. He was about to remind himself that he didn't own a Rolex, when he noticed his feet. They were dancing. Quite uncontrollably really. Rather like—

> *His feet were strutting their stuff on the drenched street. They danced, sure they danced. Jigging like drunken rain.*

Oh no, thought O'Leary.

You bet, said the Detectives.

CHAPTER EIGHT

Mrs Cuthbert let out a mortified whisper. 'Livia!'

'Yes, Mother?'

'Take that bottle away!' And she indicated with furious furtive fingers the green chilled bottle.

'Tio Pepe, Mother?'

'You can't offer the Monsignor that Spanish stuff.'

Livia sought with her eyes her daily dose of sympathy from heaven's dispensary above. 'Sherry?' she said to the Monsignor. 'Chilled?'

The Monsignor looked up quickly from the telephone. 'Chilled? Thank you, child. I have heard 'tis the modern method. The Nuncio takes it that way always. You're a credit to the parental home, Livia.'

Mrs Cuthbert huffed a moment, then bustled back into the kitchen with her tray of four Bristol Cream sherries. That girl was a liability. The sooner she was married and off her hands the better for everyone. Lock, stock and barrel. A tinker would nearly do. A tinker? She'd pay him.

She examined the soup, sniffed. It didn't seem to be

doing very much. She couldn't remember was it mushroom or tomato. It bore no particular resemblance to either. It was leftovers and something. She tasted it. It tasted of – soup, really.

Livia entered. 'I've brought you a glass of sherry, Mother.'

'What are you doing in here?'

'What are you hiding?'

'Nothing. Entertain the Monsignor.'

'Is that soup, Mother?' Livia stalked over to the range. 'Mother,' she tutted. She grabbed the soup pan and in one sweep poured the contents down the drain. 'Not for luncheon, thank you.'

'Livia!'

'See to the table, Mother. You can leave the food to me.'

Mrs Cuthbert crooked an elbow to her hip. 'It's my luncheon party,' she said.

'And I'll cry if I want to.'

'I beg your pardon, Livia?'

Livia turned. She tried not to smile. But her mother did look so comical when she was angry. 'I know it's your party, Mother. So you just go inside and enjoy yourself.' She propelled her gently out of the kitchen into the hall. 'Everything's under control in here. You have your guests to consider.'

Guests, thought Mrs Cuthbert, despairing. The one was endlessly engaged to the international operator, the other was – 'Where is he?' she said.

'I believe he's still in the lavatory.'

'Is he all right?'

'I should imagine so.'

'Did you catch his name?'

'He mumbled something. Sounded double-barrelled.'

Double-barrelled? This was happier news. A well-spoken, double-barrelled—

'Or double Dutch,' added Livia mischievously.

'Did you find out what he does?'

'He did mumble something about detective novels.'

A writer, thought Mrs Cuthbert with a doubtful jubilation, as she dispersed the place mats around the dining room table. She had read in the *Reader's Digest* that writers were extravagantly stinking. He didn't look rich. But writers were so notoriously topsy-turvy. Writers? The whole world was topsy-turvy . . . Livia and the Monsignor, herself and the writer: there, she'd laid the table. Father Michael could give Livia that sermon on the Fifth Commandment, while she herself would conduct a polite investigation into the suitor's suitability. Perfect. Meanwhile, she'd hunt out that article in the *Reader's Digest.* Apparently they all lived in extravagant luxury in the south of France . . .

Livia smiled at the lamb cutlets, shredding some caraway seed and onion over them. Terrine to precede, Stilton to follow. How convenient that she had visited Waterford yesterday. It would be mother's soup and curtains otherwise. Poor Mother. She'll have such a turn when she realizes the man's unhinged. Mind you, she added to the photograph of her father hanging between the gridirons and skillets on the wall: it'll serve her right.

Son-of-a-bitch druggist. He'd slipped him a Mickey Finn. He'd bet his wad on that. In this business you had to go by your hunches. And the way his hands were shaking like a two-bit Gospel chorus, he'd a hunch that druggist wasn't entirely kosher. Motherloving medic was not a phrase in his vocabulary. But it was no party knocking back a quarter gill of hootch. He'd get back to Downey. He'd throw the book at him.

Mrs Cuthbert heaved up her bust, and her courage, and knocked stoutly on the lavatory door. 'Are you in there?'

'Oh God,' groaned O'Leary Montagu. He allowed himself one lingering roost on his lemon jiffy, then stuffed it back in his pocket. 'Coming.'

The Monsignor wheezed. 'Well spoken, Livia,' he said. 'Save you must bear in mind that woman was created subject to the man. First there was man, and the Lord God seeing he needed a helpmeet, took one of his ribs, and made he a woman. *Genesis.* I'll help myself to the wine if that's all right with you, Mrs C.' He poured. 'And therefore shall a man leave home, and shall cleave unto his wife; and they twain shall be one. *Genesis* again.'

'Chapter two, verse twenty-four,' drawled Livia, removing some gristle from her cutlet.

'I paraphrase, of course.'

'Of course.'

'And that is why it is the duty of every woman to marry. Go forth and multiply, and all that. We must beware, Livia, the thin edge of heterodoxy.' He squinted at the label on the bottle. 'Burgundy, if I'm not mistaken?'

'Celibacy, I suppose, is a state reserved for the male gender. Meursault, Seventy-one.'

'A grand year.'

'Not too dry for your taste?'

'I like it white and dry.'

'It's from my father's cellar.'

'The Reverend Cuthbert. There was a man with a fine nose for a wine.' He squinted again at the label. 'Remoissenet,' he read aloud. 'A grand bottler.' He returned to the debate. 'You misunderstand me, Livia—'

'Actually,' she interrupted him, 'Remoissenet was the shipper. The wine was bottled at source.'

The Monsignor hesitated with a sickly smile. Then he slugged back his glass. 'This is the age of the parish priest. What use at all are monastics, this day and age? Contemplation, I ask you. Habits, Livia, wimples. Let alone convents. They all cost money.'

'Render unto Caesar,' said Livia.

'But that was years ago.'

Livia concealed her amusement under the pretence of swallowing with difficulty the morsel of meat she had been chewing. 'I quite understand, Monsignor, that as Catholics we cannot allow of predestination, but to deny God's word universality in time and space seems to me to be the thin edge of heterodoxy. How are your cutlets?'

'Heaven,' said the Monsignor. The bitch, he thought. 'Is it your own recipe?'

'I took it from the *Telegraph*.'

'A heathen paper.' He took another swig of the Meursault '71. 'So, Livia, you'd have us all turned out in mendicant orders, is that it?'

'Not I, Monsignor: Our Saviour.'

'Now, stick to the one subject, Livia.' 'A continual dropping in a very rainy day and a contentious woman are alike,' he quoted, snarling to himself.

O'Leary Montagu, across the table from Livia, endeavoured to follow the ornate, almost baroque reasoning of Livia's conversation. Handel was playing quietly in the background on the gramophone. And his eyes still gazing adoringly at Livia's disregarding face, falling every now and then to the cold-shoulder of her bosom, he entered into the sympathetic reasoning of the concerto. His fingers started tapping in time. His feet too. Except, when he glanced down it occurred to him that they were dancing to a different rhythm altogether. An African beat, like bongo drums.

So, he had a crush on this babe. You couldn't blame him. Sure as eggs is eggs, she was hell of a beauty. Easy on the eye? She was a knock-out. You'd end up pegged out, KO'd inside two seconds of the first bout. She was a stunner. Smart too.

Quietly at her place, Mrs Cuthbert was nearly crying. I can't take much more of this, she thought. They had sat to lunch at one o'clock. Now, three hours later, she glanced to her wristwatch, and it was twenty past one. Purgatory. Worse, she had found that article in the *Reader's Digest* about stinking writers, but it was so terribly short on names. Somerset Maugham had a yacht apparently. She doubted somehow this man beside her had a spare pair of shoes. She looked at his vacant face. Fool of a thing. Why didn't he say something?

It was a breach of correct table manners, she knew, but she'd have to initiate some conversation herself.

'So,' she began. But turning to O'Leary she had focused inadvertently on the scars on his cheeks. It didn't seem proper somehow to look. She glazed her eyes, continued the movement of her head, glancing to the ceiling, then down again, all in one sweep, till she landed on the priest on the other side of the table. 'Father Michael,' she ended lamely.

'Monsignor,' he corrected.

Bishop, dean, canon, pastor, rector, vicar: all decent English words. He had a treasury of them to choose from. Monsignor. It wasn't natural.

'Purgatory,' she said in despair.

And Livia, pouncing, began her theological tittle-tattle all over again.

Purgatory, thought Mrs Cuthbert. It was purgatory all right. Other people lived their life in peace and happiness and nights out at the opera and days at the races, all hats and feathers and gentlemen in morning suits and evening jackets, white gloves and manners; and it was only the centuries after that they languished in purgatory.

And Graham Greene: according to the *Reader's Digest*, he lived on the Côte d'Azur . . .

But she, for her sins, must live this hell on earth of an ungrateful daughter. It wasn't fair. She was the laughing-stock of the county. She'd married a dud – all right, he was a saint, but that buttered no toast in society – to have a nun for a daughter. The shame.

She might at least look at him. To talk to him was too much to expect: but Livia could spare him a look at least. He was no picture: but love knows no laws. He was a man, wasn't he?

And Somerset Maugham. No, she'd said him.

Mrs Cuthbert dared now a glance herself at the prospective paramour beside her. A writer, she thought. It was unchartered territory. Detective novels too, she mused exploratively. It didn't sound very grand. However. He was here. And in love. Indeed, he had the look of an adoring lap-dog, hanging on to her daughter's every word. Rather distasteful with his mouth hanging open. But certainly encouraging. And detective fiction, she was sure, was a very popular genre. And at least he was a man, dressed in a proper suit, with a nice delivery and a good name. Bugger art.

'The wife is subject to the husband!'

'Oh, tell that to the Ephesians.'

'So, Mr O'Leary Montagu,' ventured Mrs Cuthbert, in the pause that followed Livia's collapse into giggles, 'you are a writer, I believe.'

'Why yes,' said O'Leary, happily surprised.

'A writer, you say,' said the Monsignor darkly.

'He writes detective novels,' said Livia. 'Ghastly stuff. Can't abide it.'

Mrs Cuthbert rose to her feet. Family rows in public were so distasteful. She wouldn't speak, but she'd let her eyes show her anger. Except Livia was busy sipping her wine. She wouldn't look up.

'Livia,' commanded Mrs Cuthbert.

'Yes Mother?'

'Look at my eyes.'

'Good gracious, Mother. How painful. There's some witch hazel in my bathroom. I'll fetch it if you like.'

'Mr O'Leary Montagu,' sighed Mrs Cuthbert. 'Will you help me with the coffee and cheese in the kitchen?'

'Parlour, Mother.'

'Parlour,' she said.

In the library of Knight's Kilbrack, Valentine Brack stretched his long, thin arms to the topmost shelf, retrieved an ancient volume. He blew off the dust. *Sonnets,* it said, Milton. He considered it, as if weighing its weight in his hand. It would do.

He climbed down off the steps, still measuring the book in his mind. He knelt down to the broken leg of the Pembroke table. Stood on edge, the *Sonnets* was an ideal fit, almost. The table still wobbled, still leaned at a slant. But—

'It will serve,' he pronounced. 'If only in the manner of those standing and waiting.'

He was ready now for the *pièce de résistance.* He unwrapped the special oilskin covering and placed delicately the leather-bound journal on the Pembroke table. *Ill Fares the Land*, it read: *Volume XIV*. It was exactly the right effect. A small realignment here? The right angle to the window was crucial. There. Perfect. This writer fellow would know him for the cultured man he was.

But was it the right volume? One could never be certain.

It had nearly seven full pages of writing in it, only three of which had been crossed out. Of course it was the right volume.

One further appurtenance. He searched through the bureau drawer, a lifetime's detritus of rubber bands and postcards, till he found it. The silver paper-cutter with the ivory top. A bequest from his great-uncle Valentine. Or was it a memento of Bournemouth? Never mind. He positioned it beside the leather-bound volume. He was content.

He sat down at his desk, smiled expansively. 'Welcome,' he said. 'An old man, husbanding out life's taper at the close, I welcome a fellow toiler of the pen.'

It didn't sound right. So he experimented with the salutation in a lower pitch. The lower pitch was definitely better.

The curtains were half-drawn. He had tried them open, then closed, then open again, but in the end he had settled on the half-gloom of a compromise. Outside he could hear Jim still working on the flower-beds. The man had started to sneeze earlier on, complaining of the weather, but Valentine Brack had ordered him to stay put. He knew how crucial were the background sounds of manual labour to a truly intellectual conversation.

During the course of the morning, he had changed his jacket three times, his tie twice. It was so difficult achieving the desired effect. He would have changed his trousers too, but right at the beginning he had chosen perforce the black trousers that went with his black tie. They were the only ones free of dog-stain. They looked silly with boots, but he couldn't find his shoes. Besides, they wouldn't be noticed with the tweed of his jacket and his favourite yellow cardigan underneath.

He reached now into his jacket pocket for the watch with the broken strap. It was still only lunch time. He had two hours and more to wait. 'Bridie!' he called, as the library door opened and Bridie strode in.

'What d'ye want now?' she said.

'What do you want coming in here?' returned Valentine Brack.

'Didn't you call me?'

'Never mind that. You were half-way in when I called.'

'Half-way in? You have me half-way up the wall,' said Bridie.

She had left the library door open and now, nearly tripping her up, in rushed the mongrel Nancy. 'That blasted cur!'

'Which blasted cur?' Valentine Brack searched around him. 'Has Nancy invited a four-legged friend? She'll be regaling him no doubt with snippets from her intelligence.'

'Away with your nonsense.'

''Tis no nonsense at all. Sit down now Nancy and stick up for yourself properly. Describe to us the manner of a deal poor Bridie had this morning,' he said. 'Concerning the rashers,' he hinted.

And again upon the signal of the lifted finger, the dog half-growled, half-barked.

'You see?' said Valentine Brack reasonably. 'Nancy maintains it was a *rough* deal.' And he gave the mongrel a huge hug.

'I'm off,' said Bridie.

'Hold on one moment.'

'What is it?'

Valentine Brack paused for a further theatrical second. Then he nodded nonchalantly to the wall. 'Do you see the portrait of the Dadda above?'

Bridie peered up warily at the portrait of the hoary Valentine Brack that dominated the closed-up hearth. Valentine, she thought. Why were they all called Valentine? 'I dusted it last week. What about it?'

'He lived till he was ninety-nine and three-quarters years old, the Dadda did.'

'Grand man,' said Bridie dutifully.

'Grand man,' said Valentine Brack.

'What's that to do with me?' Bridie smelled a rat.

'Nothing. Nothing at all. Bridie.'

'Well?'

'Save that I've a mind I'll follow him.'

'Follow him where?'

Valentine Brack jutted forward his chin. 'Follow him till I'm ninety-nine and three-quarters years old.'

Bridie didn't scratch his eyes out, though she was close to it. 'Agh!' she cried, and she ran sobbing out of the library, wringing her poor over-worked hands in the rage and vexation that futility demanded.

'I think it would be best if you left the crockery to me,' said Mrs Cuthbert, sweeping up the last of the shards from the kitchen floor.

'I really don't know what came over me.'

'Never mind.'

'I'll be happy to replace all breakages.'

'Please sit down, Mr O'Leary Montagu. I really wouldn't hear of it.'

O'Leary sat down heavily. His hands were shaking.

Shaking like a two-bit Gospel chorus—

Yes, yes, we've had that, he moaned to himself. It was ridiculous, but he was still in the Detectives' slippery grip.

Mrs Cuthbert fussed with Livia's damned espresso contraption. How simple life would be with a maid. Or two maids, even. A maid and a cook, nothing too extravagant, simple uniforms. She was sure Graham Greene on the Côte d'Azur had maids, a host of them. 'And tell me, Mr O'Leary Montagu, are you here researching another book?'

You had to hand it to them, these jerkwater hicks. They were quick off the mark.

'Why yes,' he said. 'I am actually.'

'How interesting. Though I shouldn't have imagined the quiet waters of Kilbrack would provide much of a background for a detective novel.'

'No, Mrs Cuthbert. Actually, I gave up detective novels some years ago.'

So, he told a few white ones. In this business you had to feed the line. Sometimes. Put it down to experience.

'Will you shut up!'

'I beg your pardon?' Mrs Cuthbert turned to him from the espresso machine.

'I'm sorry. I didn't mean that.'

Diary Memo: Please help me!

It was a cry for help, said the Detectives smugly.

'I'm warning you!'

'Well really, Mr O'Leary Montagu.'

It was a case of misunderstanding. It had happened before. Sure it had. You got used to louse-ups in this line of work. You had to.

'Will you get it into your head I don't write detective novels any more!' O'Leary burst out. He was gripping the sides of his chair, rocking almost. His eyes were squeezed shut, and through his clenched teeth he repeated over and over, quietly and urgently like a prayer: 'Diary Memo, Diary Memo, Diary Memo . . .'

Well really, thought Mrs Cuthbert. She knew writers were strange, secretive with their work, but surely there was no call for this behaviour. 'Mr O'Leary Montagu,' she said sternly.

O'Leary slowly unclenched his eyes, ungripped the sides of his chair. 'You must think me an awful fool,' he muttered.

'Fool was not the word for which I searched.'

'The truth is I'm writing a biography.' He was still trying to catch his breath. 'And that's why I've come to Kilbrack.'

'I see.' Biographies she understood. Why, she even read them sometimes. Nancy Mitford on Madame – who was it? She'd even enjoyed that one. Good solid writing.

Diary Memo: I am visiting Kilbrack that I might write the biography of the Mistress, Nancy Valentine.

You bet, said the Detectives.

'Oh God,' groaned O'Leary, and buried his face in his hands.

'Is it very difficult?' asked Mrs Cuthbert, slightly more solicitously.

'Very.'

'I see.' But she still didn't quite understand why the man had to be gripped by a difficult muse in her kitchen. Perhaps she'd try a different tack. Talking about writing obviously unnerved him, unnerved the artist in him. 'Mr O'Leary Montagu,' she began.

'Hello?' he said, peeking out from between his fingers.

Mrs Cuthbert regarded him. 'I had a schoolfriend named Montagu,' she said, pleasantly. 'She was related to the Wiltshire Montagus.'

'But I told you! I have nothing to do with the Wiltshire Montagus,' O'Leary wailed, close to desperation. Why wouldn't the woman listen? She'd asked him this three times already.

'Any chance of that cheese, Mother?' called Livia from the dining room.

Mrs Cuthbert threw a harassed glance to the kitchen door. She picked up Livia's Stilton. She stared at it a moment. She tried again. 'The O'Learys of Wicklow perhaps?'

'Mrs Cuthbert, I'm all confused.'

'You're confused?'

The fat dame had confused him, butted in the Detectives, unhelpfully.

'For the last time, will you shut up!'

'Mr O'Leary Montagu!' Mrs Cuthbert banged down the cheese on the table and faced him with her stoutest stance. 'You have exhibited an interest in my daughter. I am entitled to know your antecedents.'

'I'm sorry,' he said.

'Cheese, Mother!'

'It's just that O'Leary was the name of the sister in charge of my ward. I did try to tell you.'

The smell from the cheese, the rankest and bluest of Stiltons he'd ever come across, wafted from the table to his nose. He winced. Still on edge from Downey's cure-all, he could feel his stomach begin to turn.

Hang on in there, buddy, said the Detectives.

Mrs Cuthbert fetched the cheese-board and the cheese knife. It didn't make sense. He seemed to have a consultant named Montagu and a sister in charge of a ward. 'You are the guardian of a ward?' she asked, enunciating clearly. It was something. Guardian of a ward was a responsible position.

It didn't make sense. 'How can you be the guardian of a ward?' asked O'Leary. 'O'Leary was the sister.'

'The sister of the ward? But who was the guardian?'

'It doesn't make sense!'

Mrs Cuthbert stamped her foot. 'Mr O'Leary Montagu, do I take it you have a ward?'

'I used to.'

'You used to?'

'I told you.'

Mrs Cuthbert was not certain, but it seemed that at last she had got somewhere. Where, she wasn't quite sure. Riddling it out, she arranged the Stilton on to the cheese-board.

O'Leary averted his eyes. But still everywhere he looked he could see the thin blue worms gorging their way through the fat blubber of the cheese. He closed his eyes. The room had got hot suddenly, unbearably stuffy. His stomach inched towards heaving. He must try not to think of the cheese.

Forget the stinking cheese, advised the Detectives.

'Mother, what are you doing in there with the cheese?'

Mrs Cuthbert picked up the board, put it down again. 'So, your ward has achieved her majority?'

'Mrs Cuthbert, it doesn't make sense!'

'Then your ward has died?'

'Wards don't die!'

'What do they do?'

'They don't do anything! They house patients.'

'Patience? Mr O'Leary Montagu, don't you patience me!' She looked at her hands. She was holding the cheese-board. 'For the last time, are you or are you not the guardian of a ward?'

'Mrs Cuthbert, I've been trying to tell you. I am the new barman in Miss Maguire's public house—'

'The what?'

'The barman in Miss Maguire's – Agh!'

CHAPTER NINE

'AND LOVE THAT knows no rules, whereat it falls, espies no faults, fair and free as prison is foul; conquering all, rounding the world, making a wit of a fool, and laughing at locksmiths; casting out fear, stronger than death: blind lawless love! I had tasted not once of its bloom, though forced was I to quit my home . . .'

O'Leary Montagu could feel the tears. He put away his *Ill Fares the Land* in his jacket pocket, sniffed. Poor Nancy Valentine, he thought. She had never known love, and not knowing love, she had lived but an instant.

But he was in love. He was alive.

He felt better for vomiting, his mind sailed clearer. He had flushed away the inebriety of Downey's cure-all and its concomitant Detectives. His mind was his own again, native. But he still didn't feel quite recuperated enough to face the company below. He'd convalesce a while longer in the peace and quiet of the lavatory.

That woman had a temper. No two ways about it. He had thought her an ally. He had found but a bully. Never mind: there was Livia now.

When Livia had wandered into the kitchen wondering about the commotion, she had stared at O'Leary's face, and giggled. 'What d'you call that?' she had asked. 'International cheese-board?'

'Get him out! Get him out of my house!' her mother had stormed.

But Livia, seeing he was gagging, had taken a cloth and helped wash some of the cheese off his cheeks: the Stilton that her mother, egged by her tantrum, had thrown at him. 'I think, Mr O'Leary Montagu, you should visit the little boy's room,' she had advised placidly. 'Soon.'

Then, with O'Leary still gagging, and only his hand holding back the vomit, she had wrapped an arm round his shoulder and led him up the stairs. 'You need looking after,' she'd said.

And as O'Leary vomited, barely catching the bowl, he had thought to himself: she loves me, she loves me, she loves me. She said I needed looking after.

Now, perched comfortably on the lavatory seat, he took in deep cold draughts of the fresh air from the window. Life was hardly good. But it was certainly on the upper.

There was a knock on the door. 'Who is it?' he asked tremulously.'

'You're all right. It's me, Livia.'

'Oh. Hello.'

'Come on,' she said. 'I'll walk you back. We'll have to keep you out of trouble.'

* * *

The Monsignor helped himself to the port. 'You were saying, Mrs C?'

'I was saying I may as well be talking to the birds,' said Mrs Cuthbert, slumped in her chair.

'The Assisian,' said the Monsignor. 'A true madman.'

Oh shut up, thought Mrs Cuthbert.

'Livia? She'd have us all living in the Dark Ages. She'd turn the clock back a thousand years on us, she would. Will you not have a glass of this port, Mrs C?'

Mrs Cuthbert looked up at the priest. She never honestly knew for certain. But she had a feeling niggling deep inside her, that she hated the man. She sighed. 'I think I will,' she said. 'It's been a long morning.'

''Twill do you the world of good.' He poured her a liberal measure, and one for himself too. 'And don't you worry your head about Livia. She's a good lass at heart. It's just, what she doesn't realize is: we're living in the age of the parish priest.'

'Yes,' said Mrs Cuthbert abstractedly

'Nuns. Women have no business being anything other than good wives, good mothers and obedient parishioners. Vows of poverty – sure what do we want doing with that manner of a carry-on? Poverty'd get you nowhere, Mrs C.'

'Yes.' He didn't have to tell Mrs Cuthbert about poverty. Staring her in the face, it was.

'Nuns and friars? A load of codswallop. Pardon my Gaelic. This is the age of the parish priest. Obedience. That's what we want. Lashings of it.'

'What did you say?'

'Obedience, Mrs C. Grand drop of port this.'

A light had switched on in Mrs Cuthbert's eyes. Obedience, he had said. That was it. He could forbid her daughter to become a nun. He had the power. Her daughter was a Catholic. He was a priest. Catholics always obeyed their priest. It was part of the rules. Of course it was. Persuasion had failed. It was time now for the big guns.

She reached out to hold the priest's hands in hers. She was nearly kneeling in front of him.

'Whatever is the matter, Mrs C?'

'My daughter—'

'Livia?'

'My ungrateful daughter—'

'Whatever has she done, Mrs C?'

'Monsignor.' Mrs Cuthbert blinked her beseeching eyes. 'Forbid Livia to become a nun.'

The Monsignor gulped. He forgot even to wheeze. 'Forbid her?'

'I beseech you.'

'Oh,' said the Monsignor. Absently, he released his hands from the mother's grip. Livia, he thought: a nun.

Mrs Cuthbert stared up at the priest's strong black eyes, while he raced through his brain, cataloguing his break-neck thoughts. It had never occurred to him Livia might be serious about this nun business. He had always presumed it was part of her cantankerous spirit. But if the girl was truly intent on the veil, then it was almost too good to be true. The Rectory, he knew, had been purchased by Mrs Cuthbert with the last pennies of her father's fortune. Purchased from the Church of Ireland Commissioners at the same time they had deconsecrated St Ciaran's. To buy the church would be no problem at all. An ecumenical gesture, joint services three times a year, he'd present the repaired building to the dioceses of both Churches. Out of his own funds. A centre for reconciliation, he'd call it. His own bishop would reconsecrate it, they'd have some barmy Proddy prelate present – he'd find a tame one somewhere – they were all tame, come to that. It'd be a further ecumenical gesture. No problem.

But what was a church without a priest's house to live in? If Livia took vows, she wouldn't inherit. Or Holy Mother Church would inherit for her. Livia had always been the stumbling block to his plan. She was a wily canny bitch, was Livia. But with Livia a nun and out of the way, it was all plain sailing. He'd have the most stylish Catholic church in Erin, a real old half-Norman haunt of a place, the envy of the lot of them. Mrs Cuthbert could stay on. What harm in Mrs Cuthbert? She could be his house-keeper. A parish priest would need a good house-keeper. And think of the kudos he'd gain in the Palace. The old rector's widow was the Catholic parish priest's house-keeper! A triumph.

A triumph for Rome, of course. And he'd sit out the wait – 'twould be no more than ten years at most – in comfort and style and peaceful retreat, quiet in the dying backwater of Kilbrack. They'd call him a saint to humility. Till the call to purple would rouse him, of course. Tremendous.

His fist closed on the glass of port. He lifted it to his lips. He said, 'A slice of cheese wouldn't go amiss with this port, Mrs C.'

'Cheese?'

'Stilton, for preference.'

'Come here, you,' said Livia. 'Get in under the umbrella before you're soaked through.'

O'Leary Montagu, meek as a lamb, inched under the umbrella beside her.

'You're not annoyed with me?' he asked.

'Should I be?'

'Your mother nearly fainted.'

'That's my mother. So you're really not a writer?'

'I am a writer,' he averred defensively. 'Of course I'm a writer. It's just that I haven't written any books yet.'

She strolled so slowly, languidly, that O'Leary with his long gangly legs had difficulty keeping slow-step with her. At the same time, his head kept brushing against the ceiling of the umbrella, forcing her hand up higher and higher. He started to stoop, his legs taking smaller and smaller strides till it looked like he was tip-toeing in a tunnel.

'You are a dismal idiot,' she said.

Diary Memo: She called me a dismal idiot in an ever so friendly voice . . .

'You take the umbrella. I can't have you stooping around behind me.'

So O'Leary took the umbrella and together they walked down the drive.

Diary Memo: We stepped out together . . .

'You need looking after, you do,' said Livia.

Diary Memo: And she said I needed looking after . . . again.

'Or locking up.' She giggled suddenly. 'I'm sorry,' she said. 'But I keep seeing my mother's face.'

'I didn't intend to mislead her.'

'It's her own fault. She imagined you were Croesus's long lost nephew. That's all. And you did look funny with cheese all over you. I thought I'd die laughing.'

'She did seem to go overboard rather.'

'I agree. Stilton's my favourite. And you really are only a barman at Nellie Maguire's?'

'For the time being.'

'Then what?'

'I'm writing a book.'

'A book about what?'

'It's a biography of—'

The peculiar thing was that the closer he got to Livia, or the longer he stayed in Kilbrack, or both, or neither, he wasn't sure, but anyway: the less urgent seemed the biography to him. It was still of import—

Diary Memo: Bourne of all my labours—

But it just didn't seem quite so urgent any more.

'A biography of Nancy Valentine.'

'And who's she when she's at home?'

'You've really never heard of her?'

'Should I?'

'But she wrote *Ill Fares the Land.*' He fumbled in his pocket for his copy.

Livia stopped. 'Here we are,' she said.

O'Leary turned, walked back to her. 'Where?'

'My father's church. Do you want to see inside?'

'Why, I should love to.'

'Mind the glass.'

The doors had long ago been bolted and sealed. But the hinges had come away from the rotting posts so that the ancient oak doors leaned open at the side. The floor was covered with chippings of blue glass where boys grown old years since had stoned the stained-glass windows. Some tiles had fallen from the roof, and here the rain dripped in, streaking the walls and the stone slabs on the floor. But the rain dripped quietly, tempering its downpour, as if aware of the former sanctity of the place. And there was still piety hallowing the stilled air, an aggrieved, lost, forsaken piety. One or two tablets clung to the walls, informing no one of the parish's ascendant fallen sons. O'Leary read one tablet. Balaclava, Lucknow, Khartoum, Mafeking, the wars of a lost empire. 'In Defence of Queen and Empire Freely They Gave of Their Last Breath', said the tablet. And lost their homes, thought O'Leary, tragically.

'It's beautiful,' he said.

'I often come here,' said Livia. 'To be alone. They deconsecrated it after my father died. He was rector here. But after him there were no parishioners left. It's still holy to me.'

'Yes,' said O'Leary.

'It's the dead I feel sorry for. Nobody to tend them, their memories or their graves. Nobody remembers.'

O'Leary shook his head. This surely was extinction.

'I don't trust that Father Michael, Monsignor, whatever he calls himself.'

'You don't?'

'He's up to something,' said Livia. 'I don't know what it is but I'll find out. I'll spike his wheel for him. I never liked him. They said it was his heart. But I know it wasn't my father's heart. It was Father Michael and my mother killed him.'

'Your father?' O'Leary owned it was almost too cruel to speak.

'And yet, I suppose it was his heart. For he died of shame and a heart broken in two.'

'I never liked Father Michael either.'

She looked up. 'You know him?'

'Only from the book.'

'Which book?'

'*Ill Fares the Land.*' Again he produced the book from his pocket.

She arched an eyebrow. He could see she was about to mock, so quickly he explained. 'The title contains an unfortunate printer's *error*. It should be Fares, not—'

'I should hope so.'

He could see she was still hovering on a gibe. 'It's a quote,' he said quickly.

'From Goldsmith, I know.' She took the book. 'Nancy Valentine,' she read. 'Why would anyone write a book about Father Michael?'

'You're all in it,' he explained. 'All of you. Yourself as a child, your mother, Miss Maguire, Downey, Bridie O'Toole. All of you.'

'I'm in it?'

'Everyone. Except—' He didn't know how to tell her that in the book she was dead. Dead or departed. 'You're sure you've never heard of Nancy Valentine?'

She shrugged her shoulders. 'Sounds like a pseudonym to me.'

'Whyever should you say that?'

Her lips were pursing still, trying to defeat a snicker. 'Nobody in their right minds would christen a child Nancy Valentine.'

O'Leary was about to enquire why not again, when suddenly the obvious truth of her insight quite took him. 'Of course,' he exclaimed. That's why no one could ever answer him directly. 'It's a *nom de plume.*'

'Call it what you like. For my money it's a joke.'

She could see however that he wasn't listening. He was frowning intently and his cheekbones were trembling in visible acknowledgement of the thoughts hurtling through his mind. She flicked through some pages. 'It says here that we're all dead or deported.'

'I think that should be departed.' Damn the printers.

'Well, either way, it's not true.' But he looked so downcast that she felt verbally she might coddle him slightly. 'Perhaps it's not intended as a description. Perhaps it's more of a prediction. That way it would certainly be true.'

O'Leary's face froze in amazement.

Diary Memo: Stupor mundi!

Such perspicacity, such – no wonder he had fallen so enthralled by her upon the train. 'Of course! You're right! It's a prediction.' Only that could explain the curious anomaly of a death portrayed of a still living – if hardly vibrant – village. The girl was a veritable genius.

Diary Memo: Mirabile dictu!

She was reading again. He watched her for a while, then began reading with her over her shoulder. His feet were turned inwards, his hands fiddled behind his back. His face held all the anxious expectation of a child at infants' school.

'I've come here to write a biography,' he said after a while. 'Or a memoir of my visit. A mixture, really. Containing some comments on her style, an exegesis – or perhaps even an eisegesis—'

'Never mind that now,' she said, interrupting. 'May I borrow it?'

'Of course.' But immediately he worried did he truly mean that. He'd spoken too quickly. He'd never been without the book before. What if she lost it? What if . . . There were a million possibilities.

Livia flicked through some more pages. She read a passage. The query on her face began to crack into a grin. 'Rather comical in places, don't you think?'

'It's a tragedy,' said O'Leary, hurt.

'What does "I could have believed in manacles" mean?'

'It's a typographical error. Obviously she means "miracles".'

'Obviously?'

'From the context.'

'I see. The context.'

That sealed it. He'd have to lend her the book. Reading it, she'd come around. He knew she would.

> *Diary Memo:* Nil desperandum. *She'll come round. The Mistress will see to that.*

After all, Livia was clever.

She eyed him crookedly. 'And you say you've been invited to Knight's Kilbrack?'

'Bridie O'Toole brought the message. Afternoon tea with the master of the house.'

'Where did you get those scars?' she said, suddenly.

O'Leary shuffled his feet. 'I had an accident.'

'I see.' She slipped the book into her cardigan pocket. She shivered, then pulled her cardigan closer to her. 'Come on. I'll walk you up the lane.' She stood up. 'It's cold here with the dead.'

As she watched him climb into his black sedan, a quick wave to the porch, and a quicker glance still to the church spire, Mrs Cuthbert owned to herself that things had changed. She had always felt so confident in his strong but calm, handsome presence, sure of the rightness of her course. Middle age and promotion had changed little his outward appearance. And perhaps it was only Mrs Cuthbert who had changed. But she was certain of a sudden that she disliked the man. She disliked his upstart ways. Coming into her home and half the time on the telephone – who did he think he was? She knew who he was. She knew very well what he was. He was a little upstart Christian Brother boy made good.

Monsignor! Outrageous.

The car pipped half-way down the drive and the Monsignor was gone.

Good riddance. But there was still this extraordinary suggestion of his. What did it mean? He would buy the Rectory, but she could still live on there, free of charge, spend the money as she pleased, round-the-world cruise even. What could it mean? A gesture, he had called it.

And where was Livia? At least she had shown some sense, ignoring that horrid man. She never wanted that man in her house again. She never wanted to see him again. Worming his way into her confidence with his ridiculous name and charlatan's accent. At least Livia had shown some good sense there. Where was she, Mrs Cuthbert wondered. Moping around the church again, she presumed. She was too much like her father. Too much love for him. Wasn't natural in a girl her age. She could try showing some love to her mother for a change.

She made her way into the kitchen. Where is that girl? And what does ecumenical mean?

'Interesting things, umbrellas,' said Livia, fascinated by O'Leary's champion bout with hers. A squall in the wind had taken it, blown it inside out. She spotted a clump of celandine in the hedgerow, picked two stems and added them to the agrimony in her posy.

'Are they?' said O'Leary, as a spoke ripped slowly through the cloth.

'Interesting history. In London at the start of the Napoleonic wars they were considered a Parisian fashion, and markedly effeminate.'

A spoke snapped. 'What?'

'It was felt that any man who could employ so unmanly a contraption must harbour unpatriotic sentiments.'

'Yes, I'm sure.' Why was she telling him this? Did she question his—

'Only a homosexual could be a traitor.'

Another spoke snapped. 'I'm sorry?' said O'Leary.

She toyed with a smile. 'Umbrella, effeminate, homosexual, traitor,' she recapitulated. 'Napoleonic wars.' It seemed he had forgotten about fixing the umbrella and was dangling it between two fingers as far away as possible, as though wary of contamination.

'Umbrellas?' His face was horrified.

'I'm afraid so.' She sniffed some forget-me-nots she had picked. Not much of a scent but their blue would complement the yellows already in her posy. She returned her attention to O'Leary.

He was stammering. 'But what could – what has that to do with me?'

A bruised reaction, she decided, but not altogether unexpected. 'Not to worry,' she said. 'Towards the end of the wars, with Britain's victory assured, umbrellas became something of a hearty British symbol: rather in the manner of the early Church Christianizing the pagan festivals.'

'Festivals?' repeated O'Leary. 'Pagan?'

'Or,' she added mischievously, 'the way deviant patois is often adopted by the mainstream in society.'

O'Leary shook his head at the umbrella and its entrails inside out. What did it all mean? What did she know? Or rather, he hastily corrected himself, presume?

'Forget it,' said Livia.

'I'm sorry?'

'It's stopped raining. Give it here to me. It's said,' she continued when he had released it, 'that Pitt considered taxing them even.' She tossed it into the briars. 'And ordering the bishops to pray for rain.'

O'Leary gaped at the discarded umbrella, then at Livia, then at his feet. Was there more to all this than met the eye? It was time for a Diary Memo.

Diary Memo: Sweet Livia, one night with thee, and my lips and heart my manhood shall attest.

He paused dreamily. Then he realized she had started walking on ahead. 'Wait for me,' he called, and hurried to catch up with her.

'I'll only walk with you as far as the gates,' she said. 'I've no desire for a house tumbling on top of me. Besides I think I've collected enough flowers here for a funeral.'

'Is Knight's Kilbrack truly tumbling down?'

'Worse, if anything.'

They had come to the gates. The two battered but still

gaunt magpies glared up from their fallen state beside the pillars.

O'Leary stared at them. He laughed, nervously, as if shrugging. 'Odd,' he said.

'They're magpies.'

'I can see. Rather forbidding though.'

'One for sorrow, two for mirth,' intoned Livia. She was gazing at the crownless capitals. 'What do no magpies mean?'

I don't know, thought O'Leary. And yet, there was a feeling, neither of sorrow nor of joy, nor anywhere between, but a sorrowless, joyless feeling that he was acquainted – more than acquainted – accustomed to. He didn't know what to call it. Nothingness perhaps. Could that be the answer?

'The first one fell generations ago. Nobody remembers it up even. The second fell only a few years back. Jim O'Toole maintains the old man himself knocked it down. In a rage one night. There's a local saying, you see. "One's for sorrow, two's for mirth, three's for heart and home and hearth. But no bracks upon the way, Kilbrack be Brackless e'er and a day." Brack comes from the Irish, you see. It means magpie.'

'I see.'

But it was obvious he didn't. 'He knocked it down on purpose,' Livia explained slowly. 'In a rage. He wanted for nothing. He wanted it all to end. It was soon after that we learned his son had died. They say Uncle Val's been mad ever since. But I don't believe he's mad. I think he's just lonely, purposefully so.'

O'Leary twisted his face. 'Uncle Val?' he asked.

'He's my mother's third cousin.' She stopped arranging her flowers, and looked him up and down. 'Was it a very bad accident?'

'I don't remember really.' He had explained beforehand, as they walked, as much as he could about the accident. At the time she had shown little emotion, even less interest. This was her first mention of it.

'I've never seen scars so ugly.'

'No,' confessed O'Leary, 'neither have I.'

'I remember my father in the evening. He used to sit in his armchair in the sitting room, reading his newspaper. I used to sit on the floor in front of him, leaning against his chair, my elbows resting on his knees, doing nothing, just thinking. After he died, I still used to sit there, though I no longer had his legs to support me. Then one evening, Father Michael came in. He told me a young lady must never sit on the floor. My mother said nothing. I suddenly hated her. I loved my father. It's my mother I hate. It happens.'

O'Leary had listened to this reminiscence, expecting some connection to be drawn with her previous comments. But apparently there was none. He didn't mind. She had spoken in such a distant wistful voice he had wanted only to hug her close, tell her all would be all right. Hush your troubles, Livia, all will be all right. He wanted to wrap a coat around her cold shoulders. And that feeling itself felt warming to him, heart-warming even. It was a strange, unaccustomed warmth, like a thaw. He had felt nothing like it before.

'I'm off now,' she said.

'Will you not come in with me?'

'I think it would be wiser if you met him alone.'

'Yes,' said O'Leary dreamily.

Livia picked a columbine from a crack in the wall, sniffed it, pinched it into her posy. Somehow she didn't enjoy his gaze constantly, if chastely, on her lips. 'What is it?' she said.

'Livia?'

'Yes?'

'Livia,' he said, knowing that the one word couldn't, but at the same time believing more deeply that the one word did, encompass the world. He bit his lip, searching for words, and the courage to speak them.

She said, leaning against a pillar, 'You want to marry me, is that it?'

'Yes,' said O'Leary, though he believed his mouth had only mimed it.

She looked at the lanky, soaking, scruffy, ugly man with his diffident eyes and his clumsy ways. He wants me to marry him, she thought, as one from a lofty, but not necessarily a comfortable, height might think. Men – they were always so hopeless really. They needed two things in the world: a person to push them and another to show off to. Usually, a wife filled both positions. Will I marry him? Will I marry him! Funny gangling man. He really must be unhinged, to ask even.

CHAPTER TEN

WHERE IS HE then?' said Bridie.

But the thin bent plank of Valentine Brack, concentrating over his desk, ignored her; continued filling his fountain pen.

'And don't blame me if 'tis quarter past four. I gave him the message. Half past three I said. I gave the message to Nellie Maguire herself.'

Still he ignored her.

'Can I not move?'

Nothing.

'An inch to scratch me oxters with?'

'To me more dear, congenial to my heart,' mumbled Valentine Brack at last.

'What's that?'

'One native charm, than all the gloss of art.'

'Art, is it? And me half-jaded. What am I? Where am I? I'm jaded, I am. And all done up in this get-out. Never mind your art. You have me looking a right eejit, so you have.'

Only now did Valentine Brack grant her a look. And

he winked, so that she winced. He had forced her into an old black servant's dress, with lace on the collar and hem, that he had found left over from God remembered when. And he had ordered her to wait beside the tea-tray, hands behind her back, a napkin perched on her head which he had fashioned himself into a waitress's hat; waiting in expectation of his guest. 'Did you polish your boots?'

'I did.'

'Let me see.' And she lifted one leg up so that the old man could survey it. 'Did you wash your hands?'

'I've had enough of this blether,' said Bridie. 'I'm off.'

She didn't move. And Valentine Brack didn't bother to glance up from his fountain pen to check. 'Bridie O'Toole,' he said, conversationally.

'What is it?'

'How long have you worked here, Bridie?'

Cantankerous old fart, thought Bridie, why couldn't he pass over like any normal man would? 'What time is it?' she asked.

Valentine Brack consulted his wristwatch without the strap on it. 'Eighteen minutes past five o'clock,' he said. '*Post meridiem.*'

Bridie made a brief calculation – which consisted of adding the time of the day to last midnight's tally. 'I've been working here nine years, eight months, seventeen days, seventeen hours and eighteen minutes,' she said.

'That's interesting.'

'And for why is that?' asked Bridie, though she knew the answer before he spokc it.

'Because, Bridie, I've forgotten for the moment where I

left your cards. Your employment cards, Bridie. I wondered if you'd come across them at all in your busy round of cleaning?'

'Damn you,' whispered Bridie through her pursed-up lips, quiet as a mouse when a cat is at play. She'd fix him. If it was the last thing she ever did – the last fling before ever she died – she'd fix that eagle-tailed plank of a man. And the clench of her fists behind her back italicized her resolve. See if she didn't.

Valentine Brack returned fulfilled to his fountain pen. He had charged it now. He held it over the blotting pad and squeezed out the ink into a satisfactory workmanlike spill. He allowed the spill to blot. Then he began filling his pen again. Where was the bugger?

He wandered a quick glance over the library and the preparations he had contrived. Everything was arranged. The old Pembroke table and the old book propping up the broken leg and the leather-bound journal on top: all strategically positioned for the first impression the visitor would have of the room: cultured. *Volume XIV*, he remembered. With only seven pages, was it the right volume? Nonsense, he concluded rapidly: cultured or not, seven pages was enough for any man.

He looked out of the window, abstractedly; out into the courtyard to where Jim was working on the flower-beds. 'For him light labour spread her wholesome store', he quoted to himself. 'Just gave what life required, but gave no more . . .' Oh, he thought, losing completely the threads of his poem. Oh.

He rescrewed the sheath that covered the bladder that

would suck up the ink, rescrewed the cap to his fountain pen; laid it aside.

Oh, he thought. I see, he thought. Yes, he thought. Oh. Yes . . .

Dammit!

And never shifting his gaze a moment from the lanky-legged man regarding his house outside, he carefully removed his spectacles. He set them down on the desk, wiped his eyes. Then with exaggerated care, he wiped his spectacles, and donned them again.

Oh.

He crept up from his desk, padded with a cat's danger over to the bureau, rummaged through the bureau drawer.

'What are ye up to?' asked Bridie dubiously.

'Shut up, woman!'

And Bridie recoiled.

Valentine Brack unearthed what he was looking for. He raced back to his desk, sat down. He doffed his spectacles. And peering again out the window into the courtyard, he tried his distance lenses, newly-recovered from the bureau's drawer.

Of course, they were dirty. He wiped them, spat on them, wiped them again furiously.

But it was already too late. The spectre had already passed. The lanky-legged man had disappeared from his view.

He tried his ordinary spectacles again. But that was stupid. They wouldn't see through a brick wall. He tore them off, dropped them scattering on the desk top. What should he do?

Valentine Brack brought his hands to his face. Unaccustomed to prayer and unequal to tears, there was only one thing left. He stormed out of the room, shouting 'I'll murder him!'

The rain had recommenced its downpour. Jim O'Toole leaned on his spade, dreaming of galleons and steamers and clippers that plied the distant seas.

O'Leary approached. 'Hello, Jim,' he said.

Jim woke, grudgingly, and sneezed a violent snort. He was sodden through, and his corduroy pants hung with the weight and the shape of tubular bells. O'Leary sniffed. It was the homely smell of the earth, he allowed, indulgently.

He halted there a while to view the prospect before him, the Mistress's childhood home. Knight's Kilbrack.

The façade was precisely as he had pictured it. Four storeys high, the top one barely a man's height. The servants would have slept there. Though old, it was of no particular age. And though definitely stylish, no particular style prevailed. Some few of the windows appeared Jacobean, more were in the Georgian style; most, however, had been blocked up. A verandah straddled one corner, or rather, the posts and railings of a verandah; the walkway itself had slipped one end to the ground, and had taken on the unlikely masquerade of a modern, if shaky, fire escape. Odd bricks and stone, tiles and masonry, littered the base. The intimation of the house was of a Regency mistress, once lewdly gay and with a heart of gold, now greying and repentant, pulling her skirts tighter together.

The skirts, however, in the meantime had frayed. Knight's Kilbrack was falling down.

Amongst the debris O'Leary picked out another toppled magpie, still glowering. Once, guardant, it had graced a pinnacle.

'I believe the master of the house awaits me in the library,' he said.

Jim shrugged as an indifferent frown crossed his face. Then he nodded abruptly, dismissively; and wandered off to the portico.

O'Leary followed. Remembering Downey's admonition about the Irish weather earlier that day, he remarked, 'Well Jim. 'Tis a grand soft day.'

Jim eyed him crookedly.

'Are ye mad?' he said. ''Tis pissing down.'

Lying on the floor of the library, O'Leary wondered must he always be the fool. Would there never come a time when he strove with the stream, shaved with the wool, pissed not into the wind? Must there always be bungling and botching and clumsiness? And though crosses were ladders that led to heaven, yet his clumsiness was too heavy a cross forever to bear. Must he always be the fool?

The mongrel dog was still licking his face, tail and tongue still wagging in ecstasy. O'Leary punched her snout. Yelping, the dog scurried out the door.

It had been that mangy mongrel's fault. No sooner had O'Leary entered the library than the stupid beast had jumped up, puffing rancid breath. To steady himself, he had reached out to a table in the centre of the room. But the table had stood upright apparently only with the aid of a book beneath it. O'Leary half-leaned on it. And table, dog and O'Leary Montagu had collapsed on to the floor.

He glanced up at Bridie now. She was stood to rigid attention by a tea-tray. 'The dog,' he said.

Bridie's cheeks stole clandestinely into a thin snigger.

'The dog caught me – er – off-guard.'

The snigger, though strained and thin, was too close to a welcoming grin for Bridie. She cut it.

'I've come to tea,' said O'Leary with an embarrassed smirk. He scrambled to his knees and scrabbled with the sticks of the table. 'I'm sorry about the er—' He tried to re-stand it, but with small success. 'I'm sure a touch of glue would do the trick.'

He climbed to his feet, straightened up. He smiled at Bridie, still smirking with embarrassment. He looked around him, clasped his hands behind his back; unclasped them. Bridie didn't move an inch, but she followed his every move with her electric piercing gaze.

'You were expecting me, I see.' No response. He nodded. 'The tea all set out.' Still nothing. Then doubtfully: 'You were expecting me, weren't you?'

Bridie weighed up the prospect of the lanky clumsy oaf. There was either more to him or less to him than met the eye. She'd find out one way or another.

'Sit ye down,' she said, moving at last. 'You've come for your tea.'

Thank God, thought O'Leary. He sat down on the worn scarlet leather of the sofa. 'Should we not wait for the master of the house?' he asked tentatively. But Bridie was busy rattling crockery. She said nothing.

O'Leary tried to settle back into the sofa, allowed his attention to wander over the room. And it was a beautiful room; a room in which O'Leary could feel – almost immediately did feel – at home. The four walls were lined with books: old books with leather bindings. His nostrils quivered at the earthy odour of old knowledge. The windows faced west. And it would be pleasant, thought O'Leary, to read here of an evening, bathed in an evening sun. As it was, the windows looked comfortably out on the rainsodden paddocks beyond. Above a marble chimneypiece hung a lifesize portrait of a forbidding old man; an ancient ancestor, deemed O'Leary. It wasn't named, but a gilt ribbon billowing stiffly below proclaimed, *Constans Valensque*. The family motto? Behind the desk, a table really, was a large *bergère*. Ladder-back chairs ranged between the windows. It was a beautiful comfortable room. Even the remains of the smashed Pembroke table, lying jagged in the middle of the carpet, with the old polish of the wood, even they failed to detract from the room's ambience.

'Milk?'

'I'm sorry?'

'Sugar?'

'Yes please.'

'Help yourself.' Bridie plonked the crockery on his table and returned to her vigil beside the tea-tray.

Arranging the milk and the sugar to his satisfaction, O'Leary pondered the various mysteries that gnawed through his mind. He was about to meet the master of the house.

In the book, of course, the master was wild, blind and senile. And – finally – dead. But the book, as Livia had so brilliantly surmised, was not a description, plain and simple. There were further depths, a netherland of meaning and intimation, which hitherto O'Leary had never imagined. Surely Livia was correct. The book was a prediction. And yet, who was Nancy Valentine? Did the Mistress write under a pseudonym? No one, certainly no one he had asked so far in his sojourn at Kilbrack, seemed ever to have heard of her. And Livia – sweet Livia, he remembered – had said the master had only a son, a dead son. She had mentioned nothing of any daughter. What could it mean?

Bridie eyed the visitor with the quick eyes of a cashier. She had been right all along. She knew she had. She had been clever that morning, thinking so quick on her feet, to tell the old man that there was a writer in Kilbrack. She was well aware of course that the incognito man wasn't really a writer. Only pretended to be one. But the ruse had served her purpose, though not entirely as she had expected. She'd intended only to rattle the old man when he discovered the visitor wasn't truly a writer. But things had turned out different to that. The devil they had.

For there was something truly novel here – with the old man's idiot behaviour, and his wailing into his hands, and his sudden change of mind. Wasn't it the old man himself who'd invited the fellow? And then all that carry on at the window, groaning and moaning. Sure, he hadn't even stopped to greet the visitor, but he'd jumped up and dashed out before the footsteps in the hall even. 'Get him out, Bridie!' he'd screamed. 'Get rid of him before I murder the blackguard!' The visitor had a strange effect on the old man, that was for sure. For why, though, she didn't know. But she'd find out. Of course she would. She'd keep the incognito man busy here till she'd discovered the root cause of the upset. Her name was Bridie O'Toole, after all: of course she'd find it out.

'The master,' said O'Leary, 'will he be joining us soon?'

Bridie bit on her lip, chewed the question over. Blast it, she thought; she'd make a stab in the dark. 'Yes,' she said. 'He surely will.'

'Ah,' said O'Leary. 'Good.' He sipped his tea. 'My God, but this tea is disgusting!'

''Tis stewed stone cold.'

'You knew?'

'You're late.'

'I'm sorry.' And as O'Leary forced the vile tea to his lips, he realized he was terrified of the cramped, wiry woman. If she'd blink her gaze a moment, he'd feel better. But under those unwavering eyes, he felt cornered, an animal cowed.

He picked up an old leather-bound journal that lay amongst the smithereens of the Pembroke table. 'May I?' he said to Bridie.

Bridie said nothing. She didn't know which answer to give. She waited and watched.

He opened the journal, read the title on the first page. Then he dropped the journal. Then he picked it up again. Then dropped it again. *Ill Fares the Land* – could it be true? *Volume XIV*? It couldn't be true. Could it? No. But there it was lying concrete on his lap. He grabbed at it again, his hands quivered with excitement. His heart missed a beat, then recouped, beating twice, three times as fast. Very slowly, with leaden hands no longer a-quiver, he turned the heavy leather cover.

Valentine Brack arranged the five keys so that they hung loose from the high chimneypiece in the stag room. Then, walking backwards out of the room, he counted thirty paces. He stopped. He adjusted his distance lenses to read what the tickets attached to the five keys said. Jackass that he was, in his desperate flight from the library, he had grabbed the wrong lenses, left his spectacles on the desk top. Without them, he was blind – except, of course, for thirty paces with his blasted distance lenses.

The folly itself was bad enough. What was worse was that there was humour in this carry-on. He could feel it himself as he jerked the lenses up and down on his nose, trying to purchase an unblurred image of the keys. And humour he did not want. He wanted only the undiluted blind rage that swelled inside him. He wanted blood.

He ranged his eyes over the keys and their tickets. 'Cabinet B', he read. But that was only the cabinet where he kept his marbles – the ones that probably really were agate – and the conkers his father Valentine had bequeathed him. 'Cabinet E'. But that was only for the night commode with his last will and testament in it. 'Cabinet A'. He couldn't recall for the moment its particular use; but it didn't matter because the next key along said 'cabinet D', and the D was written in bold red ink for danger. That was the one.

He stumbled back into the stag room, felt for and grabbed

the fourth key, and withdrew thirty paces again to see through his distance lenses where the lock to cabinet D might be. His hands were shaking still with the dementia of anguish as he quivered the key into the lock.

'When I inherit, I'll knock your house down!'

Valentine Brack stopped fumbling with the key. He could see in his mind in the glass of the cabinet the lanky-legged man standing before him now, hear his words even.

'And all memory of you with it!'

The old man's fist blanched to a clench. 'You're dead,' he said to the shattering spectre. And when he pulled his fist out of the smashed glass door, his hand was cut, bleeding. 'You're dead,' he said.

And if not, you soon will be. He smashed more of the glass door, elbowing it through with his leather-patched sleeve. He grabbed at a stock, the first his fingers met, yanked it out. And knocking tables and chairs and lampstands, he marched his way out of the stag room.

The sun had at last discovered a pathway through the clouds. And in the sudden warmth of the library O'Leary Montagu was reading.

And it truly was like that man in that poem Mary had read to him once. And he was that star-gazer suddenly, and a new planet swam into his ken; or he was that conquistador on a peak in Darien; and on first looking into that leathern prize, as he read, he read with a wild surmise.

And thus in the volume previous we recounted the tales and the deeds of Kilbrack in the reigns of the early

Hanoverian ['Angevin' crossed out] monarchs. And so it is we come now to Victoria ['King John' crossed out], the most illustrious, beauteous, gracious scion of that kingly if alien line. It is during this reign that written record of Kilbrack – *qua* village – is first encountered. And this mention has come down to us from the busy years of the last century ['down through the long generations, wreathed in the mists and bogs of Irish time' crossed out]. It is in an invoice, marked 'Final Demand' ['an epistle royal' crossed out], addressed to a certain J. Maguire, Esq. ['to the gallowglass sept Maguire' crossed out], from a brewery in Lismore ['from His Grace John de Gray, Bishop of Norwich, Justiciar in Dublin' crossed out], dated 1861 ['in the year of Our Lord, 1210' crossed out].

O'Leary Montagu turned the page. But all the writing on the next page was crossed out. And the next. The narrative returned on the fourth, but here the script deteriorated with so many subscript and superscript additions and corrections that it was impossible to decipher the words. He could read one sentence. It was in parentheses at the top corner of the page. 'Hopeless – have to rewrite whole shebang', it said. The final page had one legible paragraph.

But let us divagate now a moment from our necessary narrative whilst I in my gnarled dotage ['senility' crossed out] recount the sapling ['springtime' crossed out] memory of the magic that was my Victorian ['Edwardian?' pencilled in] home. I was returning upon an evening, leaf-late in August, an August of rustling russet. I stopped by a thorn tree for the catching of my breath. ['Good this bit' pencilled in.] The sun through the treetops was ['golden' crossed out] a leprechaun's pot of gold. The evening I could have believed in ['magic' crossed out, and 'miracles' pencilled in with a query]. Damn, believe I have done this bit before.

It ended abruptly there. O'Leary closed the heavy tome, and held it a moment in his arms' trembling embrace.

'Upon a peak in Darien,' he muttered, rocking slowly on the sofa. 'Upon a peak in Darien . . .' He pressed the leather-bound journal close to his heart. He said: 'The Mistress, grail of all my labours, I have found thee . . .'

'What's that?' said Bridie.

He half-woke from his reverie. He had forgotten that Bridie was in the room with him. Not only that but he'd rested unaware that any other soul breathed ever on this earth.

'Who will tell me,' he said, 'whose hand has penned this poetry?'

Bridie had witnessed closely his peculiar display. Suspicion had risen determinedly through her throat. What was he up to with his antics? 'Are you laughing at me?' she said, lowly, slowly and menacingly.

But even Bridie could not deter him now. 'Who wrote it? I must know!'

Pah, thought Bridie. 'He's here now,' she said, as the library door swung open.

O'Leary turned, stood up. 'Ah,' he said. There was wonder in his eyes. 'The Mistress—' he began, before he could check himself. 'I'm sorry,' he quickly corrected. 'It was a *nom de plume* after all!' He made to hold out a hand; couldn't. He bent to replace the journal on the sofa.

Valentine Brack didn't check his stride, but still advancing, raised the barrel of the shotgun to point in the blurred but general direction of O'Leary's chest.

O'Leary looked up. 'Ah,' he said again.

'You're dead,' said Valentine Brack.

'Bridie!' cried O'Leary.

'The table,' said Bridie.

But it was too late. Advancing still, Valentine Brack tripped over the remains of the Sheraton Pembroke table, fell flat on his face. There was a crashing report. The two barrels of the shotgun were discharged, scattering the books, the walls, the portrait with shot. The report resounded on the four walls. A dust cloud rose, whirled in the grip of the shock of a storm; then floated, calmly settling.

Valentine Brack lay still on the floor. Bridie inspected him, lifted a limp hand, then dropped it again in disgust.

'Blast,' she said.

'Is he dead?' asked O'Leary without daring to look, his grip desperate on the lemon jiffy in his pocket.

'Worse luck. He's only conked out. More tea?'

'What?' O'Leary risked his eyes peeking over the back of the scarlet leather and mahogany sofa, behind which he had dived for cover.

'There's a cup still in the pot.'

'What was he trying to do?' He stood up, still chary.

'He was going to shoot you.'

'Shoot me?' O'Leary stabbed the lemon jiffy with his finger nail.

'Kill you dead.'

'Kill me?' The juice of the lemon began trickling out into his pocket. 'But I've never seen him before.'

'He's not fond of you anyway.'

'But what have I done?'

'Maybe and he doesn't take to men coming here calling themselves writers when truly they're working incognito in a bar.'

'I'm sorry?'

'Matter a damn now,' said Bridie, delicately pouring more tea.

'What do you mean, it doesn't matter? He was trying to shoot me!'

'Sure he's blind without his spectacles.' And she nodded to the desk where his spectacles had been dropped before his flight from the library. 'And his spectacles is smashed to smithereens with shot,' she said slowly, lowly and happily – as O'Leary stumbled his way out of the library, dashed to find the nearest lavatory.

CHAPTER ELEVEN

'AND JUST WHAT did you think you were up to, my girl?'

'Gathering buds while I may.'

'Stepping out with that madman, that maniac?'

'Tautology,' said Livia.

'Don't you tautology me,' said Mrs Cuthbert. 'Tell that to the guards when he – I don't know – waylays you, ravishes you.'

'I don't ravish awfully easily, Mother,' said Livia, and she dropped a stem of agrimony into a vase.

Mrs Cuthbert sat down on her bed, stood up again, straightened the counterpane, sat down. She was close to her wits' end. She needed to escape this house; to think, to deliberate. She would go for a drive. She'd take a roundabout route, and she would visit third cousin Valentine. It was their canasta night anyway. He would be expecting her. If he didn't go on about the bats, of course. And she'd talk it over with him – Livia, and the Monsignor's bewildering offer. Third cousin Valentine might be mad, but at least he was family.

She heaved up from the depression she had made in her bed, straightened again the counterpane, found her handbag.

'Besides,' said Livia, 'I rather like him – in a ministering sort of way.'

'Like him? I'm talking about marriage – not nursing an imbecile.'

'So am I, Mother. So am I.'

Mrs Cuthbert stopped suddenly her furious navigation of her bedroom. She had been searching for her lipstick. The cherry lipstick. It was only half-used. Why was she worrying about that? She stared at her daughter, then averted her eyes. 'Don't say another word, Livia. Don't speak another syllable. Please leave my bedroom. Forget about the flowers. I don't wish for flowers. I wish to be on my own.'

'Mother—'

'Please, Livia.'

'Mother—'

'What is it?'

'Your lipstick is on the dressing table where you left it.'

'Thank you, Livia.' She picked up the lipstick, dropped it into her handbag. 'When I think – when I think—' Her powder compact was there too. She tossed it in. 'Where is my comb?'

'On the mantelpiece.'

'Chimneypiece,' she corrected automatically. 'When I think of all I've been through for you. Have you read yesterday's *Telegraph*?'

'Of course I've read yesterday's *Telegraph*.'

Mrs Cuthbert grabbed at a newspaper. She tore through

the pages. 'Read it,' she said, presenting the paper point blank before her daughter's eyes. 'Page fourteen.'

'Court and Social?' said Livia, incuriously.

'Latest wills! Bennett, Mrs Alana P. Clapham, North Yorkshire, and Kinsale, Cork: £343,662 – net!' Mrs Cuthbert stabbed her finger at the entry. 'What are they going to say when my time comes? The shame . . .'

Livia sidestepped the newspaper, and dropped a sprig of forget-me-not into the vase.

'And all you can think of is flower arranging.'

'Mother, I am not flower arranging. The very point of wild flowers is that you don't arrange them. It is their careless *déshabillé* which is the secret to their attraction.'

'What?'

'Nothing, Mother.'

Mrs Cuthbert dropped the newspaper, and picked up instead the plastic phial in the shape of the Virgin Mary that Father Michael had given her on his return from Lourdes. She brandished this before Livia's nose. 'We were county,' she said. 'County.'

'But we've grown, Mother,' reasoned Livia. Another stem of agrimony and the vase was complete. 'We're provincial now.'

'Don't provincial me. Think I'm beaten, do you? Well, Livia Cuthbert, you are mistaken. Quite mistaken.' She hated the ugly plastic phial. But it was Holy Water. She dropped it into her handbag too. If she had time she might say a prayer. Aspirin? In her bathroom.

'What do you mean, Mother?' Livia breathed in to let her mother bustle past into her bathroom.

'Never you mind.' Mrs Cuthbert popped the bottle of aspirins into her handbag. She already had a headache. She'd need them. Back into her bedroom now to find her purse.

Livia watched her mother. She didn't like this sudden busyness. Her mother looked almost in control. She'd stop that. 'Mother, I think I should tell you, I am considering marriage.'

Mrs Cuthbert busied herself with her purse. She had already smelt the ordure of that particular rat. 'To whom?'

'You had him to lunch. Mr O'Leary Montagu. You remember.'

It worked. Mrs Cuthbert, her composure fading, grabbed at some tissues from a box by her bed. 'Why, Livia, why must you torment me?'

'He showed enormous interest in St Ciaran's.'

'St Ciaran's?' She pecked at her eyes with the tissues.

'My father's church.'

'Your sainted father's church,' wept Mrs Cuthbert.

'And I'm sure it would please my father if I married a man so interested in his life's work. Don't you think?'

Mrs Cuthbert tugged a fistful of tissues from the box, stuffed them in her handbag. 'Marry him then.'

'What?'

'Out of my way, Livia.'

'Where are you going?' She pursued her mother out of her bedroom, down the stairs. The staircase shook with her mother's stout thumping. Livia could feel the earth shifting beneath her. What was she up to?

'I'm going to be on my own.' Mrs Cuthbert opened a

drawer in the hall table. She found the two decks of cards for canasta, and the booklet of rules. She needed the rules: third cousin Valentine would never play fair otherwise. And the spectacles to play with.

'But it's far too early for canasta, Mother. Uncle Val won't even have eaten. You haven't eaten yourself.'

'Food,' said Mrs Cuthbert. 'At a time like this. I'm going for a jaunt in the motor-car.'

'But you can't.'

'Just try to stop me.'

'The bills.'

'Which bills?'

'Legal bills, Mother. You always crash.'

Mrs Cuthbert snatched the car key. She grabbed another fistful of tissues from the box on the hall table, worked them on her eyes. 'And I'll tell you something else, Livia Cuthbert. Father Michael—'

'Monsignor.'

'Bugger that. Father Michael has made me a very interesting offer. A very interesting offer indeed. And it doesn't concern you, Livia Cuthbert, Mrs O'Leary Montagu or the Reverend Mother Livia – whatever you like. It doesn't concern you at all!'

And she slammed the Rectory door after her.

Valentine Brack shielded his eyes from the spectre of death, but the spectre of death was still there before him, with the streaks of blood on his cheeks like war-paint. 'No!' cried Valentine Brack. But the spectre of death laughed, laughed hideously. Unaccountably, for he was sure it had been in his own hands only seconds before, the spectre of death raised the shotgun so that it was aimed at Valentine Brack's blood-beating heart. 'No!'

'Yes,' said the spectre of death. 'You are an abomination on the earth,' said the spectre of death. 'You have brought forth a perversion of nature; your line shall cease.'

'No!' cried the old man.

And the spectre of death threw off his cloak and his dark-benighting cowl, to reveal a shabby black suit beneath. 'Hello Daddo,' said the lanky-legged spectre.

'I'll kill you,' screamed Valentine Brack, and grabbing the lapels of the shabby black suit, he squeezed and squeezed with all his ancient anguish . . .

Till the poor mongrel yelped in agony.

Valentine Brack awoke with a start. 'What?' he said.

The mongrel yelped again.

'Nancy?' said Valentine Brack. And he loosed his hold on the mongrel's throat. 'And did I hurt you, Nancy? Did I hurt you? I'm sorry.'

He reached to stroke her, but the poor old thing had had enough of the human race for the time being. Bridie had kicked her in the kitchen, her old friend had snubbed her in the library, and now her master had sought to strangle her poor thin neck. She sneaked out of the master's bedchamber. She'd try her luck elsewhere below stairs. There might even be an unsuspecting rat on the loose, who knows? She could try her own hand at a touch of torture.

'Nancy,' called Valentine Brack. 'Where are my spectacles? Nancy, come back. Where are my spectacles?' He collapsed back down on his pillows. 'What a terrible dream,' he said.

A terrible dream it was. What was he dreaming the likes of that for now? And he had a God-awful headache too. The hammer in his head would split marrow from a bone.

He sat up suddenly. And what was he doing in bed? He pulled sharply on the rope that rang the bell in the kitchen. 'Bridie,' he called weakly. 'Bridie.'

What was he doing in bed with a granddaddo of a headache and dreams the worse? And where were his spectacles?

'Bridie,' he called in a thin sickly voice. 'Bridie . . .' He soon lost his patience with that. And tugging again on the bell rope he thundered: 'Bridie O'Toole!'

'What is it?' said Bridie at the door.

'You're here?'

'And didn't you ring?'

'Is it the menopause, Bridie?'

'The what?'

'You've got very quick lately.'

'I'm busy below,' she said. 'What d'ye want?'

'Prop up my pillows for me.' And though he couldn't see her clearly without his spectacles, he could smell the rankness of her dribbles as she bent over close to him. The smell of her foul humanity reassured him somehow. 'Now tell me, Bridie, what am I doing in bed?'

'You had a fall. Meself and Jim had to fetch you up here.'

'I had a fall? But I had a fall in my dream. I dreamed it, didn't I?'

'How would I know what you was dreaming?'

Valentine Brack chewed that over. 'I have a headache too,' he said, in the voice of a schoolboy with too much homework.

'Aspirin, is it?'

'Brandy!' he exploded. 'What would I want doing with kids' play?'

'There isn't no brandy.'

'In the wash stand, of course.'

Bridie allowed herself a snigger and fetched him a glass. She'd often wondered where he kept the brandy. She was finding out a lot today. And a very interesting day it was proving.

'Where are my spectacles?'

'Smashed.'

'Smashed?'

'To smithereens.'

Valentine Brack nearly spilled his brandy. 'Who smashed my spectacles?' he demanded imperiously.

'You did.'

'I did?'

'Blasting off with a shotgun.'

'Shotgun? But that was in my dream too. Are you telling me it wasn't a dream?'

'I'm not telling you nothing. That's what I'm doing. You're not dragging me into your shenanigans.'

'Wait there,' commanded Valentine Brack, sensing she was leaving.

'I'm busy below.'

'Wait!'

He tried to reason it out. Had it not been a bad dream after all? He had dreamed certainly. But which was dream and which was truth? It was a Gordian knot and no mistake. And what of the man in the shabby black suit? He had invited a man to afternoon tea. He remembered that. But he had woken in his bed having dreamed his son had returned. What had happened in between?

Oh my God, he thought suddenly. Did I kill him? Did I murder my son again?

'Is he dead?' he asked, quavering.

'Is who dead?'

'Didn't I invite a man to tea?'

'He's not dead. He's hiding, sure.'

'Oh.' Thank God. He made to get out of bed, but fumbling his way, he banged his head on one of the posts. He collapsed back down on his pillows. 'My poor head. I'm blinded without my spectacles.'

'Carrots,' said Bridie. 'Carrots for the eyes.' But then she seemed to doubt her prognostication, for she added, 'Or is it sticks? Carrots or the stick: one or t'other.'

'It won't do!'

'What?'

Valentine Brack knew very well what wouldn't do. Without his spectacles Bridie could treat him like a blind man, like an invalid, or worst of all, like an equal. He needed to frighten her back to a respectful and distant fear. Maybe he could threaten again to fetch her employment cards. But that would pull no strings now. Sure, how could he fetch them without his spectacles to show the way? He tried to think of a quotation from *The Deserted Village*. That would surely upset her and reset the balance to his rightful favour. But his mind was too befuddled to think clearly. If Nancy was here he could ask the dog about the Toccata and Fugue in D minor. Bach, she'd answer. That would show the hag who was on top. But even the blasted dog had deserted him. What had happened him today? Which was real and which was dreaming?

'Am I dreaming, Bridie, or is it real?' he asked in a suddenly thin and hollow, aged voice. It was an appeal for sympathy. 'I feel like a man being rowed in a ferry. A reluctant emigrant, calling thin o'er the deep green river. "Let me back," I call, "let me back to my home, Bridie . . ."'

But he was crying into the wind. Bridie had heard it all many times before.

'I'm off,' she said. She had better fish to fry. She was still searching for that incognito man. She had hunted high and low, in and out, though always with her eyes on the doors. Where had he got to? She didn't know – yet. 'I'm off,' she said again. And she strode out the door.

'Bridie,' wailed Valentine Brack. 'Fetch me Nancy at least. Don't leave me alone.'

'Shut up your blether,' said Bridie.

She stopped dead in her tracks on a landing at the top of the first flight of stairs. For there he was, down at the bottom, the incognito man, almost within her grip. He was about to sneak out the door.

'Good day to you,' she called in an almost civil tone of voice.

'What is it?' called Valentine Brack from his bedchamber above.

'Shut up,' said Bridie.

O'Leary Montagu looked up the flight of stairs. 'Ah,' he said. His instinct was to run, but he didn't move. Already, he was a victim, a rabbit caught in the harridan's green gaze. 'I thought I might – er – take my leave of you. It's getting on now,' he said. He had spent the last half-hour locked in a lavatory. Only now, with his heart half-calmed, had he judged it safe to move. Under his arm he carried the leather-bound journal from the library. He had decided to sneak back to Nellie Maguire's with it, catch his breath and deliberate in peace and safety on the startling turns and revelations of the day. He smiled weakly.

'A grand day,' called Bridie from the landing, in another grotesque attempt at civility. Her voice prowled ever so slowly, almost imperceptibly, down the stairs. She wasn't about to frighten away her prey.

'Er – has the master recovered?'

Bridie twisted her mouth. He had a journal, one of the old man's dotty scribblings, under his arm. Was that a clue? Was she getting closer, warmer, colder, or what? She nodded warily. 'You're away thieving his books, are you?'

'Ah,' said O'Leary. How to explain? 'I don't know if you're aware of this – you might have heard Miss Maguire mention it – but I have a book at the pub – leastways Miss Cuthbert has it now – and I wish to check the authorship of it. Do you know the book? *Ill Fares the Land*, it's called. I want to know who wrote it. It's important to me, but of course it's of little consequence to anyone else. Not, that is, until I've completed my biography. Of Nancy Valentine, I mean.'

Why was this man always so difficult, wondered Bridie. It was like listening to a foreign language, or the way a Corkman might speak. And what manner of a test was it, anyway? Was he still on about being incognito? Nancy Valentine wrote that book. The name was on the cover, sure. Hadn't the man just admitted it even?

'Nancy Valentine wrote it,' she said slowly and mistrustfully.

'Bridie!'

It was Valentine Brack calling again from his bedchamber above.

Bridie glanced up, cursed under her breath. 'What?' she called.

O'Leary made to bolt.

'Stay!' she commanded.

'But he's out to murder me!'

'Stay!' Then more softly, 'He won't harm you now. He's blind in his bed, and I've the shotgun hidden on him.'

'Who is it?' called Valentine Brack from his bed.

'Never mind.'

'I thought I heard you say Nancy.'

''Twas Nancy Valentine I said.' She was getting confused herself now.

Why is she calling me by my first name, wondered the old man. Things were truly getting out of hand. Time to upset her good and proper. 'Say "Sit",' he called.

'Sit,' said Bridie.

'I'm sorry?' said O'Leary.

'He says he's sorry,' said Bridie. She grimaced happily. She could come to enjoy playing the medium. This way nothing could escape her close scrutiny.

'Ask am I forgiven,' said Valentine Brack.

'He wants to know is he forgiven,' said Bridie.

Have I forgiven him, wondered O'Leary. The man certainly seemed in a more civil temper. 'May I come up and talk with him?'

'He wants to come up,' said Bridie.

'Toccata and Fugue in D minor, first,' called Valentine Brack. 'Ask who wrote it.'

'Toccata and Fugue in D minor,' repeated Bridie. 'Who wrote it?'

'Now lift your finger and drop it again,' he instructed.

O'Leary was perplexed. What an odd question. Toccata and what? He remembered Mary's record collection. And the incessant, interfering stridor of it. Toccata and Fugue in D minor. 'Beethoven, I think,' he said.

'He says Beethoven,' said Bridie.

'Beethoven? How can a dog say Beethoven? It's Bach, you ignoramus!'

'You ignoramus yourself,' said Bridie, storming up and into his bedchamber. ''Tis your visitor is here. Not that blasted cur. The fellow from Nellie Maguire's place as you invited to tea!'

Valentine Brack held the threads of his dreams and his waking life in his hands. With his old fingers not as nimble as they had been, it was difficult to disentangle them, impossible almost without help, without his spectacles. 'Show him in,' he said to Bridie, fatefully. 'Show the man in.'

So you have read a volume of my history,' said Valentine Brack still sceptically. 'And you say you enjoyed it?'

It was the wind through a hollow reed, thought O'Leary Montague: 'the keen of an emigrant', he quoted to himself from *Ill Fares the Land*, 'who called reluctant from a ferry's stern, calling thin o'er the deep green sea.' It was the voice of age.

And the man was the picture too of age. His thin strands of white hair lay limply symmetrical on either side of the bolstered pillows. Sitting up in his bed, with his cardigan buttoned close and his jacket on top of that, he reminded O'Leary of someone. But, O'Leary reminded himself: what living soul lives unacquainted with the picture of old age?

Diary Memo: So feeble and failing a body, it is ridiculous that I should ever have felt intimidated by him.

Even allowing for the shotgun.

Diary Memo: So powerful, so evocative a writer as the Mistress – nay, it is the Master now; he is bound to be touched with the Muses' dementing brand.

O'Leary smiled. He stood at last before the end of all his

labours. And the end of all his labours lay in his carved and gilded four-poster bed; lay grandly, in fitting state.

'I realize what I have read is only your first draft,' he answered humbly, yet seasoned with a touch of pride at finally confronting the object of his long search. 'But I believe it the equal – in potential at least – to the best you have ever written. I bow my head to the Master.'

Valentine Brack fumbled his fingers, as if he actually did hold within them the entangled threads of dreams and reality. He could see nothing. The pitch of the voice was the same as he remembered, but the tone was of a polite, if slightly barmy, visitor.

'Who are you?' he said.

'O'Leary Montague, sir.'

'Bridie!' he snapped suddenly.

'What?' said Bridie.

'Describe to me our visitor.'

'Lanky,' she said.

The old man weighed this. Lanky would fit. 'Go on.'

'Thin as a rake.'

That too. But neither of them was conclusive.

'Clumsy with it,' continued Bridie.

Clumsy? There was nothing clumsy about the son he remembered. 'Get on with it!' he snapped.

'Scars,' said Bridie. 'On his face.'

'Scars?'

'Ugly ones.'

He didn't remember scars either. But then.

'Black suit.'

'Is it shabby?'

'It is,' said Bridie.

'Is he a ghost, Bridie? The spectre of death come to haunt me?'

'Leave off with yer crap. Says he's a writer. Writes books by the name of Nancy Valentine.'

'But I don't!' butted in O'Leary at last. 'I didn't write that book! You did!'

'I did?' growled Valentine Brack.

'Nancy Valentine! You are the Mistress – I mean—'

'Nancy, is it?' And Valentine Brack was two-fold blind: the blindness of his rage doubling his myopia.

'I've read your book, your masterpiece!' cried O'Leary. 'You are Nancy Valentine!'

'Nancy, you say?'

'The Mistress!' he blurted.

'Calling me a nancy now, are you? Mistress, too. You've come back to torment me, taunt me and haunt me? You'd think I'd put up with that? Even from a ghost? Get out! Out of my house, back to the cesspit of your own creation! Out! You hear me? Away!'

Bridie watched from the landing window the incognito man, legs flying, arms flailing, racing away down the drive. From where she watched he had the look and the shape of a stricken spider, worried from its lair.

In her hands she held a lemon jiffy. He'd dropped it in his flight. What was he doing porting jiffies about with him? It was nearly empty too. Was it a clue? Not at all.

She let it drop. It rolled outside a bedroom door. Forget it, she thought.

She had a real clue now. Thinking of it, she freed for a moment the lifetime's restraints on her work-hardened face, and smiled. It seemed that book was the hinge of all this bother. She had made up her mind about it. And she knew what she had to do.

And to test this new resolve, she subjected herself to a small catechism.

What was her name?

Her name was Bridie O'Toole.

And if it was true that Bridie O'Toole was her name, what would she do?

As true as her name was Bridie O'Toole, she'd lay her hands on that man's book. And she would read it.

Valentine Brack put down his distance lenses. He remembered a time maybe fifteen, twenty years ago. He was strolling down a street, Clonmel, he believed. He stopped. He turned. And he hollered at the boy behind him.

'Why do you always lag behind me?' he demanded. 'Are you ashamed to be seen with your father? Is that it? Prefer your nancy-boy friends, do you?'

And it was only after he had beaten the boy, and the boy's sullen, defiant eyes glinting back up, that it had occurred to him. He had looked by chance into the sheet window of a shop, and seen reflected there his own long legs and his hearty adult gait. Perhaps the boy just couldn't keep pace. Perhaps.

He sighed. Passion aroused memories, and memories pointed to what might have been. He peered through his distance lenses again at the clumsy man racing away down the drive. There seemed no defiance there, no perversity. Just lanky frightened legs and a stooping back. Perhaps he had been mistaken. Perhaps it wasn't his son after all. Nor even a ghost. Just an unlucky stranger.

Valentine Brack had shouted, he had bawled, his blood had boiled. But at least he had shouted, the heat had been in his blood. It felt odd after all these years to have raged again. He was alone once more now. Where was his dog? His dog was away.

The lanky-legged man had disappeared. Valentine Brack could see him no longer through his distance lenses. A tear had fallen, clouding the glass. He doffed the lenses, as another tear fell. Maybe it wasn't his son returned after all.

CHAPTER TWELVE

O'LEARY MONTAGU WIPED the last glass and placed it to drip down on the shelf. He had washed every glass he could find in Nellie Maguire's. None of them had been particularly dirty – a smear here and there, dusty with disuse. He had needed something to do. His brain needed resting, his hands occupying. Mary, the nurse, had told him that during the war, soldiers in their trenches had taken to knitting. O'Leary, in his own war, in this interlude in the pub, a bunker behind the lines, took to washing and drying glasses.

Had he smoked, he would have sat down now and lit a cigarette. After the vigour of his cleaning, the cigarette smoke would have curled satisfyingly lazily. He didn't smoke. He sat down. He stood up. And he set to washing the glasses all over again.

When he had raced down the drive of Knight's Kilbrack, zig-zagging haphazardly, expecting buckshot at any moment, his brain had been full to bursting. And darting through the pillars, turning on to the road, it had felt like he had entered into a dream.

The car had appeared suddenly, from nowhere. A sudden roar, the screech of brakes. Tyres skidded on the gravel, gravel crunched into the walls. O'Leary jumped, and falling, he fell to a blood-red world, bleeding, bleeding, bleeding . . .

The old Bentley disappeared up the drive into Knight's Kilbrack. A horn blared a long trail behind it. O'Leary gathered himself on the verge, brushed off the wet grass from his suit. It had felt like a dream, an accustomed, recurrent dream, but no dream he could remember having dreamt. He had hurried back to the peace and the quiet of the empty pub. He needed to think. Because, more than a dream, it had felt like a memory.

So much had happened. O'Leary, deciphering it, did not know where to begin. A jigsaw had attacked his day. It had cut Kilbrack into difficult and zany pieces. And though he was sure he had all the pieces, still he did not know how to fit them together.

There was a published masterpiece titled *Ill Fares the Land* and there was a leather-bound journal called *Ill Fares the Land, Volume XIV*. How many volumes were there? And the two that he knew of were both written by the one hand, the hand of the—

He knew a momentary doubt. Were they truly written by the same hand? He shook his head. There could be no doubt. The style of Nancy Valentine – let him continue to call her by the name he had grown to love and worship – was incomparably unique. Even the same passage was repeated. They were both the definite work of the one magnificent hand.

But whose hand was it? There was an old man in the big house. There was a dead son, but no daughter in evidence. And yet both Livia and – indeed – the book itself, both described the old man as mad. 'Lonely,' Livia had said in her caring way. 'Wild with rage,' Nancy Valentine described him. That at least tallied with his own experience. What if – and here O'Leary knew he was getting somewhere – the old man were lying. Perhaps not mendaciously, but in his obvious senility he had lost close contact with the truth. What, indeed, if he weren't the writer of either book, but was instead the father? The father of whom, he wasn't sure. Save that he had seeded a genius.

But this worry was far too esoteric. The old man had tried to murder him – twice. Why? The word seemed far too tiny for all the perplexities of questions and doubts it launched.

Diary Memo: Did Livia say truly that she would marry me?

O'Leary blinked at the *non sequitur* of the memo. He had intended a far more pertinent entry. He scrunched up his eyes to erase it. But he stopped. On the whole, he was happier with things the way they stood. *Stet.*

Did Livia say truly she would marry me?

Yes, avowed O'Leary Montagu. In all the day's torrent of abuse and revelation, there was that one surety, that safe haven. Livia and he would marry. Not immediately, she had said, when he had risked his lips for a kiss at the gates to Knight's Kilbrack. Given time. And O'Leary had time. He had time and more for Livia.

He smiled at the prospect of their happy future together.

The mother would come round. Of course she would. Though it had to be said, that woman was a bully. He reached a hand into his pocket. Then froze. The darkest, most hellish of horrors overcame his face.

'I am afraid, dear lady, we shall have to serve ourselves the pudding,' said Valentine Brack. 'I have let the serving lady away.'

'Yes, Valentine,' repeated Mrs Cuthbert, for the fifth time. 'So you have told me.'

'I would serve you willingly, dear lady, myself. But alas, my spectacles . . .'

'Yes,' said Mrs Cuthbert. 'Your spectacles.'

'Smashed.'

'So you have told me.' She served the rhubarb charlotte. The custard was cold and congealed, with a skin thick as hide on top. As such, it was exactly the way Mrs Cuthbert enjoyed her custard. There had been bacon before and cabbage. It was all the food she liked best: plain, safe, homely cooking. She had worked up a considerable appetite with her roundabout motoring and deliberations. She served herself a large helping.

'I apologize for my humble fare,' said Valentine Brack. He addressed an imaginary guest who sat to his left. Mrs Cuthbert sat to his right. 'But an old man myself, dear lady, I have the thinnest of appetites.' His three full courses of dinner lay untouched before him. He had neither appetite nor courage for Bridie O'Toole's cooking, tonight. He would sneak into the larder later.

'Don't apologize, Valentine,' said Mrs Cuthbert, her mouth full of charlotte. 'It reminds me of nanny's.'

'You like it?'

'I do.'

God damn the woman, he thought. He had no stomach for Bridie's food, but even less for prankstering. He wanted to think on his own. But the silly woman was here now; if the food wouldn't put her off, he would have to act the prankster to get rid of her. He allowed himself a low grumble, disguised as a hawking of phlegm, and changed tack. 'Perhaps afterwards, dear lady, you would take a look at the bats. There's terrible thumping from the stairs.'

Mrs Cuthbert put down her spoon. She had expected it. Indeed, she was surprised it had taken so long. Without this preliminary wrong-end-of-the-stick, it wouldn't have been a Thursday canasta evening at all. She clicked her tongue, choking back her exasperation. 'Valentine,' she said, 'you know it's Thursday. I have come to play canasta.'

'Canasta at dinner? Is it the new fashion in Paris, dear lady?' He stared blindly at the imaginary guest to his left, secure in the mists of his myopia. 'I fear we are behind the times in Kilbrack, somewhat. Or perhaps in the busy life of bat specialists the dinner table provides the only leisure for card games. Is it that way with you, dear lady?'

Mrs Cuthbert pursed her lips. On a sudden notion, she grabbed for her handbag, rummaged purposefully through the wads of used wet tissues, till she found her spectacles. 'Put these on,' she said.

'Which is these, dear lady? I'm only blind as a bat without my spectacles.'

'My playing card spectacles,' said Mrs Cuthbert, and she slipped them on the old man's face.

To his consternation Valentine Brack could see through them almost perfectly. He blinked. He was home again in a clear world. He blinked again. God damn the woman. He would have to behave half-decent to her now, else she might retrieve them in a huff. It was a thin line he must tread to rid him of her company, yet retain her spectacles with it. God damn her.

He peered at the imaginary guest to his left, his mouth gaping in puzzlement. He shrugged, turned, and recoiled. 'Ah,' he said, 'There you are.' He stared at his third cousin, beside him at the end of the dinner table. 'I had always imagined the bat lady was thin,' he said.

'I am not the bat lady.'

'You are certainly not thin. And you say you're not the lady come to see about the bats either?'

'I'm your third cousin, Valentine.'

'My third cousin Valentine? I wasn't aware I had a third cousin Valentine. Fancy that and begorrah, as the country folk hereabouts might say.'

'I am Charity Cuthbert – your third cousin.'

'My third cousin?'

'Yes.'

'You don't say.'

'I do say.'

'And what, dear lady, happened the other two, so?'

Mrs Cuthbert rose. 'If you can't see through my spectacles, Valentine, you can give them straight back to me here.'

'But I can see quite clearly through them,' he answered, retreating. He had overstepped his thin line. 'You are my third cousin.'

'Yes.'

'A Mrs Cuthbert, I believe.'

'Charity Cuthbert.' She allowed herself back into her seat.

Valentine Brack doffed the spectacles, wiped them, donned them again. 'Are you related at all to a Cuthbert I used to know, I wonder? He was rector here, in Kilbrack. A fine gentleman he was. Saintly with it.'

'My late husband of course,' said Mrs Cuthbert.

'You don't say.'

'I do say.'

Valentine Brack assumed a quizzical expression. The conundrum, however, seemed beyond him. He gave in. 'Though saintly,' he said, 'he was a very very strange man. A man singular in his pursuits. I had always believed him C of I.'

'He was Church of Ireland.'

'But they tell me, dear lady, you are of the Roman persuasion.'

'Valentine, don't let's drag that up again. I've had enough of that today.'

'Of course, dear lady. Verity, is it?'

'Charity.'

'Well, Verity.' He served her another huge helping of rhubarb charlotte, smiled graciously, then launched into his bat discourse, his favourite method of nettling her. 'So you haven't come to see about the bats. It is a great shame. For it is worse and worse the bats are getting. Thumping away the day long, and the night. What can it be the bats are up to? You'd think they'd be tired with all the thumping. There is a sound of ringing too, though so far as I can ascertain there are no bells in Knight's Kilbrack. Bats there are.'

'Valentine . . .'

'And though I have nothing in particular against our chiropteran friends, believing them the nocturnal and winged equivalent of the homely mouse, yet their incessant thumping and the sound of ringing have a value which can only be described as one of nuisance. It is a great nuisance, Faith, to have bats in one's belfry, when one was unaware of one's possession of a belfry to begin with. Furthermore—'

'Valentine . . .'

Valentine Brack glanced over at his third cousin. He had forgotten it was canasta night. No matter, he would have pretended to forget anyway. But he was annoyed she had arrived so early. He would have sent her packing to return at eight, but the silly woman had scraped her car against the portico steps. Her car – sure it was his own motor. He had lent it to her years back when he realized he'd have no further use for it. She had punctured one of the tyres. He had immediately set Jim O'Toole to repair the damage, but in the meantime he'd felt constrained to offer her dinner. And the silly woman, to his immense surprise, had accepted. It had never occurred to him that anyone would volunteer for Bridie O'Toole's cooking. But here she was at his table now.

And Valentine Brack had looked forward to a dinner on his own, a silent ponderance over the day's events. God knows, they deserved, even compelled, it.

It, however, was not to be.

He glanced at his third cousin, and her fingers wringing her napkin. She was crying. 'Why, Verity,' he said. 'You are crying.'

'I didn't mean to cry, Valentine.'

'Nonsense, Hope. The eyes need a good rinsing every now and then. I beg you, though, not to agonize quite so distractedly over the bats. It is not their extermination I have in mind, only their pacification.'

'It's Livia,' said Mrs Cuthbert, dabbing at her eyes with her napkin. 'I fear she's not interested in men.'

'Perhaps,' he mused, 'she should consider zoology as a career. Anthropology, it seems to me, is a very narrow discipline, unrewarding both materially and spiritually. However, there is a great call in these parts for specialists in the ways of bats. She might be off on the pig's back, as the country folk hereabouts would have it.'

Mrs Cuthbert shook her head into her napkin. 'I think she might be an avocado,' she said.

'An avocado?' repeated Valentine Brack. It quite shocked him out of his preoccupation. 'Avocado?'

'You know,' said Mrs Cuthbert. 'Avocados. Women who prefer, you know . . .'

'Don't be ridiculous, Patience. You mean lesbians.'

'Do I?'

'Lesbians: women of a homophilic nature.'

'Well, I get them confused. Lesbians and avocados: they both seemed to arrive in Ireland at the same time.'

Valentine Brack's lips quivered, then trembled, then collapsed into a guffaw. 'That's true,' he said. 'That's surely true.' He rose from his seat, still laughing, to fetch his Scotch. He took a long swig. He had her on the run now. He'd soon be rid of her. 'Myself,' he began, 'I have little experience of the homophilic nature. Nevertheless, I do remember a time I was staying at a house somewhere, the usual weekend business; I was still young, on holidays from school. I forget the exact where and when of my tale.'

'Yes,' said Mrs Cuthbert. She dried her eyes. Crying was no use, and trying to get sense from third cousin Valentine was worse. She found her powder compact. Her eyes were all smudged. In the mirror her face was a distorted cracked stained-glass image. Crying was no use. Her tears were wasted on this barren earth.

Meanwhile, over at the drinks tray, Valentine Brack continued his recollection. 'I was late down for breakfast, this particular morning. An unpardonable lapse, but again I was young. Consequently I sat alone at table. I was eating toast, whilst reading the London *Times*. My host arrived and asked me if I was busy reading the newspaper. I replied that I was. Would it disturb me, he enquired, if – while I read – he were to—'

'Were to what?' asked Mrs Cuthbert, looking up sharply from her compact. What mischief was the man concocting for her now?

'My host was a man deeply learned in the Classics. It seemed he was interested in what might be considered an Orphic and Hadean view of the body.'

'What happened, Valentine?'

'I stood up, leaning on the breakfast table, and continued

reading the personal columns of *The Times.* You will remember, in those days the personal columns appeared on the front page of the newspaper.'

'But what happened?'

'I really couldn't say, Faith. You must remember, Hope, I had my back to him, Charity, throughout.'

'Valentine Brack, you are a wicked old man!' stormed Mrs Cuthbert, aware at last of the enormity of his story. 'You're a wicked, wicked old man!'

'Must you leave?' asked Valentine Brack, wickedly.

'I am leaving this instant!'

'How unfortunate, dear lady.'

'Hand me back my spectacles!'

'Ah,' said the wicked Valentine Brack. 'Your spectacles.'

Bridie rose slowly from her bench, gathered together Jim's empty bottle and her own empty glass, her gaze never straying from O'Leary. She shuffled up to the bar.

'Large bottle, is it?' asked O'Leary, feigning a cheerfulness he could not feel. 'For Jim?'

But Bridie was having none of this cheerfulness lark. 'Ye shouldn't need asking,' she said.

'And a whiskey and red for you,' said O'Leary, deflated.

'Paddy. Be sure 'tis Paddy.' She watched him, eagle-eyed, fill the glass with the correct measure of whiskey, made sure he wiped the rim against the bottom of the optic, catching the smallest stray drops. 'And go easy there on the lemonade,' she said. 'Now.' She checked behind her. She was safe. Jim was nodding off again. 'Stick another measure of Paddy into that,' she said, *sotto voce*, and she landed some change on the counter.

O'Leary checked over the coins, opened the wooden drawer that served for a till. He was counting out her change, when she said, lowly, slowly and accusingly:

'Did you ever hear tell of incest?'

O'Leary looked up, astounded. 'I'm sorry?'

'You lived in the city,' said Bridie.

'You mean London?' His hand was already deep in his pocket.

'There's incest in the city. There's the incest and the drugs.'

With his free hand he inched her change on to the counter.

'There's the incest and the drugs and the all sorts in the city,' said Bridie. A leak of dribble pioneered a passage through the hairs on her chin, plopped on to the counter. 'And I know.'

He glanced over at Jim, but there was no solace there. He was asleep. His chill fingers tugged beseechingly on the loose threads in his pocket, but no, nothing would avail.

'And them no better than they should be.'

'I'm sorry?'

'And I know,' said Bridie. ''Tis in the papers even.' She blinked her gaze, and picked up her change. ''Tis tuppence cheaper in Paddy Aherne's,' she said.

'What?'

'In Waterford. Downey says so.' Her eyes narrowed again to the glint of green. 'There's the incest and the drugs and the all sorts in the city.' And slowly, excruciatingly slowly, she returned to her bench.

O'Leary fell back down on the stool behind him. My God. His pocket was a desert of desperation. Nothing at all save the hole he had made there to facilitate his talisman's emergency use. Nothing at all save that perfidious hole through which his lemon jiffy somewhere, somehow had escaped. Nothing.

Bridie sipped her drink. Maybe it wasn't incest and maybe it wasn't drugs, but there was something darkly secret about the incognito man behind the bar. The way the old man reacted, there was something very dark, very secret, very strange. The papers were full of drugs and incest in the city, but maybe it wasn't that. Murder was it? Blackmail? Whatever it was, she'd keep him on his toes, the way he might trip himself up. With Nellie Maguire upstairs and the incognito man behind the bar watching, it was impossible to sneak her way to his bedroom. But she'd get there. And she'd get her hands on that book before the night was out. See if she didn't. And she racked her brains for a suitable subterfuge.

Downey entered.

Blast him, thought Bridie. She'd enough to cope with, with Nellie and the incognito man. She didn't need that prying gobshite as well.

Downey quickly closed the door after him, and hurried the hand back into his pocket, where his knife was sharp and open. He swallowed. It was madness coming here, he knew, risking further interrogation from the Pharmaceutical Society man. But what was he to do? How else was he to lay his hands on that book he'd said he'd kept on him?

Across the road in his pharmacy, honing his Swiss-made knife, sharpening his wits as much as the blade, he had decided finally that he must fetch that book for himself. But he couldn't go up to the lanky-legged man and demand the book outright. By the Shoes and Last of Saints Crispin and Crispinian, of course he couldn't do that! He'd be found lying dead in the red-soaked grass of the verge, days later, by the roadside like a dog in a ditch. His mother had warned him of strangers.

Then Downey had smiled to himself and pocketed his Swiss-made knife. Sure couldn't he more easily, more simply and directly, just sneak up to the room himself – he knew the way – sure, what was stopping him? It was only a question of slipping into the fellow's room, stuff the book down his pants, and out again before you could say St Nicephorus of Antioch the Martyr. Easy as pie. And Downey had thought up all by himself a suitable ruse to get up to the bedroom alone. Sure, he'd been intending to do it for years, anyhow.

In the doorway of the pub, Downey swallowed again. By the Green of St Stephen, he swore in trepidation, this had better do the business.

No no! What was he saying? St Stephen's Green was a park in Dublin, the capital city of Ireland. It wasn't the saint's emblem at all. He tightened his grip on the knife in his pocket, tensed the muscles on his face. Pray God, the saint wouldn't have a down on him for that.

He tore his gaze away from the consolation of his neatly bowed shoelaces and raised his head. He addressed a spot three feet above and to the left of O'Leary. He said stonily: 'I am not here for the drink, thank you.'

'I see,' said O'Leary, glancing behind and above to check there really wasn't somebody there to whom the pharmacist might be speaking.

'I have a sheet here,' said Downey holding out a poster, but still staring doggedly beside and above O'Leary, 'that needs urgent hanging in a public place. Too long have the smaller communities in this country lived in unhappy ignorance of the true nature of St Vitus's Dance. Rheumatic chorea, to give the affliction its more precise and modern name, has often in the past been associated with the dancing mania of the Middle Ages. These ancient outbreaks, however, were almost certainly occasioned by the ravages of ergotism, St Anthony's Fire, as it was then called. It is time the country communities of Ireland were correctly informed.' Downey finished and swallowed again. His speech, he deemed, had gone well. God knows and it should have. He'd practised it for nearly a whole hour and a quarter in the pharmacy opposite.

O'Leary stared at the poster. It was a hastily drawn caricature of a child with frantic, waving, writhing limbs, at least five of each of the normal four. It was headed, 'St Vitus's Dance: The True Facts'; and in the bottom right-hand corner was the message, 'For further information, and advice on any subject, medicinal, organic or mental, contact J. D. Downey, Dispenser of Advice Only, Kilbrack.' 'Advice Only' was underlined three times.

O'Leary looked up. 'You want to hang that here?' he said.

'I do,' said Downey, with the politest stamp of his toe to indicate his pioneering resolve.

'Very well,' said O'Leary.

'What d'ye mean, very well?' demanded Downey. 'I have to ask Miss Maguire's permission.'

'I'm sure she won't mind.'

'What d'ye mean? I have to go upstairs now and ask her personally. And don't you try to fob me off with her not being upstairs, for I saw her light was on from the pharmacy – I beg your pardon – my shop across the road. 'Tis a desperate and delicate subject. I need her permission personal, so I do.'

Downey, still staring above and beside O'Leary, had edged towards the door to the stairs.

'But she told me on no account was she to be disturbed,' said O'Leary. '*She said she was tired.* Tired beyond the long endurance.'

'The what?'

'Those were her very words.'

'She's tired?'

'Yes.'

'Oh,' said Downey.

'I'm sorry,' said O'Leary.

'Well,' said Downey. His fingers, loose with sweat, let the knife fall free in his pocket.

'Perhaps she'll be down later,' said O'Leary. The poor man had such a dispirited look on his face, he felt obliged to offer some solace.

'Will she then?'

'It's possible.'

It was the Green of St Stephen had done it, thought Downey. In the heat of the moment, he'd got the saint's familiar emblem wrong. Hell and damnation. And now the saint had a down on him, had cursed his very enterprise. Lackaday, lackaday.

No two ways about it: he'd have to wait.

'Put on a pint for me,' he said, defeated. He sat down by the poster of *The All-Star Hurley Players of Ireland*. Offaly, Offaly, Cork, Waterford, he said to himself dejectedly, Derry, Derry, Cork, Dublin . . .

What was this, wondered Bridie. Regarding this place of a sudden, there was always more or there was always less to anything that met the eye. What was this? She elbowed Jim beside her a terrific jab in his stomach.

'What?' said Jim.

'Your large bottle.'

'Well,' said Jim. He poured a half a medium into his glass. He was about to pick up the glass, sup the bottled stout from it, when he fell asleep again, rolling aboard ship in the gentle Doldrums . . .

'I oughtn't to drink,' said Mrs Cuthbert. 'You can't drink your sorrows away.' And she emptied her glass in one go.

'No,' agreed Valentine Brack. 'But you can drink a damned good glass of Scotch.'

He poured another three fingers into her glass. He examined the bottle. It was empty. He shook the dregs into his own glass, but it was still empty. He returned to the drinks tray for a new bottle.

Hanging above the drinks tray was an old looking-glass losing its shimmer, in a tarnished brazed frame. He looked into it now, remembering how his father, years before, had placed it there that he might know what the guests were helping themselves to. He smiled with the memory. He saw his dirty neck, and the grimy collar to his shirt, his uncombed hair, and his third cousin's spectacles, pink with butterfly wings; and he smiled again. In the corner of the looking-glass he could see his third cousin Charity behind him, overpowering the poor armchair she sat in. She was turning her glass round and round in her fingers, weighing it and pressing it, as though it were the physical embodiment of her encircling problems, a snake eating its own tail, oroborus-like. He even smiled at this. She wasn't such a bad old bat, he thought. After the threats and the recriminations, the shouting and ranting, and finally the settling of their differences in apologies mutually accepted; after such exhausting activity, they had withdrawn to the small sitting room to recuperate and drink Scotch. Already the old bottle was finished.

He chose a malt and returned to the fire. 'Now, Charity,' he said.

He clinked his glass against hers, made her raise it. She drank, and Valentine immediately refilled her glass with the malt. 'I've been keeping this for a special occasion,' he said.

'Thank you, Valentine.'

'But damn it anyway,' he added, 'it has to be drunk some time.' He pantomimed a wide grin, so that Mrs Cuthbert allowed her mollified self a weakish simper in reply.

'You are a rascal, Valentine,' she said. 'You always were a rascal. What was it your father used to call you?'

'The rantipole of Knight's Kilbrack. A long time since, Charity, a long time since.' He eased himself into his favourite chair, his glass in his hand, the bottle of Scotch beside him; and he rested his long old legs on the brass fender. It was his favourite position, and the fender was worn smooth in that spot with the decades' rubbing of his boots. He felt quite at home. He even felt at home with third cousin Charity. In the mahogany gloom of the small sitting room, the logfire crackling the night away, he was content to share old memories with his cousin; old memories and modern complaints. 'The world was in its place then,' he said.

'Yes,' said Mrs Cuthbert. 'Nowadays . . .'

'Yes,' agreed Valentine Brack. 'Nowadays.'

They both sipped their Scotch.

'Shall I put another log on?' she asked.

'Do,' said Valentine.

And Mrs Cuthbert manoeuvred half a trunk on to the fire. 'The old house is standing up,' she said.

'It is,' said Valentine.

They both knew it wasn't. They both knew that the house was crumbling slowly about them, sinking back into the earth that had spawned it, to be now a relic, soon a shell. One day it would be a store-house for bricks for new-fangled estates in some period style. Its day, like theirs, had passed.

'I remember the balls,' said Mrs Cuthbert.

'Yes, the balls,' said Valentine Brack.

'And the orchestras, and the music.'

'The dance-music and the dances.'

'In the gallery. And all the bunting and the thousands of candles; glass everywhere, against every wall.'

'Candles and glass galore, that's right.'

'Listen to us,' said Mrs Cuthbert. 'It's an old fireside story we're telling. I don't know. The poorer we get, it seems to me, the more Irish we become.'

'Yes,' said Valentine Brack, rocking slowly an inch to and fro in his chair. '*Sea*,' he agreed in the Irish of his old nurse.

'Do you miss your son?'

'What?' said Valentine. But he relaxed back into his chair. The spell that the small sitting room had woven about them was too pleasant a thread to cut. 'You wouldn't know,' he said.

'Children,' said Mrs Cuthbert.

'Yes, children.'

'Livia . . .'

'Don't you worry about Livia. Livia's all right. She'll come through in the end. You'll see. Whatever.'

'I wish I could see.'

'She's anguished still about her father. She blames you, Charity, for his death.'

'Do you blame me, Valentine?'

'Of course I don't, Charity.'

'I didn't want him to die. I just wanted to hurt him a little; shock him, I suppose, into his senses. It was a fortune he wasted on that church of his. I didn't mean to break his heart like Livia says.'

'He was a saintly man,' said Valentine Brack. Though he knew he wasn't. He was a philanderer who glimpsing mortality had sought atonement for his sins in the restoration of St Ciaran's. He wondered did Charity know? He knew. Half the world knew. Amazing what you could keep from yourself, given the will. 'But like all saintly men, he was a pain in the arse with it.'

'You think so?'

'I do.'

'Thank you, Valentine.'

'Not at all, Charity. You were wasted on him.'

'Was I?'

'You were.'

It was a bowery combination: the shaky low wattage of the lamps, the wood glow of the fire, the warmth of the old Scotch in his veins, the night of the day. Valentine Brack felt pleasantly contemplative, intimate with the world and its ways. And he knew what Livia, because she was young, could not know: that had her father lived, by now she would hate him. She would hate him with all the vengeance she wasted now on her mother. It was always the same in families. Until perhaps the parent was old and the child was middle-aged and both had tasted a little of success, a little of failure, when memories perhaps could be shared.

After all, it was that way with his own son. He hadn't considered it before, but Livia and Valentine had so much in common. Both were perverse, perverted, given to their extremes. Livia gave out that she was worldly-wise, sardonic even. However, through her backbone, he guessed, ran a strain of tory romance. What of his son? Perhaps in the end, all they shared was their contumacy. If there was romance in his son, his son had died too soon for anyone to glimpse it. He had all the romance of a property-developer. 'When I inherit,' he'd said once, 'I'll knock your house down. And all memory of you with it.'

Did he miss his son? It was hard to say. These last years since his death and the unlooked-for death of the future with him, Valentine Brack had not thought to ask was he lonely. Kilbrack and Knight's Kilbrack had tumbled about him. At first it had consoled his own desolation. In the end, it was all a joke shared drily . . . with no one. Did he miss his son? It was a long time. And if this man was his son returned . . . ?

The lids of his eyes fell closed. And in the small world of the sitting room, the present slowly dissolved, to be replaced, if only for a moment, by the happier mood of what might have been.

He looked up. His third cousin was staring at him. 'Forgive me, Charity. I was dozing off.'

'I was thinking about your son,' she said.

'So was I.'

'I never really knew him.'

'Neither did I.'

'What was it he died of?'

'He died of a Wednesday,' said Valentine Brack. 'I remember it well.' He quaffed his glass of Scotch, stood up. 'Come on now, Charity,' he said. He smacked his hands together, quavering the gloaming. 'We've gone shocking morbid, the two of us. Drink up there. Do you know what I have a mind for? I think I'll wind up the old gramophone.

I have the records here somewhere. Let's see if we can't remember the steps. Will you give me your hand?'

'It's very late,' said Mrs Cuthbert doubtfully.

'And 'twill only get later. Will you give me your hand, Charity?'

'Valentine,' she said. The glow from the fire pinked her smile to the blush of a maiden. 'I should be delighted.'

'I'm sorry,' said O'Leary, marshalling what courage he could, 'but Miss Maguire insists we close at eleven sharp.' The grandmother clock in the corner struck quarter past eleven. 'The disturbance, she says. And it's already quarter past, as you can see. I did warn you of last orders and you did in fact order them. You've drunk them now and I must insist you depart.'

'And whyfore is that? Miss Maguire never closes shop.'

O'Leary sighed. He had racked his brains the evening through and had finally decided the only place he could have dropped his jiffy was Knight's Kilbrack itself. In his scurrying flight it had slipped through the hole in his pocket. Striving to remember, he was sure he had felt even its passage down his leg. The only thing for it, though he risked his skin, was to return to the big house and sweep the corridors. 'I intend to take a walk,' he said. 'I need some fresh air.'

Bridie's face changed immediately, from defiance to a semblance of sympathy.

'I'm going now,' she said, rising, 'that you might take your walk immediately.'

'Thank you.' He had not expected it to be so easy.

'Jim!' she called. 'Get up out of that!'

'What's that?'

'We're off!' She looked over at Downey. 'He's closed,' she said.

'I can see that,' said Downey to the laces in his shoes. And by the hokey, he had heard what the queer man had said. A stroke of luck it was. 'Thank you, St Stephen,' said Downey, glancing upwards at heaven. The saint had heard his repentant prayers, had not forsaken him after all. If the incognito man was gallivanting out in the night, he'd have plenty of time himself to sneak back into the pub – he knew the ins and outs, of course he did – and he'd steal into that bedroom and he'd steal that book. Oh, St Stephen the Protomartyr, he thought in awe: you're a saint and a half.

At the door, Bridie searched through O'Leary's eyes to assure herself of his true intention. 'A walk?' she asked.

'Yes,' said O'Leary.

'Get out,' she said to Jim.

'I'm out,' said Jim.

'Good night,' said Downey to his shoes, as O'Leary bolted the door behind him.

'Goodbye,' said O'Leary. He poured himself a long glass of water. Well, he thought, looking east. Anyway, he thought, looking west. What harm, he said to the north. What – beside his skin – had he to lose?

The old 78s were scratched slightly, and the winding mechanism of the gramophone unsound, but soon, nevertheless, the small sitting room of Knight's Kilbrack came alive – not vibrantly, but gently – to the demure and genteel strains of the bygone dances. The steps came slow and awkward at first, perhaps not as graceful as the veleta of their youth: not tripping, but hesitant still. Their expressions, however, remained straight-faced and courteous, disdaining to admit of a knock or a pull. And soon the music had worked its timeless spell. There was re-awakened in their toes the memory of grace and elegance and polish of the thousand and one balls of their season. They danced, as only they remembered they danced.

And between the rounds, they cheered each other with glasses of old malt whisky. The world, for a season, was in its place.

CHAPTER THIRTEEN

O'LEARY FLINCHED HIS eyes. For a considerable second the impulse to flee nearly triumphed. It was the same car, the old Bentley, that had narrowly missed running him over earlier that day. It was quiet now, stationary. But there seemed still to be a dream-like motivation to it; as if at any moment it might burst to automatic life, to light and roar, and attack him. It was that dream again, that dream he had no memory of dreaming.

He edged past the car, his eyes peripherally searching out danger. He climbed the steps of the portico. It was terra firma. He felt safer there.

He glanced back down the drive of Knight's Kilbrack. The moon played on the treetops. A bat squeaked. The quiet of the country night civilized his panic to a nagging doubt at the back of his mind. Ridiculous: it was only a car.

Diary Memo: Ridiculous, the small instances that will institute a panic. And yet that is the meaning of the word. An irrational fear, inspired by the god—

But this was a time too alarming for docile diary memos. Something was happening to O'Leary Montagu, and O'Leary didn't know what. There were dreams stalking him. And whatever those dreams portended, they had a slippery handle, hard to get to grips with. He squeezed his eyes. There was a demented and wild old man hunting him too, with a loaded shotgun, in all probability. He felt so naked. He had neither jiffy nor book to comfort him. From a distant room deep inside the house he could catch the tinny sound of dance-music. It was laughing at him. The jolly rhythm parodied the tremble in his legs. In his pocket, his fingers rounded fiercely on the empty air. There was nothing for it. He opened his eyes, creaked open the door, and he entered Knight's Kilbrack.

Livia let the book slip through her fingers. It fell to the floor beside her bed. Young Valentine Brack, she thought. There was a time in her childhood when every second whisper concerned that name. Then there was nothing. She had never truly understood the passion that Uncle Val had shown for his son. Only love could lie beneath it. For love alone could produce such anger, such retribution.

Now she understood. It was all in the book. 'Love was forced to quit her home . . .' She felt sick reading it. So much love wasted, perverted.

She reached for a cigarette. But without the corresponding grimace of annoyance on her mother's face, it didn't seem worth smoking.

'Where are you, Mother?' she said aloud. She counted the

chimes on the clock downstairs. It was midnight. Her mother had been gone nearly six hours. And she was driving. 'It's getting late, Mother.'

Livia stared blankly out the black window to the dark where the graveyard of her father's church would be. She remembered when she was a little girl she used to play amongst the gravestones. She had a ribbon in her hair, white ankle socks and shoes. It was summer in her childhood, holidays at home from school. The grass had the soft spring of Ireland, accepting her tread with a momentary footprint. Sheep grazed, cropping the graveyard grass. She was happy.

Later, her mother scrubbed her knees to a pinky shine in the kitchen. And in a fresh white dress, she leaned between her father's legs, soaking up the ponderous pipesmoke air. In her prayers, God blessed Father and God blessed Mother. The moon shone at night as the sun through the day, and she slept with the tang of a tangible fear of adjacent ghosts from the graveyard. She was alive and happy in Kilbrack.

Now she knew – because Livia knew nearly everything now – that she remembered her days as sunny because, had it been raining, she would not have been outside and so the weather would play no part in her memories. She knew the grass was soft and green because of the particular humidity of the Irish climate. Her mother's concern was with cleanliness and Godliness and a neighbour's unlooked-for visit. Pipesmoking carried a danger of cancer in the mouth. And ghosts, when at all physical, were St Elmo's fire or – extravagantly – an electrical luminescence quirksome as lightning. That was all.

Perhaps she should talk with her mother. She surely couldn't live her entire life this way through. They'd end up one day like the Bracks. She had accepted that man's hand in marriage. At the time it had seemed a masterstroke. If her mother was so averse to the fool, then switching tactics, accepting his hand, had seemed masterly.

'Marry him then,' her mother had said.

And this offer of the Monsignor's . . .

She lit a cigarette, then immediately stubbed it out. She did not smoke cigarettes any more, she decided.

She reached under her pillow, brought out the architectural drawings. Daddy, she said. But for once there was no tingling acknowledgement to her touch. What am I doing? The drawings were yellow and crisp. If she opened them from their folds they would crack, crumble to dust probably. The details had faded. And what remained were to her as hieroglyphics, whose key even was fading.

How clever I am, she thought. I can converse intelligently on any subject, from the sciences to the humanities and back again. My mind, as they say, is a many-roomed mansion. Yet one door is closed. I know what's behind that door. I can't think why I'm so frightened. It's just a little girl. She's called Livia.

She gazed at the hieroglyphics on her father's drawings. How little I know about myself.

And how the Bracks hated each other, father and son. She must talk with her mother. 'Where are you?' she said again. And when she heard the rattling of a key in the door, she crept down the stairs in her nightdress. 'Mother, are you all right?'

The door was still open. Mrs Cuthbert lay on the floor. She looked up, her head swaying with the effort to focus her eyes. 'The Reverend Mother Livia, is it?' she said, slurring her words. 'Don't worry about me. Don't let me disturb you from your complan.'

'Complan, Mother?'

'Or whatever office the Reverend Mother happens to be saying.'

Livia helped her to her feet. 'You mean compline,' she said.

'Thank you, Reverend Mother.'

'Where have you been all night? I've been worried. I've been thinking—'

'I've been dancing,' said Mrs Cuthbert. She bumped into the hall table.

'Mother, you really are drunk!'

'Yes,' she said. 'But as Valentine says, I shall be ugly in the morning.'

'I'll help you into bed.'

'I don't need helping. I want to dance.'

'Dance?'

And Mrs Cuthbert danced her way up the stairs. Her wake, however, was less that of a stately galleon, as the trail of destruction following a shoeless mob. Two pictures fell. Three rocked uncertainly. The remainder – glass pictures mostly, on a religious theme – hung modernistically askew. Another one fell. Livia caught it just in time. She looked up at her mother in disbelief.

At the landing, Mrs Cuthbert turned. Her lips opened and closed like a fish's, as she tried to formulate a sentence.

'Mother,' said Livia, 'we can't talk now. I can see that. But perhaps in the morning? I'd like us to talk. We never do. We're growing too far apart.'

'Reverend Mother Livia,' said Mrs Cuthbert, 'as third cousin Valentine says, you are a pain in the arse.' And she contorted her face into a grotesque wink, cackling at the enormity of what she had at last allowed herself to say. 'Good night.' And she crashed into a porcelain vase.

Livia returned to her bedroom. She was about to climb back into her bed, when she saw once more the book lying at its side.

Something had to be done. It was all getting out of hand. Kilbrack was dying just as that book predicted. So much love wasted, perverted. So many bachelors, spinsters, so many widows and widowers. Orphans all of us. And not only because Uncle Val wanted it that way. Didn't they all? Didn't she? All this reverence for her father's church. She wanted a graveyard. As though only this ruin could provide a suitable depository for her father's memory. We're all so jealous of the past, nursing old wounds and grievances. We use it not to explain the present but to pervert it. Is it the same all over Ireland? Anyone so jealous of his past must be insecure of his present. Is it the Irish in us? What are we frightened of losing?

We've turned our back on the living, she thought, as she dressed in her oldest clothes. Something had to be done. And she knew what – just – might save Kilbrack. She crept down the stairs and stole into the night.

* * *

If she could stand on that ledge, and if she could balance a moment, a split-second would nearly do, and if her hand would stretch, and her fingers would touch, then hold, get a fix, and if the guttering didn't give way, and she could pull with her strength, and if her feet could walk upwards along the wall, skid on the pebble-dash, that was all right, so long as they didn't slip too far, pushing herself upwards, heaving with all her breath, elbowing herself over the guttering . . .

The harridan sneaked her wiry body, creeping it over the pipes, on to the flat roof of the store-house. She stood up. She caught her breath. Her work-hardened hands had accepted no injury; her boots were years old anyhow. She brushed the pebble-dash off her house-coat. She smiled at the moon, her accomplice. She had known she could do it. It was a matter of her will, the strength of it. Her name, after all, was Bridie O'Toole.

She peered over at the incognito man's bedroom window. It was at the other end of the store-house roof, looking out on to it. And it was left open, the way she knew it was from her reconnoitre previously. And it was dark inside his bedroom. The book was virtually in her grasp.

Meanwhile, inside the pub, thin old Downey tested the tip of a toe on the stair. Not a sound. He risked the bottom of a toe. Nothing. He stepped on the stair. It creaked – Holy Mother of God! – and Downey blessed himself three times. He listened for an age. Still nothing stirred above. The only sound emanating from Miss Maguire's bedroom was the steady rasp of her snore. He was safe yet.

It had taken him a while to fix the lock on the yard door of the pub. The blade of his knife had nearly snapped with the intricate pressure. But it was a Swiss-made knife; of course the blade hadn't snapped. The yard door had swung open eventually. And Downey had smiled. He was a thief, a clever thief in the night.

He was at the top of the stairs now. He pressed on the handle of the incognito man's door. Saints Florus and Laurus, he said to himself, for it was now their feast day, Friday, August the eighteenth: for God's sake, protect me now. He practised a large breath. Then he opened the bedroom door.

Bridie fell in through the window, and Downey tripped over her kicking legs.

'Get off,' said Bridie.

'What is it?' said Downey.

'You?' said Bridie.

'You?' said Downey.

'Get off, you gobshite!'

'Who's calling me a gobshite?'

'Stop holding me down!'

'Stop pulling me over!'

They struggled on the floor, in the dark, rolling about, clasped in each other's jealous grip.

'Let go of me arms,' hissed Bridie.

'Leave go of me neck first,' said Downey.

'I won't.'

'Nor I, so.'

Now Downey was on top; now, with a terrific shove, Bridie got the upper hand.

'I'll cross my eyes on you.'

'And what do I care about eyes? 'Tis dark anyhow.'

That was true. Bridie had forgotten about that. Besides it wasn't Jim at all. It was Downey.

'I'll kill you, J. D. Downey,' she hissed.

'Go on, then,' said Downey. 'And I have a knife.'

But what did she care about a knife? It was buttons on the floor she feared. She made a sudden grab for Downey's jacket, to wrench off every button, to hold them tight in her fist, lest Downey somehow might know of her terror.

'What are ye up to with me buttons?'

'Never mind that.'

Downey made a snatch for her fist and in the struggle some buttons escaped her.

'Agh!' she screamed. 'Where are they?'

'On the floor,' said Downey.

'Agh!' screamed Bridie. 'How did ye know?'

'Where else would they be?'

Bridie flailed wildly till she hit on the stray buttons hideous on the linoleum. There was nothing for it. She grabbed for his shirt. How many buttons did the blasted man have? She was exhausted with the effort.

Downey too was exhausted. He collapsed a dead weight on top of her. 'You've the breath taken out of me,' he said.

'I'm winded meself.' She had his jacket and shirt ripped open now, and her fist full of the wretched wrenched buttons. She made a dive for his fly. 'What's that?' she said.

'Is it my Swiss-made knife?' asked Downey doubtfully.

''Tis no Swiss-made knife is that.'

'What is it?'

'Stop rubbing against me.'

''Tis you is rubbing.'

'Leave go of me arms.'

'Leave go of me neck first.'

'I won't.'

'Nor I, so.'

'What is it?' said Bridie, beginning to whisper.

'I don't know,' said Downey, whispering too.

'Me skirt is in the air.'

'Me shirt is around me.'

'I'll kill you, J. D. Downey.'

'I think maybe you will,' he replied between short sharp shocked breaths.

'Be quiet,' said Bridie. 'You'll waken Nellie.'

''Tis you is moaning.'

They had rolled into a golden half-light where moonbeams half-shone on the linoleum. He could make out her face. She could make out his silhouette.

'Bridie,' he said.

'What?' she asked.

'Begging your pardon,' he said and struggled a hand free to tip his bowler hat, 'but you've a grand head of hair, Bridie O'Toole. To the touch.'

'Take off your bowler hat, J. D. Downey,' said Bridie. 'There's the queer man's bed yonder. If 'tis wrestling we're at, 'tis as well to do it proper.'

'I will then, Bridie O'Toole.'

'Get on with it, J. D. Downey.'

The grandmother of Nellie Maguire got up from her bed,

prepared, then sniffed, some cocaine. And the granddaughter of Nellie Maguire stared into the swing mirror on her dressing table at the beautiful but hopeless young thing that suddenly she presented.

It wasn't her fault. If anyone's, it was his. They would have been happy together. They would have married in love and lived in love till death them did part. But he married away. She still ached for him. After all these years, she ached still for his touch or the smell of his breath, or the whisper of a kiss on her lips. She never went there, but always in her mind was the memory of the moonlit fairy glade where first they had met, embraced. But he married away. He married the Church.

Michael, she yearned. Oh, my, my, my, my Michael . . .

She sniffed, and the cocaine rushed to her throat. What was she thinking? She couldn't remember. She cocked an ear. Listen to that, she thought, and the moaning and groaning and humping out beyond. It sounded like Bridie. It sounded like Downey. You'd swear 'twas Bridie in the spare room, having it away with Downey, so you would. And she would have laughed herself to sleep with the wild comedy of that thought, save soon she had forgotten what she was laughing about.

There was a scratching at the door in Valentine Brack's bedchamber. The door creaked open, and in padded the mongrel Nancy.

'My Nancy,' said Valentine, fondling the dog. 'Is it your supper you're after? I have it here for you.' And he watched closely as the mongrel gulped down her food. It was the bacon which Bridie had prepared, which he hadn't the stomach for at dinner. He patted the dog vigorously, while Nancy sought to shake him away, all her five senses greedy with bacon. The old man gave up, and lay back down on the pillows in the bed where he was born, where he hoped he might die. He left a hand on the dog's stomach, comforted slightly by the lively jerks. Her lively jerks were all he had. And he thought about his third cousin Charity.

It had been rather a pleasant evening. Fifteen-year-old malt, memories older; the memories were old when the Scotch was still water in a Highland burn. The veleta, the St Bernard's waltz, the military two-step, all the dances their great-aunts had frowned on: it was a grand old basheen of a time, in the manner of times as they used to be. She wasn't a good-looking woman, not even a recluse could call her that. But they had things in common, after all: not only ancestry, but the sensibilities of their class. They couldn't gossip – nobody could gossip in these days – but they could talk with no call for gloss. He had a dislike, a fear almost, of women who cried. But it was so long since Valentine Brack had heard of a tear, let alone seen one; in the end, even her crying was sufferable. He might even have her to dinner again.

In the long years, it had rarely occurred to him that he might like a companion, some evening company. He had been a recluse too long. Or maybe not a recluse: maybe he had been too busy laughing with irony to notice he might be lonely. He sighed. It had been a long day.

He closed the thin white lids of his eyes. He didn't sleep, not yet.

Why had his son returned? To wreak what vengeance?

When he had slammed his car into his son, eleven years ago, in the dead of night in London, he had stayed some hours with the lifeless broken pulp on the street. It had been an accident. He was sure. He had driven to London in a rage, he knew. And he would have harangued his son, he knew that too, berated him with all the damnation of hell. But at the same time he knew beneath the driving rage was the hope of one last appeal, one final beseeching of his son to return to his home, to be – to be Valentine Brack's son, heir to Knight's Kilbrack, custodian of her past and guarantor of her future . . . to be there.

Until his teenage years, the boy had been a joy to him. After his wife's early death, he had never dared hope that the shady shrub that was his life would again bloom. But tramping the fields and the hillsides with his growing son, Valentine Brack had indeed blossomed: not extravagantly, but discreetly, like an autumn flower. He loved the boy, not only as his own fruit, but as seed for the future. Perhaps – he didn't know – but perhaps they were too close in those years. Maybe he expected too much. For the boy changed with puberty.

Contumacious was how he described him then. For he grew dark and deceitful. He could see it in his face: his eyes sunk deep and his brow always furrowed, as though ridden with unspeakable guilt. He stooped when he walked. If you found him unexpectedly in a room, he would glower from the corner. There was trouble at his school. He wouldn't mix.

'What's wrong with you?' Valentine demanded on one occasion.

The boy bowed his head. 'I've got spots,' he replied.

Peevish thing, thought Valentine. He grabbed his chin and inspected the face. It was fresh as any boy's his age. 'Spots? What about spots?' The boy had struggled his face free. 'I asked you: where are these spots?'

The boy's eyes then flared suddenly. 'Everywhere.'

It didn't make sense. Once, on a birthday, he held a great ball for his son. All the youth of the county was present. But his son was not to be found dancing or flirting, nor even experimenting with drink like his peers. He was in the kitchens, coddling some mangy pup he'd found. 'I'm keeping her,' he said sneering before Valentine had even spoken. 'Don't try to stop me.' Why should the boy believe he would wish to stop him? 'And I'm calling her Nancy in honour of your jokes.' What jokes, wondered Valentine. And why was everything the boy said spoken so fiercely, determinedly, as though always in expectation of proscription? Valentine had shrugged his shoulders and left him to the pup.

He caught him once taking potshots at the portraits of his ancestors in the hall. He tanned him that time as he tanned him on many an occasion. But still, Valentine had believed the cussedness would pass. He embarked on his great history of Kilbrack, *Ill Fares the Land* he called it, hoping thus to rekindle if not love then at least respect in the boy's heart. But while he traipsed the tapestried halls, proclaiming his twilit prose, he heard in his ears only laughter.

As the son grew his sullens changed to sniggering asides.

'You'd better hurry up with your history, Daddo,' he told him. 'For history ends with me.' Valentine was shocked, of course. Did the boy own nothing to family, stone, tradition? It was as though he did not understand the nature of his birth. He was a Brack. There had been Bracks in Kilbrack since time immemorial. He could do and say as he liked so long as he married well and produced an heir. What was wrong with him?

'I'll tell you what's wrong with me,' the boy said once. 'You're insulting to my friends.'

What friends? His son only knew popinjays and nancy-boys from the city. They were all that would put up with him. 'Is that all?'

'That's not even the beginning.'

He knew the boy hated him, and he knew that he had come to hate the boy. But he couldn't tell why it had happened, only that it continued, in rages on his part and sneers on his son's. The shady shrub that had flowered, he realized, had brought forth but dark red fruits like the berries on a yew in a graveyard, poisonous.

Then one day, he discovered in the library some drawings the boy had been working on. At first he could make nothing of them. The outlines they showed were familiar, like the picture of a well-loved friend, his face only, in silhouette. It came to him very slowly that they were plans for a reservoir, a great lake of useless water, drowning Knight's Kilbrack and all his demesne and all of Kilbrack and the valley of the Brack, a final obliteration of all the generations. The blackguard had even corresponded with some treacherous water board. This time it was too much. In a rage he ordered his son from his house, at gunpoint, with a parting warning shot never to return.

For some years there was a furious almost daily delivery of post. The envelopes all had the black scrawl of his son's writing. Valentine rarely read them. Then one day, a book arrived, two books in fact. The one was called *Murder in the Big House* and apparently had made something of a splash. Secretly, he believed, he was proud of his son. It transpired that some at least of his strain had entered the boy's blood. But after he'd read the second book, *Ill Farts the Land*, a parody of his own great history, once more his temper raged.

And it was in that rage that he drove to the night boat, drove through Wales and half of England, to meet his son head-on. He waited a while outside his lodgings, as though he needed to catch his breath. And when his son appeared he followed him to some park where in the dark night he could make out nothing.

He waited for his son's return. Then, when he reappeared in the street, he switched on his lights, raced his engine. His intention, he was certain, was to roar past only, to sully his son in a glance with a father's hurt. Then stop. Then speak. But the son, turning to the engine's roar, glimpsing his father's face, had seemed to droop his shoulders as though a weight had lifted. He smiled so wanly. It was like he stepped out into the street.

What happened then was an accident, Valentine Brack was certain. But while he stayed with the broken body he did not speak that it was an accident. He did not hug his son to him, did not beg for breath to return. He did not howl to the trees, to the sky. He could not say whether there were trees, whether the sky was starry or dark. He stared at his son as the life drained from him, staining the kerb. And he knew when finally he returned to the Bentley, purred the engine down the street, returned to his house in Ireland, he knew his own life had drained too. It remained in some unparticular London street, a stain on a kerb, to be washed away by the falling rain, obliterated.

That night he took his axe and felled the second magpie from his gates. For years there had been no joy. Now there would be no sorrow either. Now there was nothing. Kilbrack would be Brackless e'er and a day. His continued existence was an interval only. Without his son there was no meaning to the past. When he had killed him, he had killed all hope of a future. In the silence of the seasons, he realized his son had been right. 'History ends with me.'

He continued with his history, but burdened with its futility and the futility of his life, it shrivelled itself to a parody, like his son's. It was another dry joke in a long line of jokes. For Valentine Brack discovered late in life he had the keenest of wits. His rages ceased and his halls echoed instead to his own ironical laughter.

And now his son had returned. He had not killed him after all. Was he pleased, was he sad? So much had he changed he no longer knew. Such equivocation. He had come upon him late that night. He had waved goodbye to Charity and was climbing the stairs to his chamber. And in the quivering low wattage of the lights – more shadow than anything else, and all the more delusive in the light of the Scotch that glowed in his veins – he had watched.

His son was lying prone in the corridor, reaching his fingers underneath a door to retrieve something inside. He was crying, wailing to himself. Valentine Brack had shaken his head. How ugly he had grown, hideous almost; like a devil out of hell come knocking on his gate, in expectation – of what? And such equivocation.

The day's cup had been full of it. In the afternoon, that first glimpse of the man had aroused undimmed the ancient passion, the instinct of his rage. But passion awoke memories too, in the evening, the night. And with memories aroused and haunting the untravelled lanes of his mind, there had come the glimpse of a different prospect, the gentler mood of what might still be. Perhaps it wasn't vengeance his son sought. Perhaps, in his insanity, he craved only for home.

He had left his son to his devices, whatever they were, and climbed the further stairs to his chamber.

He turned over now on his side. The mongrel Nancy snuggled closer, so that they lay together like spoons. 'I'll invite old Charity to dinner again,' he said, and the mongrel thudded her tired old tail twice on the mattress. Valentine Brack could feel his beating heart pressed against her coat. Perhaps it was too late for Kilbrack, but he didn't have to die with a frown on his face. 'I'll invite her to dinner tomorrow,' he said. The old dog thumped one more time with her tail; and finally they slept.

Outside, over all Kilbrack the moon had set, and the thick black night of the country lay heavy on the land, as thick and heavy as the blanket on Valentine Brack's four-poster bed. And underneath that blanket of night, sleepless yet, the world dreamed. The untended untilled fields sprouted barley and wheat and the lush green pasture fed herds of kine. Sheep returned to graze the hillsides. A shepherd turned in his sleep, groaning his lust as the ram in the pinfold bleated his. In the scattered shells of the cottages oil lamps once more smoked, bread was baked and ale was brewed and drunk. Children as ever forgot their manners and to say their prayers in bed. A dance ended in Nellie Maguire's, and young men and their women lined up for the next. Tomorrow Downey would clean the grocery windows, Bridie would sweep her porch, church bells would ring.

The world dreamed, so that the rustle of a vixen in the hedgerow became calves nestling to their mothers' warmth. An owl that screeched overhead was the cackling of hens at roost. And the solitary lamp that burned in Valentine Brack's bedchamber lit a glittering ball in the gallery of Knight's Kilbrack.

The world dreamed so that love returned to the barren souls, jealous no more of ancient memory, but abundant instead with everyday hope.

Soon, though, the dreaming world gave up the ghost; wearied, it slept. And turning in its sleep, it turned to the east where the dawn would dissolve all trace of its dream. The night had done. The day would tell.

CHAPTER FOURTEEN

WHERE AM I? Am I home?

His left hand twisted under cover of the bedsheet, sneaked its way beneath the pillow to curl in his fingers the hollow jiffy he found there. He pressed. It was empty. Somehow it didn't matter so much. He opened his eyes. The rude panic of waking evaporated, like his breath on the chill air.

Instinctively he began a Diary Memo but oddly, he could not formulate the words. He sat up.

He was in Knight's Kilbrack. It was morning. Birds sang. He was still clothed. He was about to rise, when the obvious question struck him. He lay back down on the pillow, tried to gather together the threads of the night. How did he come to be in this bed?

Last night he had found his jiffy quite easily in the dark. It was on the first landing. He had tripped over it, in fact. He had pulled himself together, swept his hands over the floor. He must retrieve the jiffy and get out of that place as quickly as possible. But in his tripping, he soon realized, he had kicked the jiffy so that it rolled beneath a nearby door. He tried to squeeze his hand underneath but the gap would allow only his fingers. Frantically these fingers searched, then felt, then finally grasped, the jiffy. His face quickened with joy, only to collapse in the next instant. The full fist of his predicament punched him straight in the face. The gap between door and floor had become a monkey's puzzle. He was trapped. Clutching the jiffy, he could not remove his hand. Only by letting it go could he himself be free.

He struggled, he knew he did, in his mind. But in the end there was nothing he could do. Except cry. He cried himself to sleep.

To wake inside the bedroom, inside the bed even, with the jiffy beneath his pillow, refreshed.

He thought he had imagined that Livia had come to him in the night. She had supported him with all her strength and staggered him into the bedroom, on to the bed. But perhaps it wasn't imagination. He did not know.

The thought of Livia made him smile. Where was she now, he wondered. They had not arranged to meet today. Indeed, when she had left him yesterday afternoon at the gates to Knight's Kilbrack, apart from saying she would marry him, she had evinced very little enthusiasm for ever seeing him again. She was a peculiar girl. Oh, she would be fun to be with, of course. He could imagine going for long country walks with her while she counted off the flora and fauna in their Latin and common names. He could imagine a drink with her in a hotel bar and she would list the ingredients of the most unlikely of cocktails. They might visit to the town and take in a play even. She would explain the plot and characters and contrast the work with the author's previous efforts. They would be great friends, she would be the very best of company. But did he truly wish to marry her?

He shook his head. What was he thinking? Of course he would marry. He loved her. After all, she was a woman. That's what you did with women.

He reached again for his lemon jiffy. There was a faint stickiness where his thumb had pressed earlier. Somehow – he wasn't quite sure how to explain this – but some of the magic had gone. It was as though with all his weeping through the night he had exhausted a part of its potential. And with it, a part of his need.

Diary Memo: Peculiar thing occurred this morning. I—

But he felt he couldn't really be bothered with a memo just then. He found himself looking idly about the room. How elegant, he thought, surprised. He forgot about diary memos and concentrated instead on his surroundings. The dark green walls were covered with a dense display of pictures, prints, gouaches and engravings, all finely and regularly framed, though each had its layer of dust. On the chimney-piece was a clutter of souvenir treasures: champagne corks, a blue piggy-bank, fairings, photographs. Books lined a recess. On a table was a pile of correspondence, letter upon letter upon letter. Most of them had not been opened. To judge from the yellowing of their envelopes they had been dumped there and forgotten years previously. Some alabaster had fallen from the ceiling. The white chalk dappled the carpet, as though the roof had collapsed and snow had drifted in. It was chill enough for snow.

He didn't shudder, though. It was so elegant a room, faded, unwanted perhaps, he felt quite at home there. He decided to explore further. He climbed out of bed. All the photographs on the chimneypiece were of the same person. He was rather a handsome young man. His brows were knitted fiercely together, but his face was fresh, clean, immaculate nearly.

Now O'Leary shuddered. He had caught a glimpse of his own face in the mirror above. And a memory flashed through his mind. He had dreamed through the night. And this morning, the first morning ever, he remembered his dream.

He sat down on the bed.

Diary Memo: Last night—

He hesitated. It wasn't just that he could not formulate the words. There was something about diary memos this morning. They seemed not just unsuitable, but unnecessary even.

Last night I dreamed of the accident, he said to himself. It was a terrible accident. A young man left a park. A car approached. The young man stepped on to the street. The car ran him over. He fell.

O'Leary stood up. He caught his reflection in the mirror again. Except it is no longer a stranger who fell, he said fatefully: it is I.

He shuddered again. There were further details, but already the dream was fading. He could not quite catch on to it. The dream was gone. But he had remembered a moment. That was something. Something was happening. He swallowed. He was left with a feeling of distaste. In his mouth he tasted bile. Whoever he was, whomever he remembered, the memory did not feel quite wholesome. The lemon jiffy dropped from his hand, rolled under the bed. But O'Leary didn't notice. For in the corner of his eye he had spotted something. Something as familiar, though incredible, as his own walking double.

Amongst that pile of unopened letters was a book. And O'Leary Montagu recognized the cover: the green cloth cover of Nancy Valentine's *Ill Fares the Land*.

In the small rickety bed, in Nellie Maguire's guest room, inside the tangled sheets and bedclothes, Bridie O'Toole rounded her gaze, sleekly as an owl, to face the bowler hat on the pillow beside her. She spoke slowly, lowly and venomously. 'My name is dirt,' she said.

Huddled inside the gloom of his bowler hat, thin old Downey clenched his teeth. St Dympna, Patroness of the Insane, he prayed, what mad affliction did you send on me in the night?

'You'd better get me out of this, J. D. Downey,' said Bridie. 'Or I'll have the guards on to you.'

And Leonard the Hermit, the Crusaders' Saint of Prisoners, get me out of this now and I'll close for you on your every feast day, I swear it. I'll burn candles forever in my good silver stick, the one with the angels for handles, my mother got it from her mother.

'Nellie Maguire'll be in any second now banging on the door, she will.'

Saints Florus and Laurus, August the eighteenth – look kindly on a sinner on your feast day.

'And you'd better have a good excuse. Whipping wouldn't do you.'

'Agh!' cried Downey, unable any longer to withstand the rising gall of panic.

'Shut up!' hissed Bridie. 'You'll have herself in on us!'

They could hear Nellie in the hall outside, opening doors and closing them, shuffling about her business.

'What are we to do?' whispered Downey. 'By all the saints in heaven, what'll become of us?'

'Shut up yer crap! She's outside. I can hear her.'

Downey squeezed shut his eyes and held his breath, while Bridie sharpened her ears and glinted her eyes to the door. 'She's downstairs now.'

'Holy Mother of God, we're stuck in here for ever!'

Bridie thought quickly. From her close scrutiny of life in Kilbrack, she knew Nellie's routine off by heart. She would put the kettle on the hob first of all in the kitchen. Then she'd sweep the floor of the pub. Then she'd unlock the front door and the back door. Then she'd make the tea in the kitchen, or she'd sweep the pavement outside, depending on the water boiling. And that would be her chance. She'd sneak down the stairs then, and whichever end of the pub Nellie was in, she'd sneak out the other – front door or back door, whichever. Pah, she thought. Sure brains was all it took. She threw a quick shrewd look at Downey still huddled inside his bowler hat. Downey would have to look out for himself.

'We'll be caught,' moaned Downey. 'We'll be named in chapel by the priest.'

'Caught or not, you have me good name shattered on me,' said Bridie, on the pleasant side of venom.

'I'm shattered meself.'

'Father Michael himself warned me about it.'

'Father Michael? Was he expecting this?' Holy Mother, it was worse it was getting. 'How did Father Michael know?'

'I'll get no Labour nor no redundancy if 'tis sacked I am.'

'Sacked as well?'

'Nine years, eight months, eighteen days I've slaved in the big house. And all for nothing now. You've earned me the sack, so you have.'

'I haven't, I haven't! Sure, how would the old man above know what we were up to? Isn't he a heathen pagan himself?'

'I'm not talking about that. My good name, fifty years' standing, black as spades is bad enough – but lying-in till this hour! I was due working at six.'

'Oh,' said Downey.

'Oh,' aped Bridie. 'Is that all you can say?'

'Well,' said Downey, 'I'm late meself.'

'Late for what?'

'Haven't I the shop above to close?'

'Sure, isn't the shop above closed anyhow?'

'What would you know? It isn't Saint Hyacinth of Cracow's day at all now. 'Tis the feast day of Saints Florus and Laurus now.'

'And what of that?'

'I have the sign to change, of course.'

'Pah,' said Bridie.

'Pah yourself.'

Underneath the sheet, Downey ran his thumb along the sharp blade of his Swiss-made knife. He could murder Miss Maguire – that was one way out. And leave a witness? He couldn't trust Bridie O'Toole with a secret the nature of murder. What was he saying? He couldn't trust that one with the clippings of his nails. He'd have to murder her as well. It was a lot of murders for a poor Swiss-made knife. Suddenly, the blade didn't feel quite so long nor half-way sharp enough for a brace of murdered spinsters. What was he to do?

'What am I to do?' he groaned.

Bridie snorted, and shifted in the bed. 'You have me back broken too with all your wrestling,' she said.

Downey sighed. It was a poor silver lining when a cloud hung over him of murder and disgrace. But at least there was that silver lining. ''Twas a reasonable wrestle, all right,' he allowed.

Bridie grudged herself a nod. 'I'll give you that,' she said. She squeezed her fist and ran it satisfyingly along her skirt covering her thigh. She had all of Downey's buttons in her hand. Wrenched from his jacket and shirt last night, she had slept with them clenched in her fist.

'You're not the worst at the wrestling,' said Downey, nodding an odd appreciation, 'Bridie O'Toole, begging your pardon, Mam.'

Bridie's lips curled to a grin, then a grimace, then a grin again. 'You're not the worst yourself, J. D. Downey,' she said.

They met each other's eyes. For a moment there glinted a professional respect in each. Downey caught the glaze of spittle that washed her chin. Had he had the better of her? He didn't know. She surely had him shattered. 'All the same, I think I had the size of you,' he said experimentally.

'Pah,' said Bridie, and she snorted again. Looking down her side of the bed she saw a woollen-stockinged leg with a muddy laced-up boot at the end of it, sticking out from the bedclothes into the morning chill. Serve him right, she thought. Then of a sudden she realized that the chilled leg belonged to her. 'You've all the blankets to yourself,' she snapped, and she gave a terrific tug with her free hand on the bedclothes.

Downey clenched his teeth, and his fingers on the blankets. 'I'm half-frozen with your antics,' he said. 'Give me back me blankets, blast you, woman.'

'You've more than your share,' she dribbled, holding a fierce one-handed grasp on the bedclothes. 'And you no better than you should be.'

'Let go.'

'Let go yourself.'

'I won't.'

'Nor I.'

With one hand wasted clinging to his knife, the satin edge of the blankets slipped remorselessly through Downey's fingers, and Bridie for the moment had the better of him. 'Saint – Saint—' he stammered. But in the outrageous heat of the moment the names of any and every saint inexplicably escaped him. He lurched up and tore at the air for the blankets. Bridie tore back. And grappling thus, the one unloosed her hoard of buttons, the other his Swiss-made knife.

'Agh!' cried Downey.

'Agh!' cried Bridie.

They scattered on the bed in frantic search of their lost treasures. And before either of them knew it properly, he was on top of Bridie, and she was under Downey; and they had locked once more into a close and wrestling embrace. All notion of secrecy and stealth was forgotten. The bed lurched and clanged beneath them, as though it was of its own wild motivation that it humped them up and down. And their faces, though determined, looked unhappy and undignified as the Queen of England's on a gambler's spinning coin.

The door opened.

Downey looked up slowly. The brim of his bowler hat slipped with the sweat down over his brow, brimmed his eyes. He reached up a hand to peak it. 'Good morning, Miss Maguire,' he said.

Bridie O'Toole struggle her face clear from underneath him. Her cheekbones trembled into a smile. Her lips barely moved. 'Good morning, Miss Maguire.'

At the door, Nellie Maguire surveyed the two of them lying one atop the other in the tangled mess of the bed. They were both fully clothed, from bowler hat to boots, from house-coat to woollen stockings. The bed was shattered. One of the legs had given way. She wasn't surprised, the commotion, the ranting, raving and rattling, she had heard outside. The two of them seemed to be clinging both to themselves and the bedstead to stop themselves from slipping to the floor. They stared up at her, pale and scared and shocked – face-wise, anywise.

'Oh,' said Nellie, her eyes twinkling a Milky Way of cheerfulness, 'Nellie Maguire: you're only the hopeless hostess. In the wrong again – room-wise. Sure, it must be the other door I was looking for. Beg pardon, please.'

'What?' said Bridie.

'It's a lie-in you're after, is it?' she said, rattling the metal chain that waisted her yellow and black striped catsuit. 'And am I after disturbing you? Will you ever forgive me?'

'What?' said Downey.

'And isn't it the marvellous morning for a lie-in too? Marvellous only.' She smiled, then clapped her hand against her temple. 'Breakfast in bed,' she said. 'Is that what it is? I'd forget – I'd forget my – what is it now, that thing I'd forget?'

Bridie glanced at Downey, Downey glanced back. 'What?' they said together.

'And you on your holidays and all. Shan't be a sec. I'll have breakfast cooked up in no time. Will eggs and – eggs and – what is that other stuff called?'

'Bacon, is it?' said Bridie, squinting her eyes.

'That's it!' said Nellie. 'Eggs and bacon. Shan't be two secs.' She smiled at the aged holidaying couple in their single bed. How close and happy they looked together. They looked familiar too. Slightly familiar, anyhow – the way a wild flower would look when you've only seen it in the flora before. They must have been staying some while. She was losing touch with her memory, so she was. And where was that other guest, Mr Leary, was it? Kilbrack seemed very popular of a sudden – visitor-wise. Still, spice's the life.

'Don't move an inch,' she said. 'I'll be back before you know it.' And smiling courteously again and sniffing a mountain of a snort, she closed the bedroom door after her.

The two faces turned to each other on the pillow.

'What's that all about?' said Downey, half-inching his hand in the morass of the bed, half-seeking again for his pocket knife. Maybe and he'd buy another one. It wasn't right to be caught out like this.

'Bacon,' said Bridie.

'Bacon? She's after flipping her lid.' No knife, no knife anywhere.

'Bacon,' insisted Bridie as she caught the whiff of sizzling rashers from below.

'I'm off,' said Downey.

'Did you come looking for a book?' said Bridie, with a low, slow and shrewd surmise.

'Who told you that?'

'Thieving, were you?'

'Who told you that?' said Downey. 'MPSI. They wouldn't let a thief in the Pharmaceutical Society of Ireland!'

'Never mind that. Fetch down them notebooks now and we'll steal ourselves to a small read.'

'What?' said Downey.

'The bacon won't be long in coming.'

O'Leary Montagu gazed still in disbelief. The coincidence was too much to bear. It outraged him. Yes, he had found a volume of *Ill Fares the Land* by Nancy Valentine. Yes, at long last he had come across a second copy. There was a minor irritation that the printers even for this proofed edition had not corrected their typographical lapses: '*Fares*' still appeared as '*Farts*' in the title. But it was not this that gave tremors to his lips, shivers to his feet.

Impossibly, underneath it he had discovered another book. It was all too improbable. He felt hunted, as though some shady private eye was following him. Or haunted, like someone was walking on his grave. Not walking. They were dancing a Highland jig.

And although O'Leary had read this book a hundred times or more, still he turned to the flyleaf, gaped in disbelief. What was Fate playing at?

'In the big house,' he read, 'a particularly bloody and savage murder is discovered. The father is suspected. Inspector Nancy is called in to investigate.' O'Leary let the book fall to the floor. He knew the blurb off by heart. He didn't need to read it. He continued, quoting from memory. 'In the course of a tortuous enquiry, Inspector Nancy uncovers a vile and scheming fiend beneath the murdered son's façade of decency. Did the father kill his son? Was it a crime of passion? Or was his aim to rid the world of a perverted presence?'

O'Leary leant back for support against the fire surround. He grabbed the book and checked it again, as though there really could be some mistake. '*Murder in the Big House*,' the blurb continued, 'the Number One World Bestseller, is Valentine Brack's first novel. "A veritable tour de farce" – Russell Harty writing in the *Spectator*. "Lavatory humour" – the *Sunday Mirror*. "Unputdownable" – Joan Stalker.'

O'Leary put the book down.

Diary Memo: In hospital, eleven years ago—

But he couldn't concentrate. His mind was abuzz with speculation. It was difficult, impossible, to tie all this together. He felt like a child trying to do his laces. He stared at the photograph of the author on the back cover. He was a young man. Rather a good-looking fellow. The brows were knitted fiercely together, but his face was fresh, clean, immaculate nearly. Like the young man in the photographs above.

There was a rap on the door and O'Leary jumped, banging his head on the chimneypiece.

'It's only me,' came a voice from outside.

For a considerable moment he didn't recognize the voice. Was it Mary? Then the waves of a legend rolled over him.

'I've brought your breakfast,' said Livia.

CHAPTER FIFTEEN

IN HIS CARVED and gilded four-poster bed, draped with embroidered cloth-of-gold that pronounced to the world *Constans Valensque*, the family motto – it had been misread by an ancestor as meaning 'Always Valentine' so that the first-born son had been christened that name ever since – Valentine Brack, older and wiser by yet one more day, wiped the kedgeree stains from his chin. He was happily full. 'There you are, Nancy,' he said to the mongrel who nudged against him. 'You can lick the plate.'

She sniffed at the empty plate, troubled her tail uncertainly.

'What's that?' he asked. He gave her his fingers to lick. 'It's no holiday for you, is it, with Bridie away? But don't blame me. Blame the young lady yonder for cooking edible fare.'

He winked up at Livia who smiled back, enjoying his clowning. She was dressed still in her oldest clothes and they were soaked and filthy. She looked tired too, drained. He eyed her closely as she picked up the tray. Her fingers were cut and bruised.

'So,' he said.

Livia placed the tray on the side table then sat back down on his bed.

'Well,' said Valentine.

She stroked the dog. She knew the old man was curious as to why she was there. She also knew that he wouldn't give in and ask. Maybe she'd tell him. It had seemed such a good idea. And she had worked on it all night nearly, heaving and pulling and scraping. Then in the early hours she'd realized she hadn't the strength. The pillars had defeated her. Down-hearted, she had crept into the big house, slept on a sofa. And it would have been a grand idea, had it worked. 'You know the magpies, Uncle Val, at the gates?'

She watched a cloud lower on his face. It passed in a moment. She smiled to herself. She liked the old man. And even if she hadn't been certain that he liked her too, she believed still that she would visit him. 'I thought if you looked out the window this morning and saw the birds returned to their plinths—'

'Ah,' he said. So she knew this stranger was his son. Clever girl. He felt quite proud of her. 'As if by magic. And everything would be all right. Joy would have returned. We'd all live happily for e'er and a day.'

Livia shrugged slightly her shoulders. He was right, of course. In the night it had sounded a grand idea. But in the day it was all too simplistic. 'I thought you'd take it as a sign.'

Mind you, thought Valentine. She could be right there.

'But in the end they were too heavy. I couldn't shift them. I think they've sunk into the earth.' Trickery had failed, as it was bound to in the end. She wondered now why did people trust so little in words. Speech, persuasion, truth. Why had she not thought simply to speak with her uncle? She frowned, irritated by her own duplicity. She was here now. She could try. She sought his eyes, then held them. 'You know he's your son, don't you?' she said directly.

Valentine Brack drooped his jaw, squinted an eye, then chewed on some fish he found caught between his teeth, in lazy contemplation of the beautiful girl on his bed. Would she grow fat, he found himself wondering, like her mother? No, not Livia. That girl would be whatever she chose. She was in control, though as yet she probably didn't realize her strength. If only she could forget this stupidity about her father.

'Tea?' she said, filling in his silence for him.

'Please, Livia.' He watched her pour. So graceful, he thought. He shifted in his bed. 'And do you know anything about this man, my son?'

'Uncle Val—' She lifted a hand. He believed she was about to pat his knee, but it landed instead on the counterpane, limply. 'He's got this book with him. It's a parody of your journals. I've read it.'

'Oh.'

'Of course I knew that you argued. I never understood why. Not entirely. But I think I do. Now.'

'You know he wanted to ruin the place. Not ruin it. Kill it. Obliterate Kilbrack. Is that what you know?'

'That's not what I mean.'

Valentine Brack felt uncomfortable. He wanted to tell her to prop up his pillows. But he knew that wouldn't help. He glanced to the volume of his history that he had been working on yesterday. *Volume XXXII*, said the cover. He knew there was nothing in it. There were twenty-seven page ones, but no writing. He could no longer tell was that a good joke or not.

However, he was never a cowardly man. He faced Livia now. 'Go on,' he said.

'The book's a parody. But also it's something of an apologia. Not confessional, but more as though he's trying to tell you. "This is what I am and this is how I came to be here." '

'It says that?'

She nodded. How terrible, she was thinking, when nobody speaks openly. As if anything can ever be true to itself relying only on cryptic signs and coded speech, mere undulations in a vast abjuring silence. That thought, originally born of irritation, saddened her now. She decided she wanted to get this business over with. 'Do you understand what I'm saying, Uncle Val?'

'I understand the words you use.'

'Well, don't you want to know what he says?'

She watched him take a breath and hold it, as though ordering difficult thoughts in his mind before risking their articulation. Then he seemed to think better of it, or worse. He sighed. 'And what, so, does my son have to say?'

'He's gay, of course.'

'Gay?' Was that all? 'He's gay all right. Gay as a new-born lamb.'

Livia chuckled to herself. 'Oh, Uncle Val. You can't be that far behind the times.' She straightened her face. She could sense he was about to dismiss the subject, dismiss her even, so she said plainly, 'He's homosexual.'

'My son?'

'Yes.'

'Valentine?'

She nodded.

'Oh.'

'Is that all?'

He managed an interest. 'Since when?'

'Oh, Uncle Val, I don't know. Always, I should presume.'

Half of him wished she would leave now. The other half prayed she would stay. He tipped all his fingers to his chin. He needed a shave. He dismissed that thought. He wanted to say something, for Livia's benefit if nothing else. But he found himself instead remembering the night he believed he had killed his son. When he had waited outside the park for him, he had sat impatiently in the car, tapping his fingers on the steering wheel, beating some military tune with his feet. But it never crossed his mind to wonder what might his son be engaged in, all that time in the park. He had not thought to check. It was almost as though, all along, he had expected, had known even. Something that had occurred to him while talking with Charity the evening before came back. Amazing, he'd thought, what you can hide from yourself, given the will. Were we all hiding things from ourselves? Charity that her husband was a philanderer, he that his son was homophilic, Livia that her father didn't care for her. Were our expectations so high that we could not face the reality but must live in some half-light where family and fellows were but shadows of themselves? Dissimulation everywhere, like weeds in a garden, it's choking us. And what was his son hiding from? By his behaviour, it would seem he was hiding from all of creation, everything under the sun.

'All so unhappy,' he murmured.

Such a waste, Livia was thinking. All the talent, all the potential for good and happiness wasted on this drivel. And all because some people wrote in a book that an angel was buggered in a town called Sodom. As if anyone could prefer that snivelling gaping fool in the bedroom below to a man upright and proud to be himself. 'All so unnecessary,' she said.

True, thought Valentine. And yet what did it change? 'Still,' he said, 'he went against tradition. Whatever else, it was that which I could never forgive.'

'Oh, Uncle Val,' said Livia. She gesticulated reasonableness with a waving hand. 'How could he owe anything to tradition, when tradition itself decries his very existence?'

He allowed himself to smile a touch. She was clever, that girl. True too. And what did it matter in the end? Hadn't there been enough Bracks in the world already? And he was accustomed now, anyway, to the notion of dying out. Wouldn't mind, but it's not as though we contribute much. We keep our heritage all right, but who in this country wants heritage if it's not dressed up in some emerald kilt? We've had our run. Maybe I put too many pressures on the boy: to conform in an age when conformity is considered eccentric nearly. Perhaps.

He sighed. He had always believed his son was perverse,

driven by dementing demons. But now he could not be sure. Of course he'd known. He'd guessed all along. Just couldn't bring himself to say it. Couldn't raise the subject even, except in jest or ridicule. He wondered now had he wished to prod the boy into some unguarded outburst by ragging him so? Had the boy intended to hint to him, even, calling that pup Nancy? But I'm no coward, he told himself. Why didn't I talk? There wasn't time now with Livia here to think it through, but he knew eventually he would feel sorrow for his son. Not pity – he didn't fancy pity. Just sorrow; understanding maybe. Always having to hide his nature, storing up his lonely treasures like a magpie in her nest, that in itself would render a child difficult, contumacious, not perverse but perverted. All so unnecessary, really. As a man of his class and society, he was not untouched by the homophilic nature. At school, he'd had his friend, his 'special', as most of the boys did. They clasped hands hours on end. The boy had had a fondness for oranges, he remembered. It was all quite usual, expected even. Even now, caught unawares by the smell of an orange, he might be transported pleasantly to that first love. I'm a tolerant man, he thought. Why had the boy not spoken to me?

He decided to say this. 'I'm a tolerant man,' he began.

But Livia interrupted. 'Oh Uncle Val, you know you're not.'

He hovered between gainsaying her and agreeing. In the end, her smile was too beguiling and he found himself joining in. 'Of course you're right. And I'll tell you this.' He leaned up in his bed and he wagged a bony finger. 'I'm proud of it. I loved my son. I loved him deeply. And had he spoken to me I might have shouted at him. I might have raged. But I'd never have been tolerant. Tolerance is far too cheap, too damp a commodity for my taste. I don't want tolerance and neither should any man with two ears and a brain between.'

He had spoken quite agitatedly, and now he fell back on his pillows, as though the vehemence had exhausted him.

Livia stretched over and pecked him on the cheek. She started stroking the dog again. That was the trouble with the world today, she was thinking. People thought tolerance was the opposite of intolerance. Whereas in fact it was some meaningless neutrality. A child, any child, growing up, discovering herself and the nature of her deepest, most native desires – what use was tolerance to a child? It was encouragement she needed, encouragement first to be, then to love, herself. Or himself, whichever.

Valentine Brack was pondering much the same. He could never have been tolerant, he knew. And he suspected any son of his could never have wished for that. But he might have respected the boy. For respect was earned and demanded, not granted like a half-day's holiday, taken away as easily as given. He tutted. All the wasted years, he thought. How can silence be golden? What manner of a jackass ever said that? They should have talked. Was it all too late now? His hand was resting on the counterpane, Livia's fingers brushing against it as she stroked the dog. He caught hold of her now, fast of a sudden. He said, 'Is he mad, Livia? Have I driven him insane? Is that what it is?'

She decided not to mention just then how she had found his son last night crying in the corridor and had had to cart him into his old bedroom. 'He's lost his memory. So he says. I think it's some sort of excuse for not remembering his past. But he's not mad – entirely. He maintains it's something to do with an accident.'

Valentine shivered that subject away.

'Will you speak with him, Uncle Val?' She already knew he would. 'But you'll go easy with him, won't you? It'll come as a terrible shock when finally he lets himself remember. Will you? He's in his old bedroom below.'

Valentine Brack caught his chin between his fingers and thumb, and pulled down slowly, rubbing against the pale growth of hairs. His face seemed to get longer with the pulling, longer and thinner, like dirty putty stretched too far. Much tauter and the brittle skeletal frame would be seen, like winter trees through a misty windowpane. He was remembering how they had tramped the fields together, father and son, before the sullens and rages. It hadn't bothered him then how his son would turn out. He was happy with the day. With his own mud on his boots, his own breeze through his hair. And through his son's.

He was staring not at Livia, but past her through the window, to the sky where sailed the clouds that would rain on his demesne, on Knight's Kilbrack and the village of Kilbrack, rain on the just and on the unjust. The ox knoweth his owner, he thought, and the ass his master's crib. He closed his eyes and opened them again.

'We might risk a walk,' he said, 'together.'

When he walked, Valentine Brack liked to be brisk and

purposeful about it. And watching his son now peripherally as they approached the gates, he noted with some small pride that he had grown the same. They both walked with one hand behind their backs, the other stuck in their trouser pockets. They shared the same long stride. His son stooped, but then his own back too was bent, like an ivy or a vetch which climbing too high had found no support, and so reached back down to the earth again. They had fallen silent, as though in recognition of the moment. And it felt good to be strolling his own demesne, tramping the fields, father and son. And yet . . . 'The heart distrusting asks, if this be joy?'

O'Leary was trying to compose Diary Memos. He knew what he wanted to say, but for some reason, on this day, his thoughts were mutinous. Try as he might they would not form themselves into concise memoranda. The effort felt like he was holding his breath too long. In the end he desisted. He had to resort to ordinary thought.

I yet breathe, he thought. He was surprised. It wasn't so difficult. Thinking came nearly naturally to him. I yet breathe, he repeated. The old man's mood appears reasonably amicable. But I detect, I believe, a sadness underneath. Another word for sadness. Dolour? Yes, dolour. A dolour underneath. His tread is heavy on the gravel, his shadow thin and lengthy. Bit flowery all this. Try to be more straightforward. He has invited me to walk with him to Kilbrack. Very good. To the which have I complied. O'Leary shook his head. That last bit was far too formal. I agreed, I consented, what did I do? I said yes. I said yes, he thought.

In fact, he admitted, it was because Livia said I should.

A clamour of crows, disturbed from their rookery, shook the quiet. O'Leary shivered. They were approaching the gates. Something about the magpies that awaited them there, and the ferocity of their glare, unnerved him.

'So, Mr O'Leary Montagu, you must tell me about yourself.'

O'Leary coughed. 'Myself?'

Valentine Brack winced slightly. Livia had made him promise not to propel the man to remembrance, but to prod him slowly, let him discover himself. But a forthright man, and ripe with it, he found this modern hokery-pokery disagreed with his bent. However. 'Tell me, do.'

O'Leary began. But stupidly, he soon realized, he began at the wrong end. He should have started with the accident, but really he didn't like mentioning that. Dredging up old history, he called it. Avoiding things, Mary had chided. Instead he quickly became bogged down in the maze of byways that had constituted his quest for the Mistress.

Valentine Brack allowed himself a long stare at the profile of his son. What an unfortunate sight he presented. A moment ago, strolling in silence, he had seemed a reasonable-enough fellow. It transpired, however, that as soon as he opened his mouth, all semblance of manhood collapsed. His movements became ungainly as a foal's. Indeed, though the creases on his forehead and his thinning hair belied it, his attitude, his very nature, seemed a child's. So much for the dementing demons of his youth. They had obviously upped camp years since to seek some more challenging soul to torment. He didn't blame them. An imp had taken their place, a rantipoling pixie.

'Where did you get those scars?' he demanded, snapping into O'Leary's rambling.

'I'm sorry?'

'On your face.'

'I don't actually remember, sir. Leastways, I know I got them from the accident. But I don't remember the accident. Leastways, I didn't remember it until last night. But I dreamed it last night and then this morning I remembered. The dream, I mean. It's rather complicated.'

Jackass, thought Valentine Brack. A man? He was a caricature of a man. What was that word Livia had used? Gay? He was gamesome as a nonsense rhyme.

He stopped walking. O'Leary, still in the labyrinth of his explanations, continued on a pace or two. He had to hurry back.

Valentine frowned. Under the ball of his foot he was worrying a stone on the drive. He found himself wondering if throughout the years, at the back of his mind, secretly, hidden even from him, had he always hoped for – no, more than hoped, expected even – his son's return. Was that why he never called an ambulance, a doctor? Was it not fear, not guilt, but a desperate need for hope not to die utterly? If so he was sadly disabused now. A nancy son with perverted notions, heedless of stone and blood, that was one thing. But it was far far better than this simpering jackass before him. He squinted through his third cousin's pink butterfly-winged spectacles. 'Never mind that rigmarole,' he said. 'You're a man, aren't you? Pull yourself together.

For God's sake man, face up to yourself. The way you are you wouldn't know your arse from your elbow.' He kicked the stone he was worrying as hard as his boots allowed.

'Wouldn't I?' asked O'Leary, and knowing it was ridiculous, he found himself checking where his elbow and bottom actually were. I am a fool, he thought.

'You're my son,' shouted his father. And he strode off alone to the gates.

O'Leary was quite dumbstruck. Almost mechanically, he found himself composing a memo for his diary.

Diary Memo: He berates me, calling me his son. What depths of anguish and loss the calling bespeaks. Even yet, he has not despaired of a lost son returning, but turning to strangers or catching a voice, says 'my son'. Is it this loss, irrevocable in death, that has turned his mind?

But peculiarly, the less forward, the shyer portion of his mind was remembering Mary. Perhaps he'd been wrong always considering her, damning her even, as stubborn, thorough, impossibly so. Was she stubborn? Or was she more on the impatient side? Just like this man in fact, nudging him always to some inescapable conclusion that was manifest to everyone except him. Then again, not impatient so much as exasperated.

And that was strange because he hadn't remembered Mary for – he couldn't remember when last she'd encroached on his thoughts. Was Mary like this old man? He'd never really got to grips with her appearance, though he'd spent hours upon end, days and weeks, trying to imagine her. Who was Mary like? Indeed, was she like anyone or anything at all?

'Sir?' he called.

Then he stopped. The old man was striding through the gates. O'Leary stared. How familiar he looked. Like an old friend, or a heartache. Between the ivy-clad pillars, he seemed truly to be part of this place. With his battered tweed jacket and his white wisps of hair, he blended into belonging. O'Leary had never felt he belonged anywhere. In a sense it was a feeling he reserved for Nancy Valentine. He had always imagined she belonged here, her clothes made of tweed spun from the wool of sheep who grazed the nearby hills. The old man could be hewn from local stone, like the pillars that framed him. He looked – not like Mary, of course. Nor yet like Nancy Valentine. He thinks I'm his son, he remembered. And at the same moment, he could hear Mary's voice shouting at him, egging him, urging him forwards. She wasn't shouting impatiently, nor even in exasperation: she was belting, roaring her voice, only because she needed to, to be heard above the gush of air in his ears as it rushed to fill a vacuum within. What was she saying? What could it be?

'Sir,' he called. He dashed up to the old man, through the gates, past the pillars. 'Wait for me. I think I know. You're – you're—'

'What am I?' snapped Valentine Brack. He turned. But O'Leary wasn't there. He'd tripped over a fallen magpie that Livia in her endeavours had teased an inch from the soil. And he lay face up on the drive, smiling sweetly, totally unconscious, oblivious again.

* * *

'Jackass,' said Valentine Brack.

Jim O'Toole was loafing up the lane. He nodded, grudgingly.

'Where have you been the morning?'

He scratched his head. 'Miss Cuthbert sent me to—'

'Never mind that now. This jackass here—' he motioned with a disparaging thumb, 'fetch him up to the house for me.'

'The house?'

'Yes,' snapped Valentine Brack. 'It's a big place. You'll find it at the end of the drive.'

Jim frowned as a brief indifferent confusion crossed his face. 'Is he sleeping?'

'He's knocked out, of course.'

'He has the look of your son, I was thinking.'

Valentine sighed. 'Just fetch him to his bedroom for me, let him sleep it off. Thank you.' And he strode off down the lane towards Kilbrack. Unfortunately, his timing was awry. Or maybe it was just his thoughts that preoccupied him. For a sleek black sedan glided smoothly past, plashed in a puddle, and soaked him from the waist down.

CHAPTER SIXTEEN

THE GREY, AQUILINE Monsignor avoided glancing in the vanity mirror for the duration of two Hail Marys. 'Make it three,' he said to the young novice chauffeuring him. Only on its completion did the Monsignor afford himself a decent regard in the mirror. But all was well with his strong, calm, handsome face.

The novice negotiated the twists in the road with a cautious sleekness, his eyes concentrating dreadfully on the chevron of verge straight ahead. Umbellifers on either side hazed past. In a tremulous voice he ventured, 'Monsignor, is it the Catholic chapel where we're headed?'

The Monsignor pressed 'percentage point' on his calculator, scrutinized the result; he was content. 'Another Hail Mary,' he said. 'No, make it a Rosary.' And he waited till the muttering was in full flow before he settled back into his seat.

Who was this fellow, he wondered. Why, suddenly, had the Bishop insisted he needed a chauffeur? Oh, never fear, he knew who this novice was. He was the sycophantic nephew of some time-serving, green with envy, courtier at the Bishop's palace in Cashel. And why was he here? He knew that and all. He was here to spy on him.

He'd already had words with him that morning. 'Why are we going to Kilbrack?' the novice had asked before they'd even got to the car. Fuck off with yourself, he had wanted to reply. 'We are going to pray,' he had answered sternly. And he'd kept him at his prayers for the duration.

Ah, sure let him spy. I'm half-way home already. He switched off his calculator to preserve its batteries. Ham, he thought. And hamburgers. And hamburger joints. If he cornered the ham market in Ireland, they'd have no choice but to grant the fast-food franchise to his diocesan consortium. God's will be done; the Monsignor didn't waste time. He had the market already cornered.

Ad maiorem Dei Gloriam, he thought, and remembered suddenly that his Bishop was a product of the Jesuits. He was only a poor little Christian Brothers boy himself. Fuck the Bishop, he thought. He was gaga, anyway.

'Pull in here,' he said and the black sedan drew up outside the ancient ruin of St Ciaran's.

''Tis a Protestant church,' said the novice in wonder.

'Shut up. Count ten Rosaries on your beads. I'll be back.'

Nellie Maguire watched distantly from her chair at the bedroom window. She didn't ponder what a Catholic priest might be up to in a Protestant graveyard. She just stared through the grimy window, through the drizzle outside, at his torturing presence.

From the high and technicolour peak of the cocaine she had sniffed earlier, she was descending now to the ordinary world of her monochrome failing. She had loved that man. That man outside. She had wanted that man with a desire that only God could understand. But God had not understood, but had called him jealously for His own. How it had pained her when the young newly-ordained Father Michael had returned as curate to Kilbrack. Why had he returned? Could it be that he remembered her kiss when the year before she had chanced upon him in that moonlit fairy glade? Could it? She didn't know. He had returned, but not to her. Chapel ached her heart; still, she attended. If she passed him in the street, Lucifer recalling Paradise was nothing to her sadness. And even so, she would watch and wait, her legs crossed crookedly, desirously, even at the glimpse of him. He belonged to her and she to him, as Adam for all her concupiscence belonged to Eve.

And then he had left for the Bishop's Palace and she had hoped that would be an end to it. But it hadn't. His infrequent, unlooked-for visits were so much sorer to bear than the routine of his calls. And every morning, she awoke and – who knows? – perhaps today Father Michael would visit, take tea with her, even, in her kitchen.

In those young days, she had wanted him to take her. Take her where? Just take her. Now of course, she knew her Michael could take nobody anywhere. But he could come to her. You can come to me, acushla, my Michael.

Nowadays, in the odd moments she might glance sober into her mirror, she suspected it was only her addiction that kept her love alive. For, drugged two-thirds of the time, there was small space for misery. And misery unconfronted – that a sachet of powder will defer – could linger on for ever. So she suspected anyway.

Perhaps she would give it up. Perhaps she'd make a go of it. If only. Perhaps and if only. Acushla. Michael.

But not today. Wearily, she opened the drawer, took out the package, sniffed. Now, where was she? A cup of tea wouldn't go astray. A cup of tea with milk and – what was that thing called? Sugar, was it?

Thin old Downey undid the two top and bottom Chubb locks, the central Five-Lever-Insurance lock, and finally the common or garden Yale.

'Welcome, Mam,' he said, and ushered Bridie into the pharmacy. ''Tisn't much but 'tis home.'

Bridie in her usual manner checked out the situation without moving her head, darting her eyes only. ''Tis empty,' she concluded at last.

'Empty?' He looked around the gloomy room. 'Well, 'tis a bit that way all right,' he allowed. 'You could put it that way, Mam.'

He took down yesterday's 'Closed' sign, and put it on top of a pile of similar signs. 'Pardon me, Mam,' he said, 'while I check on my wall chart. 'Tis quite the complicated wall chart, as you can see. Now then, August the eighteenth,' he mumbled busily. 'Where are we? August the sixteenth, St Rock the Healer. August the seventeenth, St Hyacinth of Cracow.' He glanced behind to see if Bridie wasn't impressed by the ease with which he traversed the intricate byways of his wall chart; but to his dismay, she wasn't even looking. 'Here we are,' he said in a loud voice. 'Saints Florus and Laurus. I was right all along.' Downey's face fell. She wasn't even listening. She seemed very busy poking her fingers into the empty shelves, as if investigating their quality and strength. He picked out the top sign from another pile. *Closed for the feast day of Ss Florus and Laurus*, it said. He had known all along, of course he had. He didn't need to check on the wall chart. He knew all the saints' days off by heart. He'd learnt them at his mother's knee. His face fell lower. He could see a long task ahead of him, impressing this spinster.

'Is this a pharmacy?' said Bridie suddenly.

'Of course 'tis a pharmacy. Doesn't it say so on the sign outside?'

'The sign outside says nothing bar Advice.'

Downey muttered a curse. That blasted incognito man, unsettling him so. Sure, there wasn't even one book in his room. Never mind that, his every notebook was empty. Not a word written. What manner of fraudster was he? He'd have the guards on to him, he would. Impersonating an inspector from the Pharmaceutical Society of Ireland, it was a serious matter. There's cheats lingering in prisons the world over for crimes perpetrated of that nature. Downey was certain.

'Them're are good shelves,' announced Bridie.

'Are they?' said Downey. Then he allowed himself to beam. How pleasant it was to have good shelves in one's pharmacy.

'Good stout shelves,' she said. 'They'd take a weight or two. A carcass even.'

'A carcass? What would I be doing with a carcass in a pharmacy?'

'Why are you a pharmacist, J. D. Downey?' she asked.

'God knows,' said Downey. And it was true. Why was he a pharmacist? He didn't know. He thought it would have pleased his mother. But she wanted only a doctor in the family. Pharmacist was second best but with his mother second best was bootless as an also-ran. Truth be told, he sometimes felt there was no pleasing his mother, God rest her soul. There was no pleasing anybody. He shook his head defeatedly. 'God knows why, and the way they treat you common as trade, begging your pardon, Mam.'

'Never mind that,' said Bridie.

'What?' said Downey.

She picked up a pencil that had been left beside the wall chart. 'Give me that sign here.'

'What sign?'

'That sign.'

Downey gave her the sign. And with the pencil she crossed out everything on it, save for the word 'Closed'.

'Now,' she said.

'Now what?' said Downey. It seemed the whole world was tumbling down about him.

'No more of your saints gobbing, nor no more of your pharmacist gobbing.'

'What?' said Downey. It was unbelievable. She had tricked him, he knew that, when he had given her back the buttons and she hadn't returned his knife. And he couldn't wrestle her now because he had to keep one hand holding his trousers up and his shirt tucked in. He knew she had tricked him cruelly. But he didn't expect this. 'Give me back my knife,' he said.

'You can come and get your knife when I'm ready. First off, you can fetch a bucket of water till we rinse down them shelves.'

'Them shelves? For what?'

'Bacon,' said Bridie, lowly, slowly and blissfully. 'This shop'd make a grand pork butcher's.'

Outside the bare ruined spire of St Ciaran's, the Monsignor traced a halting but exigent finger along the illustrations of a book he carried open in his hand. Every now and then he glanced up quickly to the church, his glance becoming lengthier till it lingered on the spire in a gaze of happy appreciation.

'Spire,' he murmured. 'Spire-light? Yes. Broach, belfry, arcade? Yes. Lancet windows? One each side. Rectangular buttresses? Of course. A taste of cement, they'd stick. Built to last, they were. Balusters and cornice? Likewise. South porch arch? Yes. Keystone, impost, pilaster? Tremendous.' Everything was present and accounted for. He knew a builder, owed him a favour or two. It wouldn't be long now. The church was virtually his.

The Monsignor flexed his spare fingers. He knew the world. He knew the world very well. The world was that thing which was putty in his hands.

He turned the page of his *Observer's Book of Churches*. The outside was all accounted for. It had everything the book said it should have. Now for the inside. He knew it wasn't necessary. He was on to a sure-fire winner here and no mistake. But so taken was he with the close prospect of this church being his own, it was a thrill even to check off the fallen details.

The Catholic chapel was a disgrace. It was an insult to God. All breeze blocks and pebble-dash. That was the trouble with being an RC in Ireland. Only the people had remained faithful. The majesty of the tradition, the building blocks themselves, had passed over to the heathens. But he would change all that. Never doubt it.

As soon as he was finished in the church, he'd take a sherry in the Rectory with Mrs C. And he'd get her answer. He had no doubts about that, either. The poor woman, where else had she to turn? It was sweets from childers. He'd have the church, he'd have the Rectory, he'd have the applause of colleagues, and better still, their green envy, around the fire at the Palace. He'd be made. He could retire to peace and comfort the while, and while the days – fishing, who knows? – till the rat-tat-tat of a mitre came knock-knock-knocking on his door.

And he needed a taste of peace and quiet. God knows, he had earned it. He was ball-sore with work these last years. Baptism, confession, communion, investment, disbursement, defrayment, what have you. On constant call, he was.

Except there was this novice now, pestering him with his spying eyes and niggling questions. Ah sure, it was only a temporary nuisance. He'd see him off soon enough. And his meddlesome time-serving courtier of an uncle too if he wasn't careful.

He slid inside the leaning rotting door, and entered the south porch of St Ciaran's. 'Stoup,' he said, reading again from his *Observer's Book of Churches*. 'Usually on the right-hand side of the entrance.' He checked over to the right. 'Yes,' he said. 'Tremendous.'

Livia finished her prayer. 'Goodbye, Daddy,' she said, very softly, her voice like a draught through a window. She brushed her fingers one last time over the books. Her fingers faltered, she let them linger a moment. There was a spot of dirt on one cover. She wiped it away. There would be time enough for decay. Just this last time she wanted everything correct, the way she remembered it. Earlier that morning, she had hauled the lectern from the aumbry where it had been stored many years ago, to save it from the firewood fate of the pews. She had stood it where it had always stood, between the chancel and the nave. She could almost see her father reading there now, in his quiet canonicals, restrained as his piety. On the lectern she had placed her father's books, his bequests to her. Her father was buried without; let his memory be laid to rest within his church. Her fingers pressed into the old leathern covers: his King James Bible and his *Book of Common Prayer*. Beside them she had laid the architectural sketches she kept under her pillow.

'Perhaps you really were a saint,' she said. 'But you understand, Daddy. You must understand. We're all of us the dust of the ground. And in the midst of life . . . my mother needs me. And I need her. Goodbye, Daddy.'

She didn't know what the future held. But life in Kilbrack had changed, she was sure. And it would be nice to have a friend nearly her own age. They could go drinking together in town. They might even take a trip up to Dublin, she in search of whatever, he for whatever he could get. At least, now, there was a future. At long last, she could begin to discover herself.

She looked up at the disturbance from below. 'What are you doing here?' she demanded.

Mrs Cuthbert commiserated with her fallen self: she sighed.

She had felt so gratified – vindicated even – when third cousin Valentine had asked for a *cream* sherry, that she had almost stopped fretting about his calling when she hadn't sent out an 'At Home' card first. It was a silly worry, she knew. But as she kept saying to Livia: there might be many ways to proceed, but there was only the one procedure.

She had pictured for a moment her card being passed to Valentine on a platter, or left on a platter in the hall of Knight's Kilbrack. Except, of course, there were no platters in Knight's Kilbrack – at least none of the sheen to complement the nicety of her 'At Home' cards.

And therefore did Mrs Cuthbert sigh. The tarnish of Valentine's plate would accord with the yellowing of her gilt-edged cards stored in the Davenport – exactly.

Mrs Cuthbert gathered her thoughts together, and her

dimples into half a smile. It was pleasant enough, after all, to have somebody call.

'It's good, Charity,' ventured Valentine Brack eventually, having tasted enough to know, 'to have a good thick brown soup of a sherry to drink of.' And he raised his glass, supped to her health.

'Thank you, Valentine,' said Mrs Cuthbert.

'At our age, Charity, we deserve a cream sherry of a morning.'

'Do we?' She still suffered from a hangover. She had poured herself a glass merely to be sociable. She did not think she could stomach it.

Valentine Brack apparently shared nothing of this delicacy. He quaffed the rest of his sherry in one go, then fiddled with the stem of the glass.

'Sherry?' said Mrs Cuthbert.

'I will,' he said. And while she poured, he embarked in a tone as if he was contradicting some argument she had advanced beforehand. 'Age, Charity,' he said, 'sure it's only natural.'

He stared her momentarily in the eyes. What was up with him, she wondered. What he said, although it was definitely true, was hardly newsworthy. He seemed agitated. When next he spoke, his words tumbled out like a confession.

'What's the point moaning and groaning your days away?' he said. 'It's not all the poisoned chalice they make it out to be. Is it?'

'Is it?' said Mrs Cuthbert. She eyed her sherry. Perhaps a small sip.

'We have excuses, damn it!'

'Excuses, Valentine?'

'Excuses, Charity. For instance, we have an excuse when we're old for idling. For instance, when old we have excuses and time to do those things we've always planned – on the long finger, I mean, Charity.'

'I see. The long finger.'

'We can indulge ourselves. In deafness, for instance. Or memory, even. We can suffer of a loss of memory or of a deafness which within an eye's twinkling will prove stray and oddly selective. Are you with me?'

It seemed to Mrs Cuthbert that her poor third cousin Valentine had succumbed to the wiles of some novel evangelical cause. What did it mean, and who would look after him? Not she: she had enough on her hands already. 'Sherry?' She hadn't checked but she was sure there must be another bottle in the cellar. At this rate she'd need it.

Valentine Brack looked suspiciously at his glass, as if doubting it was he who had quaffed his second sherry. 'I will,' he said.

She poured.

'And think on it, Charity. We can be cantankerous as hell with government officials and the like, and they'll indulge us always as though we were their own darling daddos. At our age we're all ladies and gentlemen, so we can dispose if we like of our schooling and dispense our store of bile and no one'd turn a hair. Do you not see that, Charity?'

'See what exactly?'

'There's no call, no call at all, for moaning and groaning alone. It's not all doom and gloom, Charity. It isn't, is it?'

'I suppose it isn't.'

It seemed she had said the right thing. Valentine Brack relaxed back into his chair.

'Old age, Charity,' he said more easily, 'well, it seems to me, it's a time for reflection. A time, maybe, for new interests, a time perchance for old hobbies revived. But surely, above all, it's a time for companionship?'

'Companionship,' repeated Mrs Cuthbert. She took a sip of her sherry. It tasted vile. She felt better.

'It's not all the poisoned chalice they make it out to be. Sure it isn't?'

'Well . . .'

Valentine Brack leaned forward in his chair, as if about to impart a vital secret. 'At least, Charity, it doesn't have to be,' he said.

Mrs Cuthbert nodded, not quite the committed partisan. But third cousin Valentine, for all his earnestness, was in such a polite mood, even calling her Charity, she felt it would be churlish to disagree. Besides, what he said was probably true at his age. She, of course, was a good ten years younger. She had a child that cursed her. She had a position to maintain – or worse still, she had no position at all. Things were altogether different her side of seventy. 'More sherry?' she said. There was very little else she could say.

'Sherry?' He realized he had downed his third glass. 'I think I will,' he said. 'Tell me, Charity,' he continued, again leaning forward with a straining ear, 'did you enjoy yourself last night?'

'Enjoy myself?'

'I wondered.'

'Of course I enjoyed myself.'

'You did?'

'Valentine, I always look forward to our canasta evenings.'

What was he getting at? Was this some new and fanciful prank?

'But we didn't *play* canasta,' he complained.

'It's not my fault we didn't play.'

Her third cousin was leaning so far out of his seat now, it seemed he was balancing on his haunches. 'But did you enjoy yourself, Charity?' he insisted.

Enjoy myself, wondered Mrs Cuthbert. What did he mean?

Enjoyment was a concept that she rarely considered: and certainly it had little to do with her weekly canasta evenings at Knight's Kilbrack. As her Engagements Diary had slowly grown blanker and blanker – a reminder more of the unsocial life she led than of future events to look forward to – the canasta evenings had grown proportionately in importance. If her life was a busy round, then it consisted of breathless anticipation of Thursday evenings. The Brack family was far too eccentric ever to be truly considered society. But the family was landed, and old. What was more, Valentine's grandfather had been a knight of the realm. There was a time when Mrs Cuthbert would have laughed at a knighthood, for the taint of merit attached to it, never mind that the grandfather Brack had actually bought the honour from Lloyd George's parsimonious government. But these days, her predicament the way it was, playing cards once a week with the prankstering grandson of a knight was all the society she was likely to get. Unless Livia married well.

Enjoyment didn't enter into it.

And yet, she had to confess, last night had been different. 'Do you know, Valentine?'

'What's that?' he asked. He had drooped back in his chair. She had taken so long answering, he was sure she was only searching for easy words to disabuse him.

'I did enjoy myself.' It was strange, but they were such lovely words to speak, she enjoyed now even the saying of them. She smiled. 'I did enjoy myself.' She repeated it, a look of surprise on her face.

'You did?'

'I did.'

'That's grand,' said Valentine Brack.

'Yes,' said Mrs Cuthbert. 'Grand.'

'Do you know, Charity?'

'Yes, Valentine?'

'I enjoyed myself too.'

The two of them were smiling. They smiled for some time, in silence. Valentine Brack, fiddling again with the stem of his sherry glass, realized there was still sherry in it. Once more he quaffed it. He became agitated again.

'Tell me, have I disturbed you, Charity, calling all peremptory on you like this?'

'Not at all, Valentine, I'm delighted to see you.'

'I could maybe return later? Tomorrow even. Next week?'

'Nonsense. I was only reading the *Telegraph*.'

'The *Telegraph?* Do you still get newspapers here?'

'Through the post.'

'Well, fancy. I haven't seen a newspaper in years. Through the post, you say?'

'You're welcome to borrow it,' said Mrs Cuthbert doubtfully. It seemed only a moment ago that she was enjoying herself. Now, she wasn't so sure. What was he up to?

But Valentine Brack seemed genuinely taken with her ingenuity. He chuckled to himself. 'There's initiative for you. Through the post, you say. And tell me, Charity, what's the colour of the news?'

'Nothing much, Valentine. Another Barnes girl dead.'

'Another one?'

'Haemorrhage on the brain. That's the last one now.'

'Last one?'

'And she left £371,380.'

'That much?'

'Yes,' said Mrs Cuthbert. She automatically reached for a tissue and wiped the corner of her eye. 'Net,' she said.

'Why Charity,' said Valentine Brack, half-rising from his chair, 'you're crying.'

'I'm sorry. I didn't mean to.'

'Were you very fond of her? I didn't know.'

'Fond? She was a bitch.' Another tear and another tissue. 'What am I going to do? What are they going to say?'

'Who's that now?'

'When my time comes – I won't stretch to ten thousand even. And a daughter a nun, or worse still, married to that oaf.'

'Now, now, Charity,' said Valentine Brack; and he was actually out of his chair and wrapping a comforting arm around her shoulders. 'Last night you were crying because she wouldn't marry. Today it's because she might.'

'But not to that oaf.'

'Which oaf is this?'

'Tall ugly fool of a thing. He calls himself a barman in Nellie Maguire's.'

Valentine Brack's comforting hand missed a stroke. 'My son?' he said.

'What do you mean, your son?'

'With scars on his face and mad as a March hatter?'

'Hare,' said Mrs Cuthbert automatically.

'Hair?' said Valentine Brack. 'His hair is black. What's that to do with it?'

'Your son?' This time she grabbed a whole fistful of tissues. 'Valentine, this is no time for your pranks.'

'It's true, Charity.'

'But your son is dead ten years and more.'

'He's only half with us now.'

'But you said he was dead.'

'I thought he was dead. I was wrong.' He patted her shoulder distractedly. 'My son has returned.'

Mrs Cuthbert turned to her third cousin, saw that he was staring fatefully and blindly out the window. She stared there too. 'What will you do?'

'I have little choice in the matter. Not now.' He faced her. 'He's above in the house.'

Mrs Cuthbert blushed. She blushed because her mind was making the most ruthless of calculations. The river and the riparian rights, she thought; land, perhaps a thousand acres in all, mixed arable and pasture – Livia had told her; sheep-grazing on the hills; the entire village except for church, chapel, pub and Rectory; the big house, Knight's

Kilbrack . . . And Valentine, of course, was the great-grandson of a knight of the realm, an esquire . . .

And all his descendants too.

She reached for a tissue, then changed her mind, pushed the box away. Tissues were Livia's idea, and Mrs Cuthbert had suddenly realized she disliked their disposability. At her time of life she needed something to hang on to, something comforting that was always there and belonged, like a good smell, clean or otherwise. She had a hankie up her sleeve. She didn't take it out. She didn't need to now. She had stopped crying.

'So Valentine has returned,' she said.

'Yes,' said Valentine Brack, still blindly addressing the window.

A moment, then: 'More sherry?'

CHAPTER SEVENTEEN

IT WAS SUCH a long time since anything had happened in Kilbrack that Valentine Brack wasn't at all sure how to react to this sudden influx of gew-gaws and bagatelles. 'Ecumenical gesture?' he said.

'That's what he called it.'

'We'll soon put a stop to that. What does it mean?'

'Livia did tell me. But I've forgotten.'

'But Charity, you wouldn't sell the Rectory?'

'He said I could still live here.'

'A house-keeper? In your own home?'

'He said I could spend the money on a world cruise.'

'What sort of a carry-on is that? What would you be doing on a world cruise?'

'I wouldn't *go* on a world cruise, Valentine. It would just be nice to know that I could. If I wanted.'

'I see.'

'You don't see, Valentine. You don't see at all.' She cast a pained and sideways look at her *Telegraph* beside her.

'I do, Charity, I do.'

And he did. He saw everything. They lapsed again into silence. Outside in the hall, the clock struck midday. Mrs Cuthbert rose from her chair. There was a rosette of discarded tissues around where she had sat.

'Will you stay for lunch, Valentine?' she asked. 'I'm afraid the Monsignor will be joining us.'

For a woman so stout, he thought, how surprising that she was so light on her toes. And by God, she was light on her toes. She had danced him off his feet last night. He stood up himself, and warmed his backside against the fire. 'I was thinking, Charity,' he said.

'You were?'

'It's a long time now since I took a trip to Dublin. A hellish carry-on, I know, but solicitors . . .'

'Yes,' agreed Mrs Cuthbert.

'I was thinking I might take a room in the Hibernian. Do you remember the Hibernian?'

'Ah,' said Mrs Cuthbert, 'the Hibernian . . .' She sat down again. And on her face was the memory of hansom cabs and gowns and fires and bellboys bowing and the porters knowing her name.

'I was wondering, if you weren't too busy sometime – it's just that – 'tis silly, I know – but – well, I do hear they have the odd dance at the Hibernian still.' He coughed and glanced quickly at his third cousin. 'If you weren't too busy,' he mumbled apologetically.

Mrs Cuthbert's poor eyes, strained with the odd tears of the morning, focused. She found herself staring at the old man's boots. How filthy they were, on her rug. Head to toe, he needed a good scrubbing down. 'Valentine . . .' she said, and shook her head.

His face fell. 'Don't worry about the Hibernian,' he said. 'It was only an idle thought.'

She sniffed. 'Valentine . . . will you take those boots off? Those boots need a good brushing.'

'My boots?'

'Arnold's shoes are upstairs. They should fit you.' Now she smiled. 'I have his dancing shoes too,' she said. 'I've kept them all this time. I'll hunt them out. You'll need a good pair of shoes if you're taking me dancing in the Hibernian.'

The Monsignor stormed into the kitchen. With a swish of his soutane, he turned on Livia, who harried his behind. His hand hit out, emphasizing his point. 'You'll find there are no flies on me, Livia Cuthbert,' he snapped. His hand struck her on the lip.

Livia wet her lip with her tongue. There was a sharp sting where he had smitten her. 'Just bees in your bonnet,' she said.

'I'm sorry, child. That was an accident.'

'Get away from me.'

The Monsignor caught the fire in her eyes. Could he risk giving her three Hail Marys? 'Suit yourself.' he said. Idly, he glanced at the Victorian antiques that hung in rows from the kitchen shelves behind her: gridirons and skillets, roasters and trivets, fluting irons and the like. Rust. He'd soon clear away all that rubbish. The shelves would be ideal for his Capo di Monte roses.

'You won't get away with it,' said Livia.

'I already have,' he replied. 'And you'd better mend your manners. I'm afraid there'll be small room for a vixen in my presbytery. But that wouldn't upset your mother unduly, I'll be damned. Think on it. I'm to be your priest again. It'll be a sort of homecoming.'

'They'll never sell you St Ciaran's.'

'They've already accepted my deposit.'

'Mother won't sell.'

The Monsignor winked, cocking a retinal snook at her. 'We'll soon see,' he said.

'How could a priest afford a church? How would a priest afford this Rectory?'

'Ham,' said the priest. 'And hamburgers.'

'Hamburgers? You're going to sell hamburgers in my father's church?'

'Of course not. Hamburger joints are the coming craze. Get in quick, and you'll have it made. I have it made. I have the Irish ham market cornered.'

'But—' said Livia.

'But nothing,' said the Monsignor. 'Accept defeat, Livia. Join a nunnery, why don't you? That'd be best for all of us.'

'But hamburgers aren't made of ham,' said Livia. 'They're made of beef.'

But the Monsignor, with another, more exigent swish of his soutane, had stalked off. Livia followed, a smile of wondrous satisfaction forming on her face. She found him stopped short outside the drawing room.

'Who's in there with your mother?' he demanded, whispering.

'I don't know.'

'What's he saying?'

'I don't know.'

'Be still.' And they listened, watching the scene within the drawing room between the jamb and the half-open door.

Valentine Brack was down on his knees, pressing between his long thin hands his third cousin Charity's stout, pink palm.

'In short, Charity,' he was saying – and the integrity with which he invested his voice had the serrated edge of a plea – 'it is companionship that we should seek. Anything more is trinkets, or insipid, like a cake too thick with icing. But one jot less than companionship, Charity, and we're the poorer, as poor as the last of a species. The younger generations must look after themselves. We've done our duty by them. 'Tis our turn now. And though I have the gift of prophecy, and understand all mysteries, and all knowledge; and though I have all faith, so that I could remove mountains, and have not . . . Charity . . . what do you say?'

Mrs Cuthbert didn't know what to say. She didn't know what thoughts were travelling through her mind. But when she did speak, she was pleased – if not a little surprised – at her decision. She said: 'Valentine . . . I should be honoured to be your wife.'

It was too much for the Monsignor. He swung open the door, revealed himself on the threshold. No longer aquiline, he stood dark and threatening like a crow daring starlings to touch its bread. 'Charity Cuthbert,' he said in a hard sibilance of command, 'as your Father Confessor, I must advise you to let go that heathen's hand.'

It was unnecessary advice. Valentine Brack had already dropped her palm. He had stood up to his full height. 'Well, well,' he said. 'The village preacher. "At church with meek and unaffected grace, his looks adorned the venerable place." You could at least put on a pair of trousers. Bursting in here in a frock.'

The Monsignor whipped a hand out of his soutane. 'I did not save that woman's immortal soul to have her body shamed in a heathen union.'

'And where would you like her body shamed?'

'What?'

'Is it any business of yours anyway? Bursting in here like a cock of the walk.'

The Monsignor wheezed dangerously. 'Affinity's my business. Consanguinity's my business. Consummation's my business. My business is the immortal soul.'

'And hamburger joints,' added Livia.

The Monsignor rounded on her. His chin jutted, his mouth snapped open. But he could think of nothing damning to say for the moment. 'I'll deal with you later,' he muttered. He turned back to Mrs Cuthbert. 'Charity Cuthbert, you will come with me now.'

Valentine Brack began to chuckle. 'Take a look at the little cockalorum, all sounding brass and tinkling cymbal.'

'Mrs C!' shouted the Monsignor.

'Oh, go away,' said Mrs Cuthbert.

'Quarter-pounder with French fries,' said Livia.

'Hello?' said Valentine Brack.

The Monsignor started. Everybody suddenly was rounding on him. It was like a bad dream. Worse than a dream, it was like his terrible childhood all over again. 'What?' he wheezed.

Valentine Brack had taken out a dirty handkerchief. He was scrutinizing it now as if it was a note he was trying to decipher. 'Is there a Father Michael in the house?' he chanced eventually.

'Monsignor!' wheezed the Monsignor, his face purple with rage. He stamped his foot, but could make little impression on the rug he stood on by the door.

'Monsignor – that's right,' said Valentine Brack. 'I have a note here for you.'

'A note?' The Monsignor was darting looks in between times to see where the rug ended, that he might stamp his foot more effectually.

'A note,' confirmed Valentine Brack.

'What does it say?' said the Monsignor.

'It says—' Again he seemed to have some difficulty deciphering the handkerchief; he held it close, then distant, then close again to his eyes. 'It seems to say: Father Michael, you have no chance with the Rectory. Now, if you wouldn't mind, bugger off.' He looked up at the Monsignor, a gape of bewilderment on his face. 'That's what it says,' he said, shaking his head, as if in awe himself at the wondrous advances in modern communications technology.

Then he blew his nose.

In her kitchen Nellie Maguire put the kettle on the hob, took down the tea caddy, measured two spoons of tea, one for herself and one for the pot, poured them into the teapot. She sat down. She stood up, emptied and filled the kettle, returned it to the hob, cleaned the teapot and poured two spoons of tea into it. She sat down. She stood up. Perhaps I should have a cup of tea, she thought. She was only parched with the morning. No, she thought. Later perhaps. She sat down again.

In her pocket she found a package. What was it? It looked vaguely familiar. Beecham's Powders, was it? She sniffed her usual Slievenamon of a sniff. She had a fierce cold. How long had she been down with the cold? Maybe she should take a Beecham's Powder.

She decided on a cup of tea. She was cleaning the teapot to measure fresh tea into it, when the yard door opened and the Monsignor slumped in.

'Nellie,' he said.

'Michael,' said Nellie. And quick as the twinkling of a dilatant eye she was a woman in love. Michael, she thought, and closing her eyes she was transported momentarily to a woodland fairy glade and to a midnight kiss. Oh, Michael, Michael, Michael, she vowed, nor absence nor time will rust my love, my love, my Michael.

She opened her eyes. What was she thinking? She couldn't remember. Something or other. And here was Father Michael and all.

'Nellie,' said the Monsignor, sitting down heavily at the table.

'Father Michael,' she answered.

'Fetch me a whiskey, Nellie. I've had a terrible shock.'

'A whiskey, is it?'

'And an aspirin. The shock has brought on my migraine.'

'An aspirin? Will a Beecham's Powder do?'

'Anything.'

'Coming up, Father. You've a face the length of the Shannon. And the colour of a salmon off-season. Are you all right?'

The Monsignor gave her a busy look. 'I have a migraine, Nellie.'

'I'll fetch you the whiskey, so.' And she winked. 'Pronto.'

While she was gone, the Monsignor cradled his poor spasmic head in his hands. The bitch. The bitch and the bastard. Was all lost? Surely all wasn't lost? That woman's soul was lost. But he still had the ham-market cornered. He still had the church. The Church Commissioners had taken his deposit, God damn it. What harm? So he wouldn't have a Georgian rectory for a home. He'd build a presbytery. That's what he'd do. Right in front of the blasted Cuthberts, he'd build it. And he'd ruin their view. He'd show them he wasn't a man to be taken lightly. You didn't cross a Monsignor that easy. Wheat from chaff, men from boys, they'd soon find out who was boss.

Nellie returned and deposited the whiskey on the table. 'Here you are,' she said, having stirred the contents of her package into a glass of water. 'Get this down you, Father Michael.'

The Monsignor was already sufficiently revived to correct her. 'Monsignor,' he said.

'That's right,' said Nellie.

He downed the water in one go, and took a sip at his

whiskey. 'I don't often see you in chapel these days,' he said reprovingly. 'Nellie Maguire.'

'Don't you?' said Nellie. 'Ah.' And she smiled as though the fault must lie in the Monsignor's eyesight.

'Did anyone ever tell you,' said the Monsignor dreamily, 'Nellie Maguire, that you have a tremendous bosom?'

He jerked up straight in his chair, jolted his head. What was he saying? He had intended some confessorial advice as to the propriety of a higher neckline. What was he saying? He'd had a terrible shock, it was true, but hardly of the severity to unloose his wits.

Nellie was saying something back to him, but he wasn't listening. He was watching her lips move. What lovely lips they were. What a cornucopia of delights those lips, full and rosy, would hint at. She could be more discreet with the lipstick, though.

'And what tremendous lips you have, Nellie Maguire.'

What was he saying? His thoughts came cogent and clear as ever, if anything clearer, but when he spoke, some lecherous stranger chose his words for him.

'I had forgotten what a fine-looking woman you are, Nellie. Nellie Maguire.'

He gave up trying to speak. Let him concentrate on his thoughts. He had the novice outside. He must pull himself together.

Except, and it was true, she was a fine-looking woman. He had forgotten, but hadn't they kissed a small fling together once? He was only a stripling seminarian at the time. He was on a hiking holiday through the Slievenamon Mountains, in the summer vacation. *Mens sana in corpore sano*. They had kissed goodbye at midnight.

Was she the only girl he had ever kissed? He wondered now, of a sudden, was it that one illicit kiss that had prompted him to apply for the curacy of Kilbrack? Surely not. He was a man of the cloth, bred. Born, even: there were rumours that his father had been a priest, rumours only. He knew nothing of his parents. He had been brought up in an orphanage. The Christian Brothers had been the only mother and father he had known.

Was it the shock or the migraine or what was it, but he felt unbearably sad. Why was he sad? Surely it could not be because those lips across the table from him were the only lips he had ever kissed? What was a kiss compared to the meteoric rise of his career: from orphan to Monsignor – a title only bestowed by His Holiness the Pope? A Bishop even; he had been confidentially informed it was only a question of time. And thence, who might know? In this business, even the sky presented no limit.

What was a woman's kiss, compared to these inestimable – and on the other hand, these eminently estimable – benefits?

He did not know what a kiss was, but there were times, odd times, times that crept up behind on him, tapped him on his shoulders all unawares, times when the ham market of Ireland, a half-Norman haunt of a church, the rat-tat-tat of a mitre on his door even, times when these seemed less golden, insignificant like small change in a big pocket; times when he remembered what little there was of his childhood.

At the orphanage he sometimes would sit on the perimeter wall and watch the outside world at its business. And sometimes alone he imagined a home. He had a mother and a father. They had a dog called Shep. The father kept sheep. The sheep cropped the grass. The doors and the frames of the windows were painted red. The cottage faced south. The mother loved him.

He closed tight shut his eyes. Why had he remembered that? Why did he feel so sad? Surely it could not be that the fire lit by that one kiss so many years ago still glowed in embers in his heart?

Am I lonely, he thought. He said, 'Nellie,' and his hand – he saw – had inched across the table to touch hers.

'Michael . . .' said Nellie.

'Nellie . . .' said Michael.

Nellie Maguire had a tear in her eye. She had lit a cigarette. Who knows, but neglecting to blow the smoke away, it had trickled up to smart her eyes.

'Nellie,' said the Monsignor.

'Yes?' she answered dreamily.

'Come with me now till I show you the church I've a mind for.'

Bridie O'Toole appropriated her right hand from her hip, selected the index finger, pointed then pressed on the mattress. A smile forced its way to her cheeks. Just as she'd suspected. It was a horsehair mattress. A fine deep strong and comfortable horsehair mattress.

''Tis a wide bed,' she said, 'for a single man.'

'Not at all,' said Downey. 'This was my mother's bed.' Then, as if in explanation, 'She slept in it.'

'Never mind that,' said Bridie. 'Your mother's dead years since.'

'Is she?' He sounded and looked as though this was news to him. And yet it was true, after all. His mother was dead eleven years near enough. 'Ten years, nine months, three days, eleven hours approximately,' he said, 'Mam.'

'Never mind that. You've buried her, haven't you? Isn't that enough?'

What was she on about now? Oh, she was a wily creature, you had to keep an eye forever fixed on her. 'I have my own bed inside,' he said, 'if 'tis wrestling you have a mind for, Mam.'

They had argued for nearly an hour. He didn't want a pork butcher's. He was a medical man. A pork butcher's and aspirin shop, Bridie had then adventured. In the end they'd settled on a grocery. 'With a fine cabinet of household medicaments,' Downey had insisted. 'Selling three different bacons,' Bridie had maintained. 'Streaky, best back and smoked.'

'Take off your bowler hat, J. D. Downey,' she said now. She turned her head, pouted slightly, offering a crinigerous cheek. ''Tis time you kissed your wife to be.'

The young novice ticked another square in his notebook. He had Protestant churches so far. He had pubs. Now, watching the Monsignor and this painted lady of his, he had lechery too. It was enough. He stepped out from the porch shadows into the nave. 'Stop this immediately!' he called, his young voice breaking with new authority.

The Monsignor's poor legs had given way. He was resting on Nellie's shoulders, almost crying. He didn't know why, but the weight of life was on him.

'Heresy, drunkenness and lechery,' said the novice. 'This blasphemy has gone far enough.'

But the Monsignor didn't hear him. Through the scorch of his tears he was remembering a time when he was a child. It was a Saturday. It was raining. It always rained on Saturdays. He stepped out of the orphanage and into the town. He'd saved his ha'pennies to purchase ten cigarettes, Sweet Afton, at the post office. It was a child's idle experiment. Outside, he came upon some town boys arguing noisily. They were fighting for drags on the one cigarette they had between them. Shyly, the young Michael offered them one of his own. They grabbed him and bruised him and stole his whole packet of ten. 'Why?' he sobbed now. 'Why?'

'Come with me now!' The novice's voice was already straining to the dominance that knowledge of love had banished for ever from Michael's.

'Tell me why,' he sobbed.

Nellie, sober again now, as she would remain for the rest of her days, bar the odd G and T at breakfast and other difficult times like that, wrapped her human arm around his shoulders, held his head close against her bosom. 'Michael,' she said, 'Acushla, my Michael.'

'Kiss me, Nellie,' he said. 'Please love me.'

* * *

Jim O'Toole was thinking to himself. It was too late now to go to sea. That was certain. But there was nothing stopping him visiting Waterford, say. He could stroll by the docks. He could talk with the sailors and fishermen. After a while, he might even swap stories with them in the waterfront pubs. Sure, given time, they might even invite him out on a boat trip with them. Not too far to begin with. He'd have to find his sea-legs first. But. Given time.

And that was a strange thing too. Them two great stone birds from the pillars. Only a moment since, they were lying in the dirt. Who could have come and raised them, he wondered. He shook his head. Time for a nap.

CHAPTER EIGHTEEN

O'Leary Montagu was dreaming, but not of any accident. He dreamed Mary had returned to him.

'Hello, O'Leary,' she said, as though for old times' sake.

'Mary, you've come back.' He was so happy. 'I always knew you would.'

'How do you feel?' she asked, just like a nurse.

'Better,' he allowed.

'Well?' she said.

'I'm sorry?'

'You don't need to be sorry any more.'

'Well what?' he asked. It was that sort of dream.

'Well, what do you think?'

'It was a strange journey,' he admitted.

'Certainly a long one. Sometimes I doubted it would ever end.'

'So did I.' He decided he might risk it. After all, it was his dream. 'You never existed, did you, Mary.' It wasn't a question.

'I was real enough. While it lasted. You needed to let on

to yourself you were a great macho man. But the funeral was true.'

'Was it?'

'You buried me, didn't you? Though God knows what those poor people thought.'

'I needed you, Mary.'

'You don't need me any more. You know who you are.'

'Who am I?'

'Yourself. In all your nakedness, in all your armour.'

He didn't change the subject. But there was so much to say, so short a time. 'I was so cruel to you, Mary.'

'Par for the course,' she said. 'Cruelty comes from ignorance. Always has done, always will.'

'And yet you were kind to me.'

'Kindness won't defeat cruelty,' she said. She sounded wistful now, distant as an angel. 'Only knowledge can do that. Knowledge of yourself and the prospect of tomorrow. You need nothing more.' She didn't call him O'Leary. 'You have your future to face now.' Was she sighing? He couldn't tell. 'But when you wake you'll have your past to help you.'

She was fading, returning to the ethereal vacuum that had conceived her.

'Mary,' he called. 'You were never a nurse, were you?'

'There was a nurse,' she echoed, 'called Mary.'

But she kicked me out after the first week, thought O'Leary. 'You were never a nurse,' he said aloud, though he knew he spoke to himself now. Mary had gone. 'You were an angel . . .'

He drifted awake. Outside it had begun to rain again.

Below in the paddock amidst the clumps of ragwort and thistles a lone magpie settled. One's for sorrow. He remembered how as a child he would watch from this very window through the dim light of Ireland, watch and pray for another magpie to come. Two's for mirth. And he would watch, unwilling though compulsive witness, counting the tortuous seconds, until the first would fly away, and the coming of its mate rather than expiate would serve only to double his sorrow.

And one day that waiting had got too much for him. He had taken his father's gun and shot the offending magpie dead.

He stared out of his old bedroom window, watching the Bentley sweep up the drive, past the paddock. He still felt faintly groggy. But he had slept a while. He was all right.

He had read of an ancient torture where a box was fixed to the victim's head and a starving rat placed inside to gnaw into his brain. If he remembered his youth now, that was how he remembered it. Except, he had fixed the box himself, the rat was his pet.

He had walked in front of his father's car, tried to take his own life. And waking in a hospital ward, his mind could not bear to allow his memory. For eleven years he had walked in a land with no magpies at all.

And it was not Fate nor coincidence that led him to the books and finally to Kilbrack. He knew now it was nature. For nature abhors a vacuum. And that book he had scrawled of an evening to pain his father, had become – not his memory – but the closest his mind would allow.

And all because he feared his father would hate him. Why would his father hate him? Not just for his sexuality, not even for that, he suspected. His shoulders weren't strong enough for the weight of all this tradition. Perhaps that was it. He feared his father would hate him. That fear itself had spawned the hatred.

The rain was splattering on the windowpane, on his reflection. It felt comforting somehow. He shrugged. One's for sorrow, two's for mirth. What do no magpies mean?

There was a knock on his bedroom door. As he turned, he wondered had he truly glimpsed through the corner of his eye another black and white streak alight in the paddock? He did not check.

He opened the door. The three faces that greeted him were smiling. Three's for heart and home and hearth.

'Hello,' he said to Mrs Cuthbert and to Livia.

'Hello,' said Livia, her lips still languid, but different somehow, human.

He picked up the paperback book, *Murder in the Big House*. How strange, after all these years, to discover he really was a writer. Of detective fiction, too.

He looked up at Valentine Brack.

O'Leary Montagu said: 'Er – hello, I mean, I'm sorry. I didn't intend – you see, I didn't know – leastways, I didn't want to know – allow myself to know, that is – you know – I'm sorry. But I'm better now. I've – er – changed. Leastways I've changed some ways – not every way. You've changed and I've changed. And I'm sorry. I'm sorry for all the – you know – trouble. I'm sorry for everything.'

But nobody heard what O'Leary Montagu said. O'Leary Montagu had been laid to rest.

'Hello Daddo,' said the young Valentine Brack, standing tall, a mild surmise in the lean of his head.

'Welcome home, son,' said his father.

Jamie O'Neill was brought up and educated in Dún Laoghaire, Co. Dublin. He has recently returned to Ireland and now lives in Galway. He is the author of *Disturbance*, *Kilbrack* and *At Swim, Two Boys*.

A SCRIBNER READING GROUP GUIDE

Kilbrack

Discussion Points

1. Think back to your initial impression of the main character, O'Leary Montague. What were your feelings about the man during the first chapters? In what ways does the author use the first scene, the train ride to Kilbrack, to drop clues about O'Leary—his neuroses, his past, his troubled mind?
2. Talk about O'Leary's point of view in this story and how credible it may or may not be. Did you trust his version of the past and of the present? To what extent is his interpretation of the world colored by his fears, doubts, and insecurities? For example, look at O'Leary's story of how he was arrested for sexual deviance. Can we believe him when he claims to have stumbled into that situation in complete innocence? What about the other characters in this novel? Did you believe certain individuals more than others?
3. What role do O'Leary's diary memos play in the story? Why, when they do little to advance the plot, has the author included them? In what ways do these entries speak to O'Leary's state of mind and his development as a character? Why does O'Leary so desperately hold on to words for comfort?
4. It seems that just about every character in *Kilbrack* suffers from strange and/or obsessive behavior. Whether it is an unhealthy aversion to buttons or an addiction to cocaine, many characters seem to cope with their worst fears by developing peculiar aversions and behaviors. Why so many compulsive behaviors in one town? What, if anything, seems to cause these neuroses? How do these obsessions help the people in this story deal with the world around them?
5. Similarly, what role do inanimate objects play in these behaviors? A book, a lemon Jiffy, a statue of a magpie—what power and significance do objects, symbols, and talismans hold for the characters in this story? How do they use them to distance themselves from emotion, memory, and meaningful interaction? Why do they feel that they need them to survive?
6. As Livia reads *Ill Fares the Land*, she thinks back on the tumultuous relationship between Uncle Val and his son, observing, "Only love

could lie beneath it. For love alone could produce such anger, such retribution . . . So much love wasted, perverted." Discuss the nature of love in this story. What causes this perversion that Livia speaks of and how does it seem to be at the heart of a larger problem in Kilbrack?

7. "We're all so jealous of the past, nursing old wounds and grievances . . . anyone so jealous of the past must be insecure of his present. Is it the Irish in us?" In what ways does this astute observation from Livia shed light on the tension between past and present? How does history and tradition stultify the present in the world of Kilbrack? What are the dangers of living in the past? By the end of the novel, do you believe that this town has finally broken free of the past?
8. How do the characters in this story seem to fit in with the backdrop of the natural world around them? How might location and setting go hand in hand with tradition and history?
9. Does religion play a part in holding people captive to history and tradition? Monsignor Michael—with his proselytizing and his condescension—demonstrates a heightened sense of importance and entitlement that is truly staggering. Yet he is also human, a man subject to the whims of his own insecurities. What kind of a representative is he for the church? How does the battle between the two dominant religions help to keep the Irish people beholden to their faith, and therefore their past? Is this a particularly Irish phenomenon, as Livia suspects?
10. At one point, after Uncle Val criticizes his son for going "against tradition," Livia responds with, "How could he owe anything to tradition, when tradition itself decries his very existence?" Is it only his sexuality that sets O'Leary apart from tradition or is there something more? Is reconciliation possible between the traditional Irish world and the gay community?
11. What larger issues might O'Leary's amnesia speak to? On page 259, Livia observes, "He's lost his memory. So he says. I think it's some sort of excuse for not remembering his past." Keeping this quote in mind, look at the ways that O'Leary's memory loss may be a metaphor for greater self-delusion. How much do any of the characters in this story "know" themselves? What is the nature of self-knowledge, and how does one achieve it? Why does O'Leary need to invent a history through the character of Nancy Valentine and in what ways is O'Leary's journey of self-discovery further complicated by his sexuality?
12. Besides Mary, Livia seems to be the only person in O'Leary's life capable of insight and free thought. What character traits does she possess that allow her to dig beneath the surface of things to get to the truth? Is she a symbol of Ireland's future?

13. It is interesting that Mary, one of the most fascinating characters in this story, is also one of the most mysterious. At the end of the novel, in a dream, O'Leary comes to realize that Mary never existed, but Mary herself contends that she was "real enough. While it lasted." Her words are cryptic, providing as many questions as answers. What, then, should we make of Mary's presence in the novel? Was she a figment of O'Leary's imagination, an angel, his own alter ego? If O'Leary reinvents his own history through the eyes of Nancy Valentine, as Mary insists he does, then what does he do through the eyes of Mary?